Rifling Paradise

Also by Jem Poster

Courting Shadows

Jem Poster

Rifling Paradise

SCEPTRE

First published in Great Britain in 2006 by Hodder and Stoughton
A division of Hodder Headline

A Sceptre Book

A CIP catalogue record for this title is available from the British Library

ISBN 0 340 82294 5

Typeset in Sabon by Hewer Text UK Ltd, Edinburgh
Printed and bound by Clays Ltd, St Ives plc

Hodder Headline's policy is to use papers that are natural, renewable
and recyclable products and made from wood grown in sustainable
forests. The logging and manufacturing processes are expected to
conform to the environmental regulations of the country of origin.

Hodder and Stoughton Ltd
A division of Hodder Headline
338 Euston Road
London NW1 3BH

For Kay, Tom and Tobi

I

I

It occurred to me later that I must have registered their approach a minute or so before the first stone struck the window. Certainly something had disturbed me as I dozed beside the fire – a murmured word perhaps, the click of the gate latch, a shoulder brushing the overgrown laurels beside the path – and I was already out of my armchair and moving towards the window at the moment of impact. Quite a small stone by the sound of it, such as one might imagine tossed against a young girl's casement by an importunate lover. I put my face against the glass, cupping my eyes with my hands, and peered out into the night.

The second stone must have been flung with considerable force. It struck one of the panes at waist height, sending shards of glass skittering across the floorboards. I remember starting backward, my head averted and my right hand held protectively to the side of my face, and then seizing the lamp from the chiffonier and stumbling through the hallway to the front door.

In those days – why not confess it along with the rest? – I was usually half cut by the time I turned in for the night, and possibly the claret was responsible on this occasion for what might have looked to my persecutors like a display of courage. But you have to realise that when I threw open the door and stepped out into the garden I had no particular reason to consider myself in danger. I had in mind, I suppose, a gang of mischievous schoolboys up from the village, a misguided but essentially innocuous prank.

Not schoolboys. The figures hovering at the margin of the oil-lamp's muted glow were all but featureless, but I could see at once from the stance and bulk of the two nearest that I wasn't dealing with children. I hesitated. Away to my right, someone cleared his throat and spat. Nobody spoke.

It was difficult to assess the situation. I was, in the first place, uncertain of the size of the gathering. Besides the half-dozen men dimly discernible at the lamplight's edge, there were indications – a stifled cough, the crack of a snapped twig, feet scuffing the damp leaf-litter where the beeches overhung the lawn – of perhaps as many again in the deeper shadows beyond. And what had brought them to the Hall at such an hour? I could hardly interpret their visit as a conventional courtesy, though I could see, on rapid reflection, a certain wisdom in treating it as such. I forced a smile.

'You were lucky to catch me,' I said. 'Another twenty minutes and I'd have been sound asleep in bed.'

'We'd have been sorry to have had to rouse you, Mr Redbourne.' The voice was quiet and even, but not entirely reassuring. I felt my pulse quicken.

'Might the matter not have waited until morning?' I asked, peering uncertainly towards the speaker.

'Might have. But the sooner the better, we thought.'

'In that case, you'd better come directly to the point.'

'I'll come to it soon enough. We were in the Dog, drinking a drop to poor Daniel's memory – you'll remember Daniel Rosewell – and it came to us that, living such a tidy step from the village, you mightn't have heard of his passing and that you needed to be told.'

'Daniel dead? How?'

'Six foot of rope and a milking stool. Hanged hisself last night in Waller's barn. Janie Waller found him this morning when she went out for kindling – his toes not two inches off the ground, she says, but two inches or twelve, it makes no difference.'

I was silent, thinking, I confess, less of the dead youth than of the trail that must have led this dubious company to my door.

'That'll grieve Mr Redbourne, we said. Or if it doesn't, it ought to.' Just the faintest hint of venom now. It was vital, I knew, to keep the discussion on a civilised footing.

'Thank you,' I said. 'It was good of you to bring the

news. Would you convey my condolences to the boy's mother?'

'Thanks and convey be damned.' A second voice, less measured than the first and with a harder edge to it, speaking out of the shadows to my left. 'You're to blame for the lad's death, Mr Redbourne, and you know it.'

'But that's absurd. I barely knew him.'

'That's not true. Five years back you fed and lodged him at your own expense for a month and more. The whole village knows it.'

'I gave him such employment as he was capable of and quartered him in one of my cottages while he worked for me. I'm accommodating three labourers in a similar fashion at this very moment.'

'Yes, but you visited him.'

I stared into the murk, wondering how much more my faceless accuser might know.

'At night. He told Nathan Farr. He said you put your arms about him.'

'Daniel was a troubled soul, and I offered him such consolation as I could. I may have embraced him on occasion.'

'Other things too. It wasn't only what you'd call embracing.' I thought I heard the trace of a sneer in the speaker's precise articulation of the word.

'What kind of things?' I asked. There was, I could see, a degree of risk in pressing for greater specificity, but I needed to know exactly how matters stood.

'That's not for us to say. You know better than we do what kind of mischief you visited on the lad.'

'You touched him, Mr Redbourne.' A third voice

cutting in now, reedy, distinctive. I listened intently, trying to place it. 'Wrongfully. Like you touched Nathan Farr.'

'Nathan? Is Nathan here?' I lifted my lamp and leaned forward, scanning the shadows. It was as though I had bent suddenly over a rock pool: the same instantaneous spasm of alarm, the same collective recoil.

'Not with us tonight, Mr Redbourne. But he'd take an oath on it. The touching. And the photographs. He told us about those too.'

I had it now. 'Maddocks,' I said sharply. 'Maddocks, is that you?'

A strained silence suggested that I had hit the mark. When the voice resumed, it was with a shade less aggression.

'It makes no matter who, sir. What I have to say goes for us all. For the whole village.'

'I doubt that,' I said, my spirits rising. Maddocks – a wastrel, a petty schemer, a hen-pecked nonentity. Who was he to set himself up as my inquisitor? 'I very much doubt it, Maddocks. And in any case, you've had your say and I've heard you out. Now I suggest that we all get to our beds.'

'You may have heard us, Mr Redbourne, but you've not heeded us.'

I hadn't had a word from Samuel Blaney, civil or uncivil, since he had left my employ, but I should have recognised his voice anywhere. He must have known as much. He strode forward and stood squarely in front of me, his massive head thrust defiantly forward into the lamplight.

'It's a subtle distinction,' I said.

'I've heard you out.' Blaney's mimicry of my own clipped tones was at once inaccurate and offensive. 'I've heard you out. That's what you told me when you dismissed me. My children will go hungry, I said – and so they did, believe me, for a good twelvemonth after – but you wouldn't heed my words. Hearing and heeding, Mr Redbourne – they're not the same thing, now, are they?'

'I had others to consider, Blaney. I'll not have my workforce intimidated, by you or by anyone else. And I'll not have you sneaking in now to settle old scores under cover of other business.'

I'm a tall man myself, but Blaney stands a good couple of inches taller. He reared himself to his full height and stepped up to within a yard of me. I edged back, bringing the lamp between his body and my own.

'Sneaking, is it?' he breathed. 'Well, you'd know all about that, wouldn't you? Creeping like a thief around your own grounds after nightfall, dodging in where you'd no call to be. That's sneaking, Mr Redbourne, the way a man acts when he doesn't want to be seen.'

I gestured out to the shadowy figures behind him. 'And this?' I asked. 'What's this?'

'Samuel's right, Mr Redbourne.' I tried to locate the voice, anxious to re-establish connection with the group from which Blaney had so pointedly and menacingly detached himself. 'If you'd heeded what we've told you tonight, you'd be weeping now – weeping for the lad and for what you brought him to.'

This was outrageous. I sidestepped Blaney and thrust

myself angrily forward, feeling the blood rise to my face. 'A man doesn't grieve to the orders of a mob,' I said heatedly. 'And I'll not be held responsible for what the lad chose to do to himself.'

'But why did he choose it?' the voice insisted. 'Why would a young man want to do away with himself? And as a child – well, you'd not have found a happier face for ten miles around. Bright as an April morning till he fell in with you.'

'Daniel?' I felt my self-control slipping, heard my own voice as though from someone else's mouth, shrill with incredulity. 'That's nonsense. The child was beaten black and blue from the time he could walk. Go and stand outside his mother's door if you want an answer to your questions.'

'A mother strikes her child to keep him on the straight and narrow. That's natural, and what's natural does no harm to a youngster. But what you've done—'

'Listen,' I said, 'I'll not stand for any more of this. Let me advise you, as a magistrate, that your accusations and innuendo amount to slander, and furthermore' – I glared around me as though my gaze could penetrate the enveloping darkness – 'that I could have the whole pack of you charged with trespass and malicious damage. Now get back to your homes and leave me in peace.'

I swung round and, as I did so, Blaney took a step to his left, positioning himself between me and my doorway.

'The Farr boy,' he said softly. 'He'll take an oath, remember. In the witness box if need be.'

'Let me pass.' I made a move to circumvent him, but he was too quick for me.

'You'll pass when I give you leave,' he said. And he reached forward and laid the flat of his hand against the lapel of my smoking-jacket.

It was a surprisingly unemphatic gesture, casual, almost caressing, but I knew at that moment that Blaney was prepared to steer us all into deeper and more dangerous waters. The men at my back knew it too, I could tell, sensing in their stillness a new expectancy, a sharpened focus. 'When I give you leave,' he repeated, slowly withdrawing his hand but without yielding ground. He was staring into my face with an expression of such malevolent intensity that I was obliged to avert my eyes. And as I did so, I was aware of some faint stir, subtle but unmistakable, in the group behind me. Nothing, I remember thinking – not a word, not a glance, not the smallest gesture – would be lost on this audience. I looked up at Blaney again, forcing myself to answer his gaze.

'With or without your leave,' I said, as firmly as I could, 'I intend to retire to my bed. You must excuse me.'

His silence made me think momentarily that I had retrieved the situation; then he reached forward again and gripped me by the right wrist, pressing his thumb sharply into the flesh just beneath the edge of my cuff and making the glass chimney of the lamp jitter in its housing. I tried to pull away but he held me fast and drew me, with a horrible suggestion of intimacy, to his breast.

'I could put you on the ground,' he whispered, the stink of ale coming off his breath, 'as easy as I could put out that lamp.' And then, after a tense pause, viciously, gratuitously: 'You've hands like a girl's, Mr Redbourne. I hate that in a man.'

'You can't threaten me like that, Blaney. The law doesn't allow it. And no one, let me remind you, is beyond reach of the law.'

'Just so, Mr Redbourne. No one. That's a lesson you've still to learn. A lesson' – his gaze flickered briefly outward – 'we're here to teach you. Because there are those who learn of their own accord, and there are those who won't learn until they're taught. And you' – he released my wrist and, before I had time to step back or even to register his intention, struck me across the cheek – 'you need teaching.'

Blaney was, I knew, capable of considerable brutality, but this was not in essence a brutal action. It was, rather, a finely calculated insolence, delivered without force and with a knowing eye on his audience.

'How dare you!' I was trembling violently now, caught between rage and fear. 'I could have you charged with assault.'

'Assault? How do you make that out, Mr Redbourne?'

'You just struck me in the face. I don't imagine you're going to deny it.'

'A tap, that's all. A friendly tap.'

'An unprovoked act of aggression, and in the presence of witnesses.'

'Witnesses, sir?' He was playing shamelessly to the gallery now, grinning hugely, sweeping the shadows with exaggerated movements of his heavy head. 'I can't see any witnesses.'

'Don't act the fool, Blaney. There must be a dozen

men out there, any one of whose testimony would be enough to convict you.'

The grin faded. He leaned close, his mouth against my ear. 'We'll see who's the fool,' he said quietly. And then, lifting his head and voice: 'Did anyone see me assault this man?'

There was a long, uneasy silence. Blaney bent towards me again. 'Like I said, Mr Redbourne. No witnesses.'

In my father's time, a cry would have brought a dozen servants running from the house and its outbuildings, but those days were long gone. Under my own straitened regime, the groom and the cook, man and wife, lived in a cottage at the far side of the estate, housework was attended to on an irregular basis by a girl who came up from the village as required, and only Latham slept on the premises. Well into his seventies, deaf as an adder and barely able to carry out his routine duties, he was hardly a man to be counted on in a crisis, and I could have nourished no realistic hope of assistance from that quarter. Even so, I found myself, in my agitation, turning helplessly towards the house. Blaney was quick to spot the movement.

'The old man won't hear you,' he said. 'Not even if he was awake, which I doubt. And don't go fancying you might make a break for it neither. I'd have you before your foot was off the ground.'

A sudden gust of wind, raindrops spattering the laurels. I spread my hands in a gesture of appeasement. 'What do you want of me?' I asked.

The question seemed to catch him off guard. He glanced outward as though in need of a prompt.

'After all,' I continued, heartened by his momentary discomfiture, 'we can't stand around talking in the garden all night.'

My attempt at levity was clearly a misjudgement. He turned slowly back to me, his eyes glittering dangerously. 'You're in no position to say what can or can't be done, Mr Redbourne. I'll do what I damn well like, on or off your blasted property.' And, as though to reinforce the point, he lunged clumsily towards me.

I stepped sideways, anticipating another slap, and felt my right heel sink deep in the freshly turned soil of the flowerbed. I might have retained my balance; but Blaney, seeing me stagger, put out his hand, fingers extended, and prodded me in the chest. The barest touch, but it was enough. I fell awkwardly on my side among the lavender bushes with the lamp beneath me. I heard the glass crack against my ribs, felt the heat of the wick and its fitting through my jacket. In the darkness that engulfed us, I imagined Blaney towering above me, poised to deliver whatever kicks or blows would satisfy his appetite for revenge.

In my sometimes confused memory of the events of that night, this stands out with the most extraordinary clarity. You have to think of me huddled there among the crushed foliage, knees drawn up to protect my midriff, the side of my face hard against the damp earth. Whatever faint hope I might have entertained up to that moment – hope of rescue, some vestigial trust in the essential humanity of my tormentors – had been extinguished with the lamplight. And yet out of my very hopelessness, something – grace is the word that comes

13

to mind, though I find myself more comfortable with the notion of some profound form of resignation – rose like the fragrance from the bruised lavender, stilling my agitation; and I lay quietly in that merciful state of suspension, waiting incuriously for events to unfold around me.

I remember the strangest sense of leisure, of time frozen or protracted, but in actuality my trance could hardly have lasted more than a few seconds, broken, I think, by the voice of one of the men.

'Let him be now, Samuel.' There was a nervous urgency in the man's tone, as though he were calling back a vicious and intractable dog. I looked up. Blaney still stood above me, his broad frame silhouetted against the sky, but I thought I detected a certain irresoluteness in his stance.

'We came here to teach him a lesson,' he said.

'You've given him lesson enough, Samuel.'

Blaney seemed to consider this for a moment.

'He'll not tell,' he said at last. 'Not with what we know about him.'

'You lay into him the way you laid into Arthur Cotteridge that time and there'll be no hiding it, whether he wants to tell or no.'

There was another long pause. I saw Blaney shift position but was unprepared for the kick he aimed at my legs as he turned. His boot struck my left shin a little below the knee, glancingly but not without force. I rolled sideways, anxious to avoid worse, but he was already moving away down the slope of the lawn to rejoin his companions.

'You just mind that,' he called over his shoulder, 'next time you're thinking of putting your milksop hands where they've no right to be.'

I lay still until I was sure the men had all left the grounds. Then I limped back to the house and groped my way painfully up the stairs to my bedroom.

2

My leg throbbed and my hands shook so violently that I was scarcely able to light the lamp. I removed my shoes and my muddied jacket and threw myself face down among my pillows, trying to compose myself sufficiently to summon Latham. But as my breathing returned to normal and the trembling subsided, it struck me that it would be unwise to make more of the incident than was absolutely necessary; and having satisfied myself that my injuries were essentially superficial, I eased myself from the bed, drew a chair to the fire, raked up the embers and settled back to consider my situation.

The decision I reached as a result of my deliberations seemed at the time to involve some radical shift of perspective, yet the plan I formulated that night was really nothing new. From childhood on, I had been fascinated by the exploits of those naturalists who, with scant regard for their own personal comfort and safety, had obstinately pursued their quarry – their specimens, their theories – to the most remote corners of the earth. Throughout my youth and early manhood, I had dreamed almost daily of following, more or less literally, in the footsteps of Darwin or Waterton; and though my own travels had been considerably more modest than theirs, I had made forays sufficiently gruelling and fruitful – into the Camargue, across the Pyrenees – to convince myself that my ambition wasn't entirely unrealistic.

What I suppose I lacked was precisely that obstinacy I so much admired in my heroes. At all events, in the years after my parents' early deaths I lapsed first into trivial habits of mind and then into a form of melancholia – a deep-seated ache or longing that I learned to dull with occasional doses of laudanum and regular recourse to the good red wines laid down by my father for a future he had no doubt imagined he would live to enjoy. I continued to add new specimens to my collection, I contributed notes and articles to minor periodicals; but the invigorating dreams – those vivid fantasies of exploration and discovery – were put aside like childhood toys.

I might ascribe my loss of vision to the more sombre

view of reality that comes with experience or, more specifically, to the responsibilities I rather unwillingly shouldered when I inherited the estate. Neither explanation is misleading in itself, but both skirt the darker truths of my inward life – the passions nursed in secret, the delicate liaisons screened from public view. What had begun as a sentimental camaraderie tinged with philanthropy (I would give the boys this, I thought, I would give them that – a few shillings, an education, eternal friendship) became an obsession, drawing me deep into some shadowy world of troubled pleasure and stifled aspiration.

What was I looking for, stalking my prey across the bright meadows or leaning over the bridge with assumed nonchalance, waiting in breathless ambush while the waters churned and boiled beneath me? The cynic's answer is too simple, too obvious. I was, after all, the gentlest of predators, subsisting for long periods on the most rarefied diet – a glance, a greeting, an inept pleasantry (Nathan Farr, lazing in the March sunlight with his back against the churchyard wall, looking up at me from beneath his unruly fringe: 'We're alike, Mr Redbourne, gentlemen of leisure' – the suggestion of fraternity, of easy complicity, haunting me for days). What was it – I mean, what was it precisely – that I had in mind? And what outcome could I possibly have anticipated but humiliation and disgrace?

Despite the pain from my leg, my thinking seemed unusually lucid, as though the shock of the night's events had purged my mind of its customary clutter. I could see clearly that my situation was all but untenable and that decisive action was required; it followed from that – since staying put could hardly be accounted decisive unless I were prepared to face my accusers in the open – that I should have to distance myself from the village, almost certainly for some appreciable time. And the moment the idea presented itself, I was gripped by a subdued but unmistakable excitement: the old ambition again, but now in more resolute form. I should travel, I should add significantly to my collection and I should contribute my quota to the sum of human knowledge. That was how I formulated my intentions; and as I did so, I was struck by the thought that what had been a bright but insubstantial dream had now transformed itself into a plan of action.

I saw at once that there were practical matters to be addressed. Firstly, and most importantly, I had no available funds; and secondly, I should have to find a competent steward to manage the estate in my absence. However, I had some confidence that the necessary finances could be found reasonably close to home, while the fact that my own management of the estate had in recent years proved considerably less than competent inclined me to view the second matter as an opportunity rather than an impediment.

I was so taken by the apt simplicity of it all that I began, in imagination, to pack for my voyage. That to be left, this to be taken – and this, and this, nets and collecting-boxes, coats and collar-studs, books and papers, my mind running freely over my belongings until, quite unexpectedly, it faltered and stuck.

The photographs. What about the photographs? I rose

awkwardly to my feet, limped over to the wardrobe and took the heavy portfolio from its hiding-place. *Village Types: a Photographic Record* – the title, neatly inscribed in violet ink on the front cover, was intentionally misleading. There had been half a dozen sitters but, in truth, only one type: a young man somewhere between fifteen and eighteen years of age, well muscled and firm-featured, with a certain unreflective openness in his gaze. A representative record had never, in fact, been my aim. I was, as collectors phrase it, a specialist.

I set the portfolio on my bedside table and untied the fastening, feeling again the familiar quickening of the pulse, the flickering thrill of guilty anticipation. Yet the portraits were, I reminded myself as I leafed through them, innocuous enough. Luke Wainwright, perhaps divining something of the nature of my interest but more probably prompted by his own notorious self-regard, had stripped to the waist for his sitting, squaring up to the camera like a prizefighter; but all the others sat or stood in their shirt-sleeves, informally posed against the plain white wall which, I had realised from the beginning, set off to perfection their tanned features and the strong outlines of their lightly clothed bodies.

No, the meaning of the portraits wasn't to be found in the images themselves, but in the memories they enshrined: the sharp reek of sweat as I helped Matty Turner out of his jacket, my face so close to his sunburned neck that I might easily have put my lips to it; my fingers resting lightly on Luke's shoulder as I showed him how to look through the view lens or, more audaciously, brushing the inside of Nathan Farr's thigh as I leaned over him to adjust the angle of his chair.

I'd touched Nathan, yes, and one or two others besides, but neither those fleeting moments of physical contact nor the earnest, oblique and largely one-sided discussions that had led up to them would have been sufficient in themselves to keep me in thrall to Blaney and his mob. Whatever power my persecutors might have exercised under cover of darkness, I should probably have faced them down in public if it hadn't been for Daniel.

Daniel, poor, bewildered Daniel, skulking aimlessly in all weathers through the narrow lanes around the village, afraid to return to a house in which cuffs, punches and worse were meted out more regularly than meals by a mother whose name was a local byword for erratic and unreasonable behaviour; Daniel, whose hooded gaze and pinched, melancholy features had drawn me into territory far darker and more dangerous than any I had negotiated in the company of his handsome confreres. The fact that those boys hadn't needed me had been a perverse part of their charm; Daniel's need, on the other hand, had been urgent, palpable. He had clung to me – sometimes literally – like a frightened child in a storm and I, for my part, had responded with a tenderness of which I had not, up to that point, believed myself capable.

Tenderness? That's the word that comes most readily to mind, though I sense how much it leaves unacknowledged – the relentless cycles of longing and shame, the corrosive despair undermining every look, protestation or act. And yet the word holds good.

I had set him apart from the others, folded in a sheet of cream-coloured paper at the back of the portfolio, and now I searched him out: a single portrait, a little under-exposed, emphasising the hollows beneath the sharp cheekbones, the shadows around the deep-set eyes. The photograph had been taken at Daniel's instigation, not my own, and had borne out my intuitive suspicion that his beauty was a thing too delicate and equivocal to be captured by the camera. Sullen, tense and slightly stooped, he looked out at me with the fixed stare that had always seemed to hold some unspoken challenge or reproach, and now frankly unsettled me. Smudged death's-head: Daniel as *memento mori*, Daniel leaning forward, thin lips parted, to remind me of the night I'd let him go.

A foul night, rain sluicing down, the wind thrashing the untended laurels in the shrubbery and buffeting the house. I had been dozing in front of the fire, a book open on my lap, when I heard a soft tapping at the window. Daniel peering in, his white face an inch from the blurred pane. I lurched to my feet and hurried to open the front door.

'What is it, Daniel? What are you doing here?'

No answer. He stood blinking in the muted light of the hallway, his black locks plastered to his cheeks, rain-water pooling at his feet. I could hear Latham moving slowly along the corridor at the back of the house.

'Come through.' I ushered Daniel into the study and helped him out of his sodden greatcoat. His shirt, scarcely less wet than the coat, clung to his thin shoulders. He moved over to the fire and stood on the hearthrug staring into the flames, pale and tremulous, his arms folded across his chest. I draped his coat over the back of the nearest chair.

'Are you ill?' I asked.

'I'm well enough. No thanks to you, though, treating me the way you do.'

I was taken aback, both by the accusation itself and the asperity of his tone.

'What do you mean?'

'You know what I mean. You keep me out there like an old dog in a kennel.'

'Hardly a kennel, Daniel. The cottage is more than large enough for you. You've coals in the grate, food on the table, a warm bed—'

'And not much else. It's no life for a human soul, holed up out there in the woods with no company but owls and flittermice.'

'A better life, I'd have thought, than the alternative. Would you rather be back with your mother?'

A long silence and then, surlily: 'I was waiting for you. You hadn't said you weren't coming.'

'The weather, Daniel. Surely you weren't expecting me to come out on a night like this?'

He spread his hands, holding them wide and a little towards me, a gesture all the more poignant for its clumsy theatricality. 'Why not? After all, I came out to see you.'

I stepped forward, meaning to take him in my arms, but a sudden clattering from the far end of the house reminded me of Latham's presence and I started guiltily, stifled the impulse. Daniel eyed me narrowly. 'You don't want me in here, do you? Not where you live. Only out there, where you can choose to visit me or not, as you see fit.'

The observation was more accurately perceptive than I cared to admit. I hesitated an instant too long, and Daniel pounced. 'It's true, isn't it? Even now, you're wondering how to get me out of the house.'

'Come now, Daniel. You know that's nonsense.'

'Is it?' He fixed me with his challenging stare. 'In that case, I'll stay.'

'It's not as easy as that. I shall have to make arrangements.'

'Arrangements? What arrangements would you have to make? You live alone in a house with more rooms than a family of ten could make use of, and you can't find space for a friend.'

He was working himself into a passion, a hint of colour rising to his cheeks. I could see clearly enough the risks involved in letting him stay, but I could see, too, that outright rejection might well fan his anger to an uncontrollable blaze.

'Some other time,' I said. 'Maybe next week.'

'Tonight,' he said fiercely. 'I want to stay tonight.'

It struck me then that Daniel had determined, perhaps long before setting out for the Hall that night, to put me to a test I could hardly be expected to pass. His dark eyes glittered with a wild exultation and I sensed that nothing would please him more, at that particular moment, than to tear apart the delicate, precarious structure we had created. Youth tends to seek resolution and truth; maturity knows with what compromises and half-truths our irresolute lives must be shored up. I reached out and gently touched his arm.

'Leave it now, Daniel. We can talk tomorrow.'

'You're sending me away, aren't you? Just like I said.' He brushed my hand aside, gestured towards the streaming panes. 'Sending me out in weather you'd not walk abroad in yourself – not for my sake, anyway. And if I catch my death—'

'Keep your voice down. Listen, I'll walk back with you.'

'Damned if I'll let you.' He lunged forward, snatched his wet coat from the chair-back and was out in the hallway before I had time to think of stopping him. I followed, to find him wrestling with the heavy bolt on the front door.

Even now, it cuts me clean to the heart to think of it. As the bolt slammed back in its groove, he half turned and looked up at me over his shoulder. The dangerous glitter was gone from his eyes, replaced by an expression of bewilderment and helpless entreaty. If I had wanted to hold him back, to hold him close, that was the moment to do so.

Anything would have served – a word, a gesture, the merest touch. I did nothing; I said nothing. And Daniel turned away again, wrenched open the door and stepped out into the dark.

I set the portrait to one side and turned my attention to the others. In retrospect my action seems freighted with significance, yet I'm not aware of having given a great deal of thought to it. I simply leaned forward and fed the photographs into the fire, singly at first and then, as the flames took hold, in thin sheaves. I remember the heat on the back of my outstretched hand, the smell of singed hair in the air; yes, and the way the lovely faces warped and darkened in the instant before the flames consumed them.

As the blaze died down, I turned back to Daniel's photograph. I should like to be able to say that what followed was a gesture of love, or at least of loyalty; but in preserving something of the image – a little oval, roughly snipped out with my mother's rusted sewing scissors, head and shoulders, like a ragged cameo – I was actually responding to darker promptings. Treat me as you treated them, the rigid stare seemed to say, and you'll be sorry. I'm not sure that I saw the matter so clearly at the time, but this was an act of propitiation, a sop to Daniel's aggrieved and possibly vengeful spirit. I slipped the scrap between the leaves of my pocket-book before consigning the remainder of the photograph to the flames.

There was more to be done. I returned to the wardrobe and withdrew the negative plates – six small maroon boxes, each representing a different sitting, a new obsession. I opened each box in turn, tipping its contents into the hearth; then I set to with the handle of the poker, methodically at first but with increasing wildness, the shards of dark glass flying about my hands as I worked. Only when every plate had been shattered beyond hope of recognition or repair did I pause for breath.

It was then that I began to cry, the tears coursing down my face as I squatted there in the hot afterglow of the blaze. Crying for Daniel, of course, for the poor soul lost in the drenching dark, but not for him alone. My tears were for myself too, for the chastened dreamer hunkered among the splinters of his own unsustainable illusions; and for those other lost ones, the beautiful boys already slipping away into unremarkable manhood in worlds utterly remote from my own.

The throbbing in my leg had become almost intolerable. I took the hearth-brush and shovel from the stand and tidied up as best I could. Then I poured myself a generous measure of brandy, knocked it quickly back and retired to bed.

3

I remember hearing the clock in the hallway strike four as I slipped between the sheets, and then nothing more until Latham came up with my shaving-water at eight. I rose on my elbow as he entered, and a flash of pain shot through my leg from shin to hip. I groaned softly and sank back against the pillows.

'If you'd prefer to sleep a little longer, sir . . .'

'Thank you, Latham, but I have matters to attend to. Is there any post?'

'No, sir, but an odd thing . . .' He set down the ewer, fumbled in his pocket and produced, with as much of a flourish as his stiff joints allowed, my silver cigarette case. 'From the garden. The girl found it by the flowerbed when she arrived for her duties this morning. And one of the lamps out there too, smashed to smithereens. I thought the house must have been burgled – there's a pane broken in the study – but we've gone over the downstairs rooms from end to end, and there's no sign anything's been so much as breathed on.'

'No, it was a matter of far less consequence – just a few lads up from the village looking for mischief. One of them shied a stone through the window and when I gave chase I stumbled and fell. No great harm done, though I imagine the flowerbed may be looking a little the worse for wear.'

'Your smoking-jacket too, sir – caked with mud. I'll have it seen to.' He placed the cigarette case gently on the bedside table and reached the jacket down from the back of the door. 'Look at this,' he said, lifting the sleeve between finger and thumb and holding up the filthy underside for my inspection. There was a hint of reproach in his voice, as though I were still the troublesome child he had once had to swab down in the stableyard after a wet afternoon's fossil-hunting in the local quarry.

'Get Mrs Garrett to attend to it after breakfast.' I eased myself gingerly up the bed and leaned back against the headboard. 'And I'd be grateful if you'd ask the girl to make arrangements for the reglazing when she returns to the village. I have business in London and I don't expect to be back before Friday.'

Latham stepped over to the window and drew back

the curtains. I leaned forward, swivelling towards the light, and the pain flared again, making me grimace and catch my breath. He returned to my bedside and stared down at me, his thin face creased with concern. 'With respect, sir, I think you should postpone your journey. You don't look fit to travel.'

'I'm well enough. Perhaps a little more shaken by my fall than I'd thought.'

'If you'd like me to send for Dr Griffiths—'

'There's no need. I shall leave immediately after breakfast.'

'You'll miss the early train, sir.'

'Then I shall take the next.'

'If you insist, sir.' He draped my jacket carefully over his forearm and withdrew without another word.

My uncle's house was barely fifteen minutes' walk from my hotel, but my leg was aching and the sky threatened rain, and it seemed sensible to take a cab. The city, I thought, as we bowled down Tottenham Court Road, was even more crowded and more frenetically busy than I remembered, and I was glad when the cab swung off down Bedford Avenue and into the quieter reaches of Bloomsbury.

The exterior of the house gave little indication of my uncle's wealth and status. Less recently painted than either of its immediate neighbours, it seemed to give off a faint air of gloom although, looking up as I stepped down from the cab, I could see the soft flicker of firelight reflected from the ceiling of a first-floor room. I paid the driver, limped up the front steps and rang the bell, hearing its muffled clang reverberating upward from some basement room or passage.

My uncle Joshua – my father's younger brother – was a banker by profession, but had accumulated most of his considerable fortune through shrewd investment in land and housing on the northern fringe of the expanding city. More successful than my father, he was also generally reckoned to be appreciably less scrupulous. A vicious scoundrel, my mother once called him in the course of an ill-tempered conversation with my father as we awaited his arrival one summer afternoon, and I remember very clearly the shock of her uncharacteristically scathing judgement, as well as the subsequent loosening of a family connection I had imagined, in my childish innocence, to be unshakeable. My uncle was never, I think, barred from the house, but he must have recognised at some point that he was unwelcome there. At all events, some time around my sixteenth year his visits ceased altogether.

Yet this sketch, I realise, misses the essential point. For, whatever else he may have been, my uncle was also the man who fanned to a flame my childhood interest in the natural world, taking me with him on his long, meandering excursions, answering my incessant questions with genuine erudition and exemplary patience, revealing what lay hidden behind the dazzling surfaces of things. I can see him now, twisting back a spray of privet to show me the hawk-moth larva clasping the stem, or withdrawing from the dark interior of a hawthorn hedge the pale, translucent egg of a linnet.

For two or three years after he had ceased to visit, we

maintained a regular correspondence. I remember the impatience, faintly tinged with guilt, with which I used to wait for his long, detailed letters – meticulous descriptions of specimens newly received from collectors in remote regions, affectionate recollections of our own excursions and general advice more accessible and more pertinent than any I can recall hearing from my father. And my replies were equally warm and full, quite different in tone from the dutiful letters I dispatched to my parents during the school term or the flippant chronicles of home life sent, during the vacations, to my schoolfellows. Only in writing to my uncle did I feel that the words on the page were in harmony with my deepest and most serious thoughts.

And perhaps it was some subtle embarrassment at my own openness with him which, as I grew to manhood, insinuated itself between us. At all events our correspondence shrank, during the course of my nineteenth or twentieth year, from a flow to a bare trickle, and the fault undoubtedly lay with me. I would put aside his letters to be answered later and then forget them for weeks on end, eventually responding with a hasty note and the promise of a fuller reply when time allowed. But time, for reasons my uncle may have understood more clearly than I, never did allow.

The door was opened by a manservant so coldly formal in his bearing and so supercilious in his manner that I wondered for a moment whether the telegram I had sent to announce my visit might have gone astray. 'I'm Charles Redbourne,' I said. 'I believe – I hope – that my uncle is expecting me.'

'Indeed.' He led me up the stairway, stopped outside one of the front rooms and knocked gently. There was a brief pause, and then the door swung open.

I hadn't seen my uncle since the day of my father's funeral, and though I should have recognised him anywhere, it was apparent that the intervening years had not dealt kindly with him. His tall frame was stooped, and he seemed to hold up his head with difficulty. The skin of his face was slack, and pale as tallow; his eyes were dark in their hollow sockets. As he took my hand I could feel the distortion of his arthritic fingers and the weakness of their grip. He drew me forward and pushed the door shut behind me.

The room was large and well lit, furnished richly but with the restraint characteristic of an earlier and less assertive age. No clutter: just two fireside chairs, a low mahogany tea-table, an inlaid bureau and a wooden chest carved in high relief with scenes from the Greek myths. The carpet, I noticed, as my uncle propelled me gently towards the hearth, was unusually soft and thick.

'You're limping, Charles. Not your father's trouble, I hope.'

'I've been spared the gout. The limp is the result of a recent gardening accident. Nothing serious.'

'Apt punishment for undermining the order of things. If you want my advice, I suggest you leave the gardening to those who are employed to do it. Half of society's ills might be averted if men knew their appointed places, and it's our duty – the duty of our class – to lead by example. When I ring this bell' – he leaned over and tugged at the tasselled bell-pull beside the chimney-breast – 'Mrs

Fraser will put three spoonfuls of Darjeeling into the pot and fill it with scalding water. There's nothing difficult about the task, and I'm perfectly capable of doing it myself. I've no doubt that, if I were obliged to do so, I could eventually lay my hands on the milk-jug, the sugar-bowl and the best china. But my point is that nobody's interests would be served by such an intervention, neither Mrs Fraser's nor mine. Gardening is for garden-ers, Charles; our part is to enjoy the fruits of their labours.'

He motioned me to one of the chairs and seated himself in the other, holding his crooked hands to the blaze. 'And what brings you,' he asked abruptly, with a hint of asperity, 'knocking on my door?'

'It struck me that we had become strangers to one another. And because I regard you as pre-eminent among those who influenced my early intellectual develop-ment—'

'Thank you, but perhaps a little plain speaking would be in order. As you can imagine, your visit comes as something of a surprise.'

'Not too much of a surprise, I hope. My telegram—'

'Come now, Charles, your visit can hardly be ac-counted less surprising for having been announced five hours in advance. You don't write to me – not a word in the past three years and no more than half a dozen carelessly scrawled pages in the past fifteen – and then you turn up on my doorstep with the air of a man who wants something. I'll tell you now, my will has already been drawn up.'

The barb, delivered with only the faintest suggestion

of humour, struck sufficiently close to the mark to disturb my composure. I sank back into my chair and cleared my throat.

'It's true,' I began carefully, 'that I'm here to request a favour, but I'm also offering something in return.'

'Forgive me, Charles, but when you've spent as many years in the world of business as I have, you develop a peculiarly sensitive nose for what's in the wind. I can tell without hearing another word that, whatever you're offering, your proposal is likely to serve your own interests far better than it will serve mine. That said, I'm willing to listen. Tell me what you have in mind.'

This was not at all the conversation I had imagined as I travelled up. I had convinced myself that my uncle, delighted to see me after so many years, would be doubly delighted when he heard my proposal. The idea that the man who had set me on the path of scientific enquiry should subsequently provide me with the funds for an important collecting trip had seemed so apposite that I had scarcely troubled to examine it. Now I was mumbling, stammering, losing my thread, like a schoolboy called upon to explain himself to an unsympathetic master.

'And of course,' I heard myself saying, 'the specimens – such as you needed for your own collection . . . I mean, it's understood that I should be collecting on your behalf as well as my own, and any significant discovery—'

'Have you no funds of your own? Your father left you tolerably well provided for.'

'He left me the estate.'

'And, if I remember correctly, a substantial proportion of his savings.'

I shifted uncomfortably beneath his gaze. 'The fact is,' I said, 'that I've handled my financial affairs rather badly. The sum in question has been seriously depleted.'

'Depleted?'

I felt my face grow hot. 'There's nothing left,' I said. 'Nothing at all. And the income from my tenants barely pays my bills.'

'Then your proposed journey would seem singularly ill-timed.' He leaned suddenly towards me, his eyes searching mine. 'You're not in any kind of trouble, are you, Charles?'

The particular predicament in which I found myself would not, perhaps, have diminished my standing in my uncle's eyes and it might have been preferable in some respects to have made a clean breast of it, but I could see that anything less than a firm denial risked leading our discussion off at a tangent to my central concern. 'No,' I said. 'I've decided that this is the moment to go. That's all there is to it.'

A soft tapping at the door heralded the arrival of the tea, borne on a silver tray by a diminutive maidservant. The girl placed her burden on the table and stood at my uncle's elbow, her eyes downcast. He looked up sharply and waved her away. 'That will be all, thank you, Alice. We'll attend to it.'

She gave a little bob and withdrew, her footfall almost silent on the thick carpet. As the door clicked shut behind her, my uncle turned back to me and resumed his questioning. 'Has it occurred to you that you might sell part of the estate?'

'I'd rather not.'

'Of course you'd rather not. But when the alternative is to come cap in hand to relatives who have managed their affairs more wisely than you appear to have done, selling would seem perhaps the sounder option and certainly the more gentlemanly one. I'm sorry, Charles, but I'm at a loss to understand your thinking on this matter. And besides . . .' He lifted the lid of the teapot and stirred the brew. 'Will you take milk with your tea?'

I nodded. 'You were about to say something.'

He was silent, apparently preoccupied with the matter in hand. I sat back and waited.

'There was a time,' he said at last, handing me my cup, 'when I dreamed of being able to help you in some way – of being in a position to offer you the support a father might offer his son. But in those days you were not fatherless, and by the time you were, you had turned your back on me.'

His phrasing was a little melodramatic for my taste, but it was impossible to dispute the essential fact. I sat staring into my teacup, listening to the rain driving against the window-panes. After a moment, my uncle rose to his feet and crossed to the bureau. He opened the top drawer and drew out a bulging file.

'Do you know what these are?' he asked, bending back the cover to reveal a thick sheaf of papers. He returned to his seat and flicked through them, eventually extracting two sheets, held together at the corner by a rusted dressmaker's pin. He leaned forward with an odd, tight-lipped smile and handed them to me.

There is something strangely disconcerting about being confronted with one's own letters, particularly when those letters belong to the period of childhood or youth. The careful schoolroom script seemed simultaneously alien and familiar, and though I knew at once that I was holding a fragment of my own past, I was slow to acknowledge the fact.

'Do you remember writing that?' He was staring intently at my face. 'Look at the second page.'

I folded back the top sheet and scanned it quickly.

. . . deserving of my gratitude, since you have been a second father to me, a second father and more. More, because you have also been friend and tutor, and I dare say that what you have taught me on our walks together will prove more important to my future life than anything I have learned in school. If I ever make a name for myself as a natural scientist – and I am more than ever convinced that that is my true vocation – my success will be due in large measure to you.

There was another paragraph in similar vein. The whole passage, I noticed, had been marked with two parallel pencil-lines in the right-hand margin of the page. 'Yes,' I said uneasily. 'Yes, I remember.'

He tapped the file. 'They're all here,' he said. 'All of your letters to me, from the first to the last. An object lesson in the callous ways of the world.'

'That seems a little harsh,' I said, struggling to suppress my anger.

He shrugged. 'Life is harsh,' he answered, and with the words he sagged suddenly in his chair, his sallow face creased with grief. Tears gathered and fell, the slow, unimpassioned tears of the old.

'I meant what I wrote,' I said. And then, with regret, sympathy and cunning so finely blended as to confuse even myself: 'I'm sorry to have disappointed you, Uncle, but the arrangement I'm proposing may go some way towards making amends. I should be glad to think that in adding to your collection I was also doing something to restore the connection between us.'

He drew a large linen handkerchief from his pocket and dabbed at his eyes. 'The collection,' he said quietly, 'is neither here nor there. Think about it, Charles. I'm seventy-one years old. There's not a single organ in my body that works as it should, and the various passions that serve to keep a man alive are all gone. Sometimes at night, when the house is quiet, I drift upstairs like the ghost of my younger self and take a few choice specimens from my cabinets. I stare at them, I finger them, I put them back again. Whatever glamour they once seemed to possess is lost. Dead matter, Charles – rows of stiffened skins in an old man's attic. Why should I add to their number?'

'Then you won't help me?'

In the stillness I could hear the cluck and gurgle of rainwater from the gutters below. My uncle placed his gnarled hands on his knees and gazed down at them for a long time as though lost in contemplation of his own decrepitude.

'I'm prepared to pay your passage to Australia,' he said at last.

It was not a destination I had considered. Although I had not thought very carefully about the matter, it was South America I had had in mind. I was about to say as much when it struck me that I would do better to hold my tongue.

'I know a fellow,' he continued, 'who can help you. Edward Vane – owns a substantial property just outside Sydney. A very substantial property indeed. Large house, extensive grounds, acres of grazing. He's made more in twenty years – mainly from coal and shale-oil – than I've made in a lifetime. But the point is' – he lowered his voice, though it was inconceivable that any of the servants could have overheard him – 'that he owes his fortune to me.'

He leaned back in his chair and ran his hand wearily across his eyes. 'I'll leave if you're tired,' I said. 'I can return tomorrow.'

He gave no indication of having heard me. 'We were close in those days,' he said, 'Vane and I. I mean, during his early months in London. He had come to the city with the express intention of making his fortune here, and I've no doubt his life would have unfolded exactly as he'd planned it if he hadn't been knocked off course by a woman. The usual story – passion, pregnancy, a hasty marriage on an inadequate income. She was a Cornish girl, a sweet enough thing but very dreamy and delicate, and not the slightest use to him. And, of course, she brought no money with her, none at all.'

'But you provided for them?'

'Eventually, yes. I don't mind telling you, Charles, I felt betrayed. I'd given Vane my friendship and assistance, introducing him into circles that would otherwise have remained closed to him, and it seemed to me he'd proved himself unworthy of my attentions. For a while I refused to have anything to do with him. But as time went on, I began to realise that I might have been unduly hard on him. And one morning I met him in the street, very pale and downcast, with his wife on his arm, and for the first and perhaps the only time in my life I was moved to an act of charity. There and then I told him that I would put a sum of money at his disposal so that he might make a fresh start elsewhere. That sum of money was the cornerstone of his fortune, and though he repaid it long ago, I know for a fact that he still considers himself in debt to me. When do you propose to leave?'

The question, characteristically incisive and practical, caught me completely off my guard. 'As soon as I've made the necessary arrangements,' I answered evasively.

'Two months? Three?'

I was suddenly and acutely aware of my own unpreparedness for the venture. Twenty-four hours earlier I had had no notion of going anywhere; now I was poised to embark on a voyage to the far side of the world. I felt my innards tighten, tasted the tea's bitterness at the back of my tongue.

'Longer,' I said. 'I shall need longer.'

'Well, let me know when matters become clearer and I'll write to Vane, informing him of your plans. I've no doubt that you'll benefit both from his hospitality and his connections.' He leaned back in his chair as though to suggest that our business was at an end.

'Thank you, Uncle.' I glanced through the window at

the darkening sky. 'It's time I left,' I said, rising to my feet. He rose with me, moving beside me through the gloom, but stopped at the door as though loath to let me go.

'I'm sorry we've become such strangers to one another,' he said.

'That can be remedied in time.'

'Perhaps, though time isn't a commodity I'd care to speculate on these days. You're no longer so very young yourself, Charles, if I may say so. I take it you're still a bachelor.'

'Yes. I've thought now and then that a wife and family would give direction to my life, but I've never met a woman I felt I might be able to love. Over the years, I've come to regard myself as temperamentally unsuited to marriage.'

'Love,' he said with a dismissive little gesture, 'is neither here nor there. A man is not obliged to love his wife. He provides for her, and she for him. And those of us who resist marriage – because they can't love, because they value their liberty, because they consider themselves unsuited – would do well to think carefully about the alternative while they're still in a position to make choices. Companionless old age, Charles – I don't recommend it. Naturally, I try to convince myself that I chose wisely, but if I could turn back the clock, knowing what I know now, I believe I should choose differently.'

'It may be that in matters of that kind the choice isn't ours to make.'

He seemed to consider this for a moment, his head drooping on his thin neck. I felt the grief and loneliness coming off him like the stink from a street-beggar, and I shifted uncomfortably to and fro until he raised his eyes again.

'You may stay here if you wish,' he said. 'The guest-room's not much used nowadays but I could have it made ready in no time.'

'Thank you, Uncle, but I've left my belongings at the hotel. I shall call again on Friday, if I may, before I leave town.'

It struck me, as we walked down to the hallway, that my refusal might have offended him; but as we reached the door his face broke into a weary smile, and he ushered me out with a gesture as delicately solicitous as if the linnet's egg still nestled there in the hollow of his upturned palm.

II

4

A little over an hour's ride from the harbour and set in spacious, well-managed grounds, Tresillian Villa amply confirmed my uncle's claim that Edward Vane was a man of substance. Meeting me on the quayside, he had seemed awkward and unimpressive, and our conversation as we journeyed out of Sydney had been strained, but as the carriage entered the drive and approached the house he seemed to puff up like a courting pigeon, suddenly amiable and expansive, his broad features animated by a boyish eagerness. He barely gave the horses time to come to a standstill before flinging back the door and leaping out, appreciably nimbler on his feet than, considering his bulk, one might have expected.

Standing on the quayside earlier, in the shadow of the rust-coloured warehouses, I had hardly been aware of the heat and we had travelled, rather to my disappointment, with the blinds half down; now, stepping from the carriage on to the shimmering drive, I felt the full force of the December sun. I stood blinking, a little unsteady, the perspiration breaking out on my face and body.

Vane turned to give instructions to a pair of servants and then took me by the elbow and walked me down the sloping lawn. 'This is the finest view of the villa,' he said, turning me so that we looked back up the slope towards the front entrance, 'and for my money the finest view in the colony.' The remark was accompanied by a sidelong smile in my direction, but I sensed that it would be unwise to treat it simply as a joke.

Certainly the villa was imposing, though not entirely to my taste. It was an odd hybrid, the house itself brick-built along essentially modern lines, but fronted by an incongruous stucco portico in the Palladian style. The effect of structural incoherence was heightened by the stable-block, which had been tacked on to the side of the house in such a way as to unbalance the whole of the front elevation. Even so, the building had its attractions: I was particularly taken by the generous proportions of the windows and by the railed verandah, raised a couple of feet above the level of the terrace and festooned with swags of mauve wisteria flowers.

I sensed that my host was waiting for my response.

'What a house,' I said, 'and what a prospect. You're a fortunate man, Vane.'

He turned to face me, beaming broadly. 'Well, Redbourne,' he said, 'we're a long way from England but I think we can offer you something of what you're accustomed to.'

There was, in fact, all the difference in the world between this luminous panorama – the wide lawns washed in sunlight, the little grove of citrus trees, the elegant eucalypts shimmering beyond – and my own shadowy wilderness of an estate, but I saw no reason to say so.

'I'm sure I shall be very comfortable here. If your men have finished attending to my luggage, I wonder if you'd be good enough to show me to my room? I'm in need of a wash and a change of clothing.'

'I've asked Mrs Denman to prepare a bath. If you'll follow me . . .' He led the way towards the house and was about to usher me up the front steps when the door was flung back and a girl stepped out and stood in front of us, staring down, her eyes narrowed against the sunlight.

If it hadn't been for the assurance of her stance and her unabashed gaze, I might have taken her for one of the servants. Her face was tanned, and her thick brown hair had been pinned back with a carelessness that, if not exactly slatternly, hardly suggested good breeding. Her clothing, though clean and reasonably neat, had evidently been chosen for comfort rather than elegance, and as she came down the steps towards us, I was struck by the natural fluency of her movements. Although she seemed, to judge from her face and figure, to stand on the threshold of womanhood, she moved with the ease of a child, swaying a little from the waist, her feet light and quick on the hot steps.

'My daughter, Eleanor,' said Vane.

Eleanor came to a halt on the bottom step and placed her hand fleetingly in mine. 'I'm pleased to meet you, Mr Redbourne,' she said. 'I hope you've had a good journey.' And then, barely waiting for my answer and with the air of having discharged a slightly tiresome duty, she made off across the lawn towards the citrus grove.

'You'll find Eleanor somewhat lacking in the social graces,' said Vane apologetically as he ushered me into the house, 'but I hope you'll make allowances.' He guided me up the staircase and along a dim corridor, stopping outside the last of four identical doors and pushing it open. 'This is your room,' he said. 'Mrs Denham will let you know when your bath is ready. I need hardly say that I should like you to be as easy here as if you were in your own home. If there's anything you need, you've only to ask. I shall look forward to continuing our conversation in due course.'

I could see at once that my new quarters were remarkably spacious, and not merely by comparison with the cramped and dingy cabin I had grown accustomed to over the preceding weeks. The room was, in fact, considerably larger than my bedroom at home, and far more pleasingly appointed. The bed was high and wide, the coverlet printed with a bold, modern design. Between the two large windows stood a writing-desk, equipped with ink, blotter and an array of pens; against the opposite wall, a heavy washstand, topped with a thick slab of pale, veined marble. The lower sashes of the windows had been raised, and the scent of flowers, sweet and faintly peppery, wafted in on the warm air, mingling with the smell of the polished furniture and floorboards. I sat on the edge of the bed, breathing deeply and waiting, without impatience, for Mrs Denham to call me.

I took my time over my bath, and then shaved with particular care, leaning close to the wall-mirror and persisting with the task until I was satisfied that my skin was as smooth as the razor could make it. And as I stepped away, wiping the blade on my towel, I was struck by something unexpected in my own reflected image, something that drew me back to examine it more carefully.

It had been a long time since I had looked at my face with any pleasure. As a schoolboy I had considered myself tolerably handsome, but my appearance had not, by and large, improved with age. True, I had been blessed with the Redbourne brow – an ample forehead which, still clear and unfurrowed in middle life, had continued to give my face some semblance of nobility; but my jawline, never a strong feature, had grown increasingly fleshy and indeterminate with the passing years, while my eyes had lost the gleam of youth without acquiring any of the compensatory qualities usually associated with maturity. Now, however, no doubt as a result of the abstemious regimen I had adopted during the voyage – a sparer diet, enforced at first by seasickness and continued by choice, the daily bottle or two of claret reduced to a single glass – my features had become leaner and more resolute, my gaze clear and steady. My hair, untrimmed since my departure, had thickened into a leonine mane, the streaks of grey at the temples barely discernible among the mass of darker curls; and looking into the mirror in the sharp white light of that uncluttered bathroom I felt a surge of elation as though I were re-encountering, after long separation, a well-loved but half-forgotten companion.

There was more to it than this, of course. Although I had come to realise, during the months of planning and preparation following my visit to my uncle, that I was in no further danger from Blaney and his mob, there were signs that my standing in the village had been seriously undermined. Sitting in my pew on a Sunday morning or strolling through the lanes around the Hall, I had noticed how reluctantly the villagers' eyes met mine, how hollowly their greetings rang in my ears. Imagination? In part, perhaps; but little by little I had become obsessed by the notion that I should need to refashion myself, heart and soul, if I were ever to regain any degree of authority in the one corner of the world I could call my own. Australia was to be the crucible in which I should be made new. My arrival there was an event of extraordinary personal significance and my elation a natural response to the beguiling suggestion that, after years of inertia, I was once more in command of my own destiny.

I dressed with what I imagined was appropriate informality but, emerging on to the veranda, I discovered that Vane had divested himself of his jacket and necktie and was sitting at ease with his waistcoat unbuttoned.

He raised his eyes from his newspaper as I approached and looked me up and down as though appraising the cut of my suit.

'I'm not a man who stands on ceremony,' he said simply, giving me leave, as I took it, to remove my own jacket. I did so, and sat down beside him.

He was, I guessed, a little above my own age, though his face was scarcely lined and his lightly oiled hair almost untouched with grey. He might have been described as distinguished but there was a certain brutality in the set of his mouth and chin, noticeably at odds with the lively intelligence of his eyes. Almost a gentleman, as my father used to say of certain acquaintances: the double-edged phrase came back to me as my host wiped his shirt-sleeve across his brow and drew a monogrammed cigarette case from his waistcoat pocket.

'Will you have one?' he asked, flipping open the case and holding it out to me.

I shook my head. 'I haven't touched tobacco since leaving England,' I said, 'and I feel much the better for it.'

'My daughter would approve.' He glanced down the garden to where the girl reclined in the shade of a lemon tree, propped on one elbow, her book open on the grass before her. 'A filthy habit, she says, and one I should have had the strength of will to abandon years ago.' He lit up and drew deeply on his cigarette before resuming.

'Eleanor is an outspoken young lady, Redbourne, and I must warn you now not to expect genteel conversation from her. She's quick and clever – some might say too clever for her own good – but she presumes on the privileges of an indulged childhood. In the aftermath of her mother's death she seemed to need those privileges, but I've had cause in recent years to regret what I now see to have been a damaging lack of firmness in her upbringing. To put it bluntly, she appears to have no idea how to conduct herself in polite society, and no intention of learning.'

'There's plenty of time, Vane. She's still very young.'

'She's twenty years old.'

'Twenty? I must say, that surprises me. I'd have taken her to be three or four years younger.'

'You're not the first to be misled. And if she'd learn to bear herself more like a lady—'

'No, it's not that. Or not that alone. There's something about her features – some brightness or clarity of a kind that rarely persists far beyond childhood.'

'She has her mother's looks. I mean she's the very image. Sometimes, when I glance up suddenly from my work and she's there, reading perhaps, or just gazing into the air the way she does, it's my wife I see. That's really how it feels – as though I'd slipped back into the past and found her there waiting for me, just as she used to be.' He stubbed his cigarette savagely against the leg of his chair and flicked it away over the veranda rail. 'Believe me, Redbourne, it's no easy matter sharing the house with a girl who might be the walking spirit of her dead mother.'

'Even so,' I said, sensing his agitation and anxious to steer our conversation into calmer waters, 'you must be thankful that she has inherited those looks. Beauty isn't everything, but it's not a negligible gift.'

He shot me a swift glance. 'Joshua gave me to understand,' he said sharply, 'that you're not a ladies' man.'

It had not occurred to me either that my well-intentioned remark could have been construed as indicative of an unseemly interest in the girl, or that my uncle might have discussed my character in his correspondence with Vane. Caught off balance, I mumbled and stammered until my host, doubtless regretting both his rudeness and his indiscretion, came to my rescue. 'He also told me,' he said, tacking neatly about, 'that I should benefit greatly from your company and conversation, and I can see already that we shall hit it off together. Let me tell you, Redbourne, I consider myself extremely fortunate to have you here as my guest.' And at that moment, as if on cue, one of the maidservants stepped up behind us and announced that luncheon was served.

5

Luncheon was a protracted affair. Eleanor stayed only long enough to satisfy her hunger before returning to her reading in the shade of the citrus trees, but Vane clearly wanted to make an occasion of the meal, toasting my arrival in good wine and maintaining a constant and eventually exhausting flow of conversation. I sensed something of the emigrant's homesickness in his insistent questions about the country he had last seen more than twenty years earlier, and though I was naturally disposed to respond fully to his enquiries, I was relieved when he pushed away his coffee-cup and rose to his feet.

'I have business to attend to,' he said. 'It might wait until tomorrow but procrastination, as your uncle was fond of telling me, is the thief of time. It's a maxim I've lived by for many years, and I've found no reason' – he spread his hands in a gesture I understood to embrace the villa, the gardens and a good deal more besides – 'to doubt its essential wisdom.'

'Of course. Please don't disturb your routines on my account. I'm used to fending for myself, and I have business of my own. Assuming that my rifle is in reasonable order, I may as well begin this afternoon.'

'I wish you luck, but I'm afraid you'll find nothing remarkable hereabouts. Tomorrow I shall introduce you to Bullen. He'll take you further afield and show you what's what.' He chuckled softly, as if at some private joke. 'Quite a character, our Mr Bullen.'

'A local naturalist?'

'I don't know whether you'd call him a naturalist. He's not a particularly well educated man – not, by any stretch of the imagination, a scientist – but he has an eye for a rarity, and I know for a fact that several of the big collectors in Sydney regularly buy from him. He has made something of a name for himself in the region, though the Grail, as he calls it, has so far eluded him.'

'The Grail?'

'He wants to discover a new species of bird or mammal – thinks they'll name it after him. I can't understand it myself, but for him it's an obsession.'

I might have tried to explain, on Bullen's behalf, the nature and power of an obsession I understood only too well, but I sensed that my efforts would be wasted on

Vane. 'I'm sure,' I said, 'that we shall find we have a good deal in common, Mr Bullen and I. I look forward to meeting him.'

How easy it is, I thought, reflecting on Vane's words as I strolled later among the eucalypts, to dismiss as unremarkable the marvels that lie most immediately about us. To me, everything was new, and everything a source of wonder, from the vivid green mantis rocking slowly back and forth on its twig to the cockatoos that rose at my approach, lifting into the bright air like a host of raucous angels, their wings suffused with sunlight. There was brilliance there but also, I realised as I began to examine my surroundings more carefully, a remarkable subtlety: I was particularly struck by the delicate coloration of the woodland foliage – the greens more muted than ours but no less various, interfused with soft shades of grey and touched with pale metallic lustres. I was so entranced by my discoveries that for some considerable time I was content simply to observe, and it was with something like regret that, coming upon a small group of parrots feeding in the undergrowth, I eventually unslung my rifle.

My shot was not, I confess, a particularly good one, but one of the birds sat tight as the others scattered, and I knew at once that it had been hit. As I approached, it tried to launch itself into the air but fell flapping to the ground, beating the dust until it died. I lifted it up and wiped the blood from its beak with a leaf.

I had always felt a degree of confusion at such moments, but on this occasion the combination of sorrow and excitement was peculiarly unsettling. I remember pacing up and down, gazing through a film of tears at the curve of the slack neck, the brilliance of the ruffled plumage. Breast upward, the bird glowed rich crimson, its throat patched with blue of an almost equal intensity; as I turned it on to its front, letting its head hang forward over the edge of my palm, I saw how the crimson seemed to bleed between the darker wing-feathers, accentuating their contours with a boldness that reminded me of an Egyptian wall-painting I had once coveted.

'We call them lories,' said Vane when I showed him the bird on my return. He had evidently completed his business and was sitting on the veranda steps cleaning his nails with a small pocket-knife. 'Crimson lories. Ten a penny round these parts – though they're handsome enough creatures, I grant you.'

I replaced the body carefully in my satchel. 'I shall have to presume further on your hospitality,' I said. 'Do you have an outhouse where I might prepare my specimens?'

'There's the barn. Ideal for your purposes, though I shall have to conduct some rather delicate negotiations on your behalf.' He folded his knife, slipped it into his waistcoat pocket and hauled himself to his feet. 'Leave the matter in my hands.'

'When you say negotiations . . .?'

'With Eleanor. The barn is her studio.'

'She's an artist?'

'She likes to think so and, to tell the truth, she has a certain talent – though, as with so many things, she makes too much of it. Young women need something to keep their hands and minds busy – patchwork, sketching, embroidery, it doesn't matter what – and I've always encouraged her. But in recent years her art, as she insists on calling it, has become an unhealthy preoccupation. When the mood takes her she'll spend the entire day in the barn, refusing to let anyone in, hardly bothering to come out. She misses meals, or she comes to the table but won't speak, bolts her food and scampers away again, like a half-tamed animal.'

'It doesn't sound as though she'll welcome my company.'

'I can guarantee that she'll accept it. And it's just possible' – he gave a wry smile – 'that your presence will exert a civilising influence. Heaven knows, she's in need of it.'

'You flatter me,' I said lightly, 'but civilising influences certainly exist. Indeed, I shouldn't be at all surprised if she were to be taken off your hands within a year or two and exposed to the civilising influence of matrimony.'

I had intended the remark to be simultaneously humorous and reassuring, but Vane's expression darkened suddenly and I realised at once that I had struck entirely the wrong note. 'What I suggest,' he said abruptly, 'is that you leave me to settle matters with Eleanor. You might like to continue your exploration of the estate and return in twenty minutes or so.' He gestured vaguely up the drive, turned on his heel and marched into the house.

Twenty minutes would have seemed time enough, but as I turned the corner of the house and stepped up to the veranda, I heard Eleanor's voice ring out, shrill and raw, through the open windows of the day-room. 'If you won't listen to what I say, then why trouble to ask me? I'm telling you, I shan't be able to work with him sitting there.'

And then Vane's voice, half angry, half cajoling: 'He has work of his own, Eleanor. He'll not trouble you. And besides—'

'It's my studio. I'll not have it turned into a poulterer's shop.'

'Don't be absurd. And let me remind you that the barn was handed over to you with certain conditions attached. I've told you before, either you respect those conditions or—'

'Just try it,' she cut in viciously, lowering her voice so that I had to strain to catch the words. 'Just you try keeping me out.'

One hears of families in which the children are perpetually at loggerheads with their parents, but my own upbringing had impressed upon me the importance of filial obedience. 'You may disagree with me,' my father had told me on one occasion, 'but while you're under my roof you do as I say.' As I grew to manhood, I found myself dissenting more and more frequently from his opinions, but it would never have occurred to me to express my opposition in any but the mildest terms. Eleanor's words shocked me into embarrassed retreat, but as I walked back up the drive I found myself re-examining them with what I can only describe as a kind of excitement. I imagined the unseen tableau with vivid precision – the girl backed, quite literally, into a corner, but staring directly into her father's face as she spat defiance at him – and I was almost sorry when, a good ten minutes later, Vane strode out to where I was loitering in the shade at the edge of the garden and told me that Eleanor would be delighted to share her studio with me for the duration of my stay.

Predictably enough, our conversation at dinner that evening was not leavened by any expression of delight on the girl's part. Vane talked loudly and a little wildly, as though he were desperate to distract my attention from Eleanor's sullen silence, while I did my best to follow, through a haze of fatigue, the twists and turns of his rambling discourse. Only at the end of the meal, as the maidservant cleared away the dessert plates, did he change his tactics, leaning over to address his daughter directly. 'I'm sure Mr Redbourne will be interested to see your work, Eleanor. Tell him what your instructor said about it.'

'My instructor was a fool,' said Eleanor curtly.

Vane turned apologetically to me. 'There was a falling out,' he explained. 'But Mr Rourke is an artist of some local reputation and he told Eleanor in my presence' – he glanced sideways as though for corroboration – 'that she had a rare talent as a watercolourist.'

'What he admired in my work,' said Eleanor, scratching irritably with her fingernail at a small stain on the tablecloth, 'were the very qualities I despised in his. My father doesn't agree with me, Mr Redbourne, but I'm certain that I paint a good deal better without Mr Rourke's guidance than I ever did with it.'

'You owe him a considerable debt,' said Vane sharply, 'and it's neither kind nor honest to pretend otherwise.'

Both glanced my way at precisely the same moment, and I saw with sudden clarity that their argument was an old one, now being rehearsed for my benefit. I wanted no part in it. I lowered my gaze and sat staring stupidly at my empty wineglass until Vane, rising abruptly from his chair, drew the uncomfortable proceedings to a close.

6

The barn had been built in the English style, plain and sturdy, with thick walls of rough-hewn stone and a tiled roof. It would scarcely have looked out of place in a Cotswold village, I thought, setting down my satchel and instruments beside the pathway and shading my eyes against the early morning sunlight. The front wall was pierced by four small unglazed windows, two on either side of the double doors; the aperture in the gable – originally, I supposed, the loft doorway – had been incongruously fitted with a large, rectangular sash, while two square skylights, evidently of recent construction, had been inserted in the roof.

Eleanor was there before me. Seated at a trestle table just inside the building, she was clearly asserting ownership both of the space she occupied and the light that fell on her through the open doorway. She raised her head as I entered, lifting her paintbrush and fixing me momentarily with a vague, unseeing gaze; then, without a word, she returned to her work.

As promised by Vane, I had been supplied with a trestle of my own but, whether accidentally or through Eleanor's machinations, it had been placed against the wall beneath one of the small windows. The light that fell on its surface was adequate for my purposes, but I could see at once that its positioning was significant: I should be working under Eleanor's eye, but without the opportunity of observing her activities. It crossed my mind that I might simply move the trestle to a more favourable position but, on reflection, I decided against it. There would be time later, I told myself, for such adjustments.

I unbuckled my satchel, took out the lory and laid it belly upward on the rough surface. 'Is there a chair?' I asked.

For some time she said nothing, her gaze flickering between the paper pinned to her drawing-board and the bright orange nasturtium flower on the table in front of her. She continued to paint, but I sensed something faintly suspect in her concentration, a subtle hint of the theatrical. 'Under the hayloft,' she said at last, jerking her head sideways without looking up at me. 'In the corner.'

The battered chair I discovered there among the debris was hardly ideal – a little low for the table and with curving arm-rests that impeded my movements – but by placing a thick plank beneath its back legs, I was able to adapt it to my needs. I untied my canvas roll and laid it flat on the table, with the handles of the instruments towards me; then I drew out a scalpel and set to work, parting the crimson breast-feathers with my fingers before running the narrow blade down the body from throat to vent.

There is nothing particularly difficult about skinning a bird, but the job requires immense patience. The thickness of the plumage is deceptive: the skin itself is thin and delicate, and separating it from the flesh is a necessarily slow process. I've learned by experience not to apply undue pressure but simply to use the end of the blade to tease the skin free of the tissue that binds it to the body. It's not an entirely agreeable task, but I've always found it an absorbing one, and I'm apt, when engaged in it, to lose all sense of my surroundings.

I don't know how long Eleanor had been standing there when I became aware of her, close behind me, paintbrush in hand, looking over my shoulder at my handiwork. I started violently, sending the scalpel clattering across the table-top, and twisted round in my seat. 'Don't do that,' I snapped.

She backed away, but without taking her eyes off mine. 'I've a right to do as I please in my own studio,' she said. 'Haven't I?'

I was at a disadvantage, embarrassed by my own

outburst. 'You frightened me,' I said lamely. 'I mean, I'd forgotten where I was.'

'It happens to me too. I hate it when anyone comes in while I'm drawing or painting.'

'How am I to take that, Eleanor?'

She shrugged. 'Take it as you please. You told me how you felt. I'm telling you how I feel.'

'Would you rather I found somewhere else to work?'

'My father says you're to work here. I've no choice in the matter.'

'I'm sorry. I'd never intended—'

'It's not your fault. But it isn't easy for me, having you here. I don't like being disturbed in my own work, and I don't like the look of yours.' She glanced down at the exposed flesh of the bird's breast. 'What's it all for, anyway, this killing and skinning?'

'All science,' I said, easing my chair round so that I faced her directly, 'is grounded in facts. A collector's cabinet is a repository of facts from which important scientific truths may be deduced, and new theories constructed. We need these collections, Eleanor, if we're to understand the world we live in – it's as simple as that.'

'You're talking to me as though I were a schoolgirl. I know what science is, and I know what collectors think they're doing. But what kind of a fact is it, your dead lory? You'll take the skin back to England with you and you'll lay it in your cabinet with a label round its neck. Now and again you might bring it out, perhaps for your own private satisfaction or to take a few notes on it, or perhaps to show it to another collector. This is a crimson lory, you'll say. But it won't be true. You know that as well as I do, Mr Redbourne. Whatever it is you imagine you're laying hold of – for yourself, for your precious science – it's gone the moment you pull the trigger.'

I knew what she was driving at, and might have acknowledged as much, but she was working herself into a state of high excitement, the words tumbling out in a breathless torrent, and there seemed no opportunity to respond.

'What you're left with is a handful of skin and feathers – the sort of thing a milliner might use to dress a hat. It's dead stuff, dry as dust, and nothing's going to bring back the bird you had in your sights when you took aim. You'd do better,' she added, turning nimbly and darting back to her table, 'to try to catch something of its life. This' – I saw her dip her brush twice and lunge at the paper on her drawing-board – 'is a lory. And' – another quick flourish – 'so is this.' She tilted the board to show me two running streaks of red slashed diagonally across the paper.

'You've spoiled your painting.'

She let the board fall to the table and put down her brush. 'I don't care,' she said, but her jaw was set hard and tight as though she were biting back some unallowable grief. 'Anyway, it was already spoiled.'

'Let me see.' I rose from my chair and stepped over to examine the painting more closely. I saw her move protectively towards it, one hand outstretched; then, with a little shrug, she stepped back and let me by.

It was not, I saw at once, the kind of study that might

have graced the pages of a botanical handbook. Bounded by the two bright slashes of red pigment, it glowed with a similar brilliance, rich and vibrant, but it notably lacked the precision we conventionally associate with scientific illustration. Yet the longer I gazed at the work, the more clearly I recognised in it something of the vital essence of the flower – the extravagance of the flared petals, bright as flame but stained and streaked with darkness, the honeyed light far down in the throat, the cool translucence of the stem.

'It's lovely,' I said encouragingly. 'Truly lovely.'

'Oh, lovely,' she said scornfully, reaching over and tugging the paper roughly from the board. 'I've had enough of lovely.' And then, with a quick, angry movement, she ripped the sheet across and flung the two halves to the earthen floor.

If it had been an act of pure spitefulness, I should no doubt have been well advised to ignore it and return to my work. But something in the girl's face – distress, I thought, and a kind of bewilderment, as though she had been caught unawares by her own action – held me there. I stooped and picked up the pieces.

'There was no call for that,' I said gently. 'If you didn't want the painting, you might have offered it to me. I should have been glad of it.'

'You said it was spoiled.'

'I didn't mean—'

'Then it's yours. Have it.' It was gracelessly done and I, for my part, had no time to thank her before she turned away and stalked out into the sunlight.

*　　*　　*

I was sitting in my room early that evening, aligning the two halves of the painting on my writing-desk, when I heard Vane call my name softly outside the door. With an obscure feeling of guilt, I gathered up the pieces and slipped them into the left-hand drawer.

'Are you there, Redbourne?'

I opened the door just as he was readying himself to rap on the panel. 'Bullen has arrived,' he said. 'He'll be at dinner tonight, but I thought it advisable to have the two of you meet in advance. That way you'll be able to address matters of business before our other guests arrive.'

'Business?'

'Bullen is more than willing to act as your guide, but he has made it clear to me that he'll be obliged to treat any excursion as a professional engagement.' He glanced uneasily down the corridor. 'The fact is,' he went on, lowering his voice to a murmur, 'that the man has fallen on hard times. A few years ago he owned seventy-five acres of good grazing, but he's been brought to the brink of ruin by unwise speculation. Sugar plantations, the hotel business – knows nothing about either, of course. If it weren't for his collecting he'd have gone under. I tell you, Redbourne, your arrival is a godsend for him.'

Vane's account fell some way short, it seemed to me, of a reassuring character reference. 'I assume,' I said, 'that the arrangement will be equally beneficial to me?'

'No doubt of it,' he said hastily, 'no doubt at all. He's already planning an itinerary for you – local excursions first, and then a trip out to the mountains. Come down and let him tell you about it.' He turned, evidently expecting me to follow at once. I hesitated for a moment, then fell into step behind him.

Bullen was sprawled at ease on the sofa in the day-room, his hat beside him on the padded arm-rest. He sprang up as I entered and advanced to meet me, a tall man, big-boned without any hint of fleshiness, his features hard and angular above a full brown beard. His handshake was firm and his voice, as he greeted me, deep and resonant, but there was something in his demeanour – the hunched shoulders, the evasive eyes – that disconcertingly offset the initial impression of physical strength. Vane had no sooner introduced us than he withdrew, pleading business of his own.

'And what,' asked Bullen, reseating himself on the sofa, 'made you fix on Australia?'

'I'm not sure that the decision was entirely mine.'

I could see him weighing up my reply. 'I mean,' I explained, 'that matters seemed to fall into place without a great deal of effort on my part.'

'You're a believer in the workings of a divine provi-dence, Mr Redbourne?'

I laughed. 'That's a very serious interpretation of a casual observation.'

'Speaking for myself,' he said, for all the world as though I had pressed him to give me an account of his personal philosophy, 'I believe that our destiny lies in our own hands. And once we recognise that fact, our power is virtually unlimited.'

I thought of the man's failed business ventures and wondered what his philosophy made of those. 'I under-stand,' I said, shifting ground with more firmness than

71

tact, 'that you've offered to act as my guide to the region. Perhaps we might discuss practicalities.'

Reflecting later on the moment, I realised that I had decisively undermined Bullen's attempts to engage with me on terms of equality – to present himself as civilised conversationalist and fellow gentleman – but if he resented my less than dextrous manipulation of our discussion, he gave no sign of it, turning his attention immediately to matters of business. We easily agreed terms for the local excursions, but it quickly became apparent that his real interest lay in the possibility of accompanying me on longer expeditions, at my expense.

'But no fee,' he added quickly, 'apart from this: of the specimens killed on any of those expeditions, five go to me. My choice.'

It might have seemed a small enough matter, but I could see at once that his proposal had serious implications. By creaming off the best of our bag – and I had a fleeting vision of him out there in some shadowy wilderness, gloating over his cache of rarities – Bullen would seriously diminish the quality of my own collection. I resisted, diplomatically at first but then more vigorously, and we were still debating the point when I heard Vane returning, his footsteps ringing out on the bare boards of the hallway. 'Three specimens,' said Bullen quickly as the door opened and our host entered.

I have often noticed that an angry conversation seems to leave some residual stain on the air and, even if he had not overheard our altercation, Vane must have realised as he stepped into the room that my first meeting with Bullen was not proving a success. I saw his eyes flicker between the two of us as though he were assessing the situation.

'Well,' he said lightly, gesturing towards the deepening shadows outside, 'at least we shall all be a little cooler now. We'll be dining in half an hour.'

'You mentioned other company,' I said.

'The Merivales. The family has farmed the opposite slope of the valley for three generations. Walter Merivale died last year, but his widow and son have kept things running smoothly enough. An admirable family, Redbourne – I can guarantee that you'll enjoy their society.'

I took leave to doubt it, though I naturally kept my opinion to myself. Vane had presumably imagined that Bullen – a man prepared to haggle like a fairground huckster in pursuit of his own dubious ends – was fit company for me, and I saw no reason to suppose that his other guests would impress me any more favourably. I excused myself, perhaps a shade abruptly, and went up to dress for dinner.

7

I could hardly have been further from the mark. From the moment Mrs Merivale stepped over the threshold, sweeping into the house a few paces ahead of her son and daughter, I realised that Vane's neighbours were people of considerable distinction and refinement. Mrs Merivale herself was thin and strikingly tall, but with none of the awkwardness that so often afflicts women of unusual height. On the contrary, she held herself imposingly erect, her shoulders back and her head high so that, as we were introduced, she looked me directly in the eye. She was dressed in widow's black and this, together with her angular features, gave an immediate impression of austerity; but as she offered me her hand, her face relaxed into a smile so warm and engaging that I felt as though I had been embraced.

'And this is William,' she said, standing aside. 'My son.'

Handsome and sturdily built, Merivale was almost as striking as his mother, but his face had about it the flush and fullness that come with high living and, though he couldn't have been above twenty-five years old, the hair had already begun to recede from his wide brow. He bowed formally from the waist as he gripped my hand.

I could see Miss Merivale out of the corner of my eye as I exchanged conventional courtesies with her brother, but I had no strong sense of her presence until she moved in on us, placing her hand on Merivale's sleeve but addressing herself to me. 'William,' she smiled, 'would be the perfect gentleman if he could only be persuaded to treat his sister with the consideration he extends to every other lady of his acquaintance. If I wait for him to introduce us, I may be obliged to stand here for another twenty minutes.'

I have never met anyone who could more aptly be described as exquisite. Her face resembled her mother's but was more delicately proportioned and of a milder cast – the high cheekbones less prominent, the fine jawline more unequivocally feminine. Her neck was long and slender, her fair skin almost translucent in its clarity. Although she had something of her mother's erect bearing, she stood a good six inches shorter, the top of her elegantly coiffed head barely above the level of my shoulder.

Merivale laughed quietly, a little easier, it struck me, for his sister's intervention. 'I am reproached,' he said with playful gravity. And then, with an odd, archaic flourish: 'My sister, Miss Esther Merivale.'

Miss Merivale proved to be as charming as she was beautiful, an accomplished conversationalist with a quick but unmalicious sense of humour and a flattering quality of attentiveness. Her questions about my life in England seemed neither intrusive nor superficial, and I responded with uncharacteristic warmth and openness, while she for her part spoke so engrossingly about her own circumstances that, by the time the dinner-gong sounded, I felt as if I had been granted privileged access to her family circle.

'This way, if you would,' called Vane, shepherding us towards the dining room. Merivale stepped up to Eleanor as though to escort her in. As he did so, Vane half turned and, evidently with the intention of blocking the manoeuvre, interposed himself between his daughter and the young man. I saw the blood rise to Merivale's face; saw Eleanor stiffen against the subtle pressure of her father's hand, placed momentarily against her slender waist as he guided her through the doorway ahead of him.

Vane occupied the seat at the head of the table, setting Mrs Merivale at his right hand and her daughter at his left. I had hoped that I might be seated next to Miss Merivale, but Vane motioned me to sit with the mother, while Bullen was accorded the honour I had coveted.

With Eleanor at his other elbow, he sat directly across the table from me, stroking his beard and grinning broadly as if at some stupendous joke.

Eleanor, I thought, was trying to catch Merivale's eye, but as the soup was brought Bullen began to engage her in conversation, while Merivale leaned sideways and addressed himself to me. 'I understand,' he said, 'that you're here on a scientific mission.'

I smiled. 'You make it sound rather grand. I'm collecting specimens, but I'm an amateur in the field.'

'Nothing to be ashamed of in that. From the little I know of the subject, I'd say that a spirit of informed amateurism has always been the driving force behind the discoveries of natural science. The world is changing, Mr Redbourne, changing with dizzying speed, and the days of the amateur may well be numbered; but that doesn't invalidate either your own enterprise or the achievements of your predecessors.'

Merivale had been unduly modest: I realised as we continued to talk that he actually knew a good deal about the subject, and before long we were deeply immersed in a discussion that ranged from the theories of Darwin, through hybridism in plants and animals, to the shooting of hawks and owls. I had long been of the opinion that English gamekeepers were too vigorous and undiscriminating in their persecution of our native birds of prey, and I was delighted to find Merivale expressing comparable views in relation to his own country. 'Even if,' he said, leaning back to let the maidservant remove his plate, 'it were to turn out that these birds really were responsible for all the crimes laid at their door, imagine the loss to us when the whole tribe has finally been shot out of the skies. If I had my way, they'd be protected by law. When I look up and see a pair of wedge-tails soaring in the air above me, my heart soars with them – really, Mr Redbourne, that's the way it feels, as though I were up there alongside them, riding the updraughts. And though I'm not, properly speaking, a religious man, that's the way I'm able to imagine the experiences the mystics speak of – as uplift, the mind or spirit rising like an eagle into a clear sky.'

He paused, visibly excited and perhaps a little embarrassed at having expressed himself so unguardedly; and at that moment Bullen, who had evidently been eavesdropping on our conversation, leaned across the table, slapping the surface with his open palm.

'I don't imagine,' he said, 'that you spend much time giving your fellow farmers the benefit of your views. You'd get short shrift from anyone who's lost stock to the creatures.'

'I was speaking to Mr Redbourne,' answered Merivale, colouring.

I was doubtful whether Bullen had had time to drink more than two or three glasses of wine, but he'd certainly downed more than was good for his manners. As the rest of the party fell silent, he leaned back and addressed himself to the company at large, his face flushed and his voice appreciably louder and more emphatic than the circumstances seemed to require. 'It's the bane of our age,' he said. 'Sentimentalism. Looking for mysteries when the facts are staring us in the face. Turning aside from reality in order to indulge our finer feelings. Do you imagine the eagles share your finer feelings, Merivale? Not a bit of it. While you're busy examining the world through your tinted prism, they'll be dropping out of the sky to take one of your lambs.'

Vane was looking round the table with an expression of mild bewilderment, but Eleanor had clearly grasped the situation and, while Merivale blushed and stammered beside me, she cut in, quick and cold: 'What you call sentimentalism,' she said, barely troubling to glance at Bullen, 'may be a refinement of the human spirit too subtle for your understanding.'

Vane gave her a withering stare. I would have intervened, but it was Bullen himself who restored a degree of order to the proceedings, breaking the silence with a high, barking laugh, as if to show that Eleanor's barb had failed to penetrate his thick skin. 'Your daughter's as sharp as a tin-tack,' he said, raising his wine-glass with mock ceremony and tilting it in Vane's direction. 'I'll wager she keeps you on your toes.' Eleanor glowered but said nothing, and the moment was past.

I should have liked to return to my discussion with Merivale but he had grown awkward and uncommunicative, as though Bullen's intervention had left him inwardly bruised. Bullen himself seemed oblivious to the young man's discomfiture, and as I listened to him holding forth loudly on a variety of topics about which he seemed to know next to nothing, I was struck by the sheer vulgarity of the fellow. By the time the coffee was brought, I was considering how best to ensure that our unfinished negotiations were not resumed.

'That was a grand dinner,' said Bullen, leaning back in

his chair and wiping his beard with his napkin. 'I'll say this, Vane, you've done us proud.'

Vane smiled. 'At all events,' he said, 'it will be a dinner for you and Redbourne to remember when you're out in the bush snacking on frogs and lizards.'

'Nothing wrong with lizard,' said Bullen. 'But' – he gave me a conspiratorial wink – 'I doubt it will come to that. Trust me, Mr Redbourne, we'll eat well enough.'

'I'm sure we shall. And now, if you'll all excuse me, I'd like to take a turn in the garden.' I placed my napkin on the table and withdrew, leaning above Vane as I passed him. 'Perhaps you'd be good enough to join me,' I murmured, 'when circumstances permit.'

He looked up at me, his brow furrowed. 'I'll come right away,' he said.

The air of the terrace was barely cooler than that of the dining-room, but it was sweet with the mingled scents of the garden. As Vane caught up with me, I turned to make sure that Bullen had not followed us out, and caught a glimpse of him through the window, his head thrown back and his mouth wide. A yawp of laughter reached me on the fragrant air. Vane gave me a sidelong glance.

'I take it you've something on your mind, Redbourne.'

'Indeed. Listen, I'm grateful to you for introducing me to Mr Bullen, but you both seem to imagine that I've come to a decision on the matter of his employment. In fact, I'm not at all sure that he and I are likely to hit it off.'

Vane gave a throaty chuckle. 'So that's it,' he said. 'Well, I don't imagine that the pair of you are going to forge a lasting friendship, but the plain truth is that Bullen has precisely the experience needed for an expedition of this kind. He's not the most civilised of companions, I grant you; but then, you're not going to the most civilised of places. He's the right man for the job, depend upon it.'

Another outburst of laughter from the house, more prolonged this time. Vane tilted his head towards the sound. 'Look here,' he said, 'Bullen knows his way around the region. He knows many of the old trails – paths followed by the aboriginal tribes – and where he doesn't, he knows people who do. And he's a skilled hunter into the bargain. You might find a more congenial travelling companion, but you'd look a long time before you found a more useful one.'

I was silent for a moment, conscious of the force of his argument, but not entirely convinced. I should like to be able to claim that I had already recognised the brittleness beneath the rugged façade, but I believe that my unease owed more to a potent combination of resentment and snobbery than to any clear understanding of Bullen's character.

'You may be right,' I said at last. 'I'll sleep on it.'

'But not yet, I hope. Esther – Miss Merivale – has agreed to play for us. She's a talented pianist, Redbourne, genuinely talented – quite a favourite in the drawing-rooms of Sydney. I'm not a musical man myself but I know fine playing when I hear it. I can tell you, you're in for a treat.'

He turned and began to walk back towards the house. Bullen had put me severely out of humour and I should have preferred to plead fatigue and send my excuses to the company, but it was clearly impossible to absent myself without causing offence and, after a few seconds' hesitation, I followed.

I entered the drawing-room to find Miss Merivale already seated at the piano, while her brother busied himself with arranging the chairs in a shallow arc around one side of the instrument. As soon as he had finished, Eleanor made for the centre of the arc and sat down, motioning me to join her. 'You'll see her hands from here,' she said. 'Her nimble little fingers.'

Some quality of mischief in her tone and phrasing put me on my guard. 'I understand from your father that she has acquired quite a reputation round about,' I said, settling myself beside her.

'Oh, yes. She's clever girl, no doubt of it. And she knows it.'

I glanced at Miss Merivale to see whether she had overheard but if she had, she gave no sign of it. She was dusting the keyboard with a small lace handkerchief, her head slightly bowed. Someone had placed a lamp on the piano's polished lid, and her features shone in the soft light with something of the delicate translucency of a cameo portrait. She tucked the handkerchief into her sleeve and straightened her back, very calm and self-possessed. The room fell suddenly silent and she began to play.

François Couperin had been a favourite of my mother's, and I recognised the minuet at once. But whereas my mother's attempts had been stiff and hesitant, the work's intricacies always seeming a little beyond her grasp, Miss Merivale's rendition shimmered and flowed, its phrasing immaculate, its tone bright and confident. She played with gentle precision, perfectly evoking an age less frenetic than our own, an age still capable of celebrating, without irony or embarrassment, the ideals of harmony and just proportion. Each note was accorded its proper value; nothing was rushed, nothing snatched or fumbled. Even the trills – and her fingerwork was indeed extraordinary – gave an impression of spaciousness, as though she had all the time in the world to execute them. As she played, she half closed her eyes and tilted back her head so that you saw the long line of her throat; her slender body moved gracefully, swaying a little from the waist in time to the music.

She was playing from memory and as she reached the end of the piece, she moved seamlessly on to another. As she began the third, Eleanor leaned inward, her shoulder touching mine, her face so close I smelt the faint perfume of her skin. 'You do realise,' she whispered, 'that she's memorised dozens of these things? She might go on for hours.'

More mischief, I thought, edging away. I tried to return to the music but my concentration had been broken, and I was almost relieved when Miss Merivale, with an elegant flourish, brought the sequence to a close and turned to acknowledge our applause. I leaned behind Eleanor to address Mrs Merivale. 'You must be very proud of your daughter,' I said.

'Indeed, though I can take very little of the credit for her accomplishments. I have no musical talent of my own.'

'Then her achievement is all the more remarkable.'

Eleanor was shifting uncomfortably on her seat between us. Mrs Merivale reached out and placed her hand gently on the girl's shoulder. 'Of course,' she said, 'you know that Eleanor is musically gifted too.'

'Really? What instrument does she play?'

Eleanor whipped round to face me, her eyes flashing. 'Anyone would think you were discussing a clever five-year-old,' she said. 'I sing.'

'And very well too,' said Mrs Merivale soothingly. 'I'm sure Mr Redbourne would like to hear something from you.'

'I doubt it,' said Eleanor sullenly.

'Believe me,' I said, with as much conviction as I could muster, 'nothing would give me greater pleasure.'

'In that case,' said Mrs Merivale, 'Eleanor must sing. I know that Esther' – she beckoned imperiously to her daughter – 'will be more than happy to accompany her.'

Just a little less than happy, I thought, scrutinising Miss Merivale's delicately expressive features as her mother enlisted her services, but she made no objection. She returned to the piano, Eleanor following at her heels.

'I'm going to sing,' announced Eleanor bluntly, as though defying the company to stop her. She lifted the hinged lid of the piano stool and withdrew a slim clothbound folio.

'Schubert,' she said, letting the lid fall with a bang. 'We'll have a Schubert song.' She opened the songbook and bent it back on itself so sharply that I heard the glue crack in the spine; then she placed it firmly on the rack.

Miss Merivale seated herself on the stool and peered at the music. 'Not this one,' she said.

Eleanor stared down at her. 'Why not? she asked coldly.

'I don't like it.'

'Don't like or can't play?' Scarcely above a whisper, but I don't imagine that any member of the company could have missed either the words themselves or the sting they carried.

Vane leaned forward. 'You'll mind your tongue, Eleanor,' he said quietly.

Miss Merivale turned to him with a thin smile, her slender hand raised. 'Please,' she said. 'If Eleanor particularly wants the song, I'm willing to accompany her.' She deftly flicked up the bottom corner of the page and half turned, lifting her eyes to meet Eleanor's. 'Are you ready?' she asked. Eleanor gave an almost imperceptible nod, and Miss Merivale began to play.

I had heard the song on a number of occasions, but the legend of the Erlking was in any case familiar to me from my childhood: indeed, I had at one stage become so morbidly obsessed by the little volume of folk-tales in which it appeared – and in particular by the sinister engravings that accompanied the text – that my father had eventually taken the unprecedented step of transferring the book to a shelf beyond my reach. Miss Merivale's performance compared favourably with others I had heard, but it was Eleanor's singing, thrusting me back into a shadowy world of half-remembered nightmare, that gripped my imagination that evening.

I don't want to give the wrong impression: Eleanor

was, in strictly musical terms, comprehensively out-classed by her accompanist, and she certainly began very badly indeed. Miss Merivale, elegantly poised above the keyboard, held the rhythms – the right hand's percussive beat, the insistent growling of the bass – with exemplary precision, while Eleanor's rich but evidently untrained voice stumbled behind like an unseated rider. I saw a smile pass across Miss Merivale's face, a smile so signally devoid of warmth that it might have been construed as a smirk; and then everything changed.

I can locate it precisely, that moment of transition. As the frantic hoofbeats slacken, the Erlking moves in, creating a stillness at the heart of the storm, his mouth so close, it seems, to the ear of the panicky child that he barely needs to raise his voice. That was where Eleanor found what she was looking for, or where it found her. '*Du liebes Kind, komm, geh mit mir*' – that terrible, unrefusable invitation, the words welling from her throat as sweet as honey but laced with menace and, more subtly, with the sick yearning of the demonic for a world of human warmth and love.

Then off again, Eleanor utterly present now in the song, her voice – the child's voice – soaring in terror against the gathering pulse of the accompaniment, the quickening hoofs; and the father's words infused, in her interpretation, with the same terror, their sensible, humane reassurance so thrillingly subverted by that unspeakable otherness that I felt the hairs prickle at my nape. I was back there in the library, the book open in front of me in a pool of yellow lamplight, a small boy lost among the nightmare images: the father crouching low in the saddle, his hair flying in the wind, his cloak half concealing the wild-eyed child huddled in the crook of his left arm; and emerging from the tangle of briars and branches behind them, one long-fingered hand outstretched, the Erlking himself. He is crowned as a king should be, but his clothes hang in tatters from his wasted body; his mouth is set in a famished grin. He doesn't seem to be moving with particular speed, but his narrowed eyes are lit with a terrifying certainty, as though he can already envisage the end of the story, the end of the hopeless, hectic ride. I heard the final words of the song ring out, stark and raw, in the space left by the suspended accompaniment; and then Miss Merivale, with studied understatement, struck the closing chords.

As the notes died away, Miss Merivale dropped her hands to her lap and drooped her head. She looked suddenly small and lost, her poise gone; in her face there was a kind of subdued panic, as though the song had told her something she would have preferred not to hear. Eleanor stood erect, staring out over our heads, her eyes brimming with tears. There was a long, uneasy silence, broken at last by Merivale.

'Bravo, ladies,' he called out, beating his thigh with the flat of his hand. 'That was splendid. Really splendid.' His sister looked up with a grateful smile, and the applause became general. I leaned back in my chair, feeling the tension begin to evaporate from my body, from the room. And then Eleanor's eyes met mine.

What did it signify, the gaze she turned on me then? Too intense for our surroundings, it might have reflected the frightful exhilaration of a night-ride whose hammering rhythms seemed still to echo in the air around us, yet it was focused on me, and on me alone, with a directness bordering on indelicacy. Recognition, was it? Accusation? Desire? For an instant that seemed an age I was transfixed, held like an insect on a pin; then she turned abruptly away and let me fall.

8

I had fallen asleep with Eleanor's singing still
echoing in my mind but it was Daniel who visited
my dreams, visible as a vague thickening of the
darkness at my bedside, his voice sweeter and clearer
than in life. *Come with me* he fluted, taking up the
Erlking's theme, wheedling, coaxing. He moved in
close and I felt his fingertips play lightly over my
face, his lips brush my ear. *Come.* I started back
from his touch and woke drenched in sweat, trembling with desire and dread. I lay in bed until the
darkness began to draw off; then I rose and towelled

my damp skin before dressing and making my way downstairs.

The eastern horizon was brightening as I left the house, and the air was ringing with bird-calls. Not the sweet tones of an English dawn chorus, but something altogether wilder and more disquieting – a babble of contending shrieks, whistles and warblings with an undercurrent of lighter piping sounds. More than anything I had yet experienced, those cries spoke to me of the distance I had travelled from my native soil, and as I walked out through the gates I was gripped by a spasm of something like vertigo and my heart lurched in my chest.

Once at a reasonable distance from the villa, I positioned myself among the shrubs at the edge of the track and waited, my gun at the ready. Vane had mentioned the passage, at dawn and dusk, of small groups of waterfowl, and I was eager to try my luck. I had barely settled back when a dozen or so duck winged over, low and fast. I jerked the rifle clumsily forward, fired both barrels and, as the second shot rang out, saw the hindmost bird stagger and drop.

I thought at first that I had lost it, but after a few minutes' searching I discovered the body half buried in a clump of low scrub, one wing twisted stiffly upward like a flag marking the spot. It was a beautiful thing, I saw, as I tugged it clear, its underparts a deep cinnamon-brown, flecked with darker mottling, and the gleam of its bottle-green head-feathers shifting with the loose swing of its neck. I placed it carefully in my satchel and returned to my makeshift hide.

I had no further success but I was pleased enough with

my prize, and after a hasty breakfast I hurried down to the barn to skin the bird. Eleanor was there before me but her glance, as I entered, seemed less unfriendly than before, and I had no sooner placed the duck on the table than she set down her brushes and stepped over to my side.

'Teal,' she said. 'Chestnut teal.' She stretched out her hand and gently touched the bird's breast with the backs of her fingers. Something in the gesture – some quality of hesitant tenderness – stirred and confused me.

'So soft,' she said, with a little catch in her voice. 'Do you remember what Milton says about the waterbirds – bathing their downy breasts on silver lakes?'

'You've read Milton?'

She must have caught the note of surprise in my question. She bridled, glared. 'Why shouldn't I have done? You take me for a dunce, don't you? A little colonial flibbertigibbet.'

'Of course I don't. But I always think of Milton as a peculiarly masculine writer. I imagine that young ladies tend, as a rule, to prefer something a little less—'

'Perhaps,' she interrupted rudely, 'you need to widen the circle of your acquaintance.'

There was a moment of tense silence. Then she reached out and touched my arm, half propitiatory, half coercive.

'Come with me,' she said. 'I want to show you something.'

She marched over to the hayloft ladder, hitched up the front of her skirt and began to climb. I hung back, inhibited by a faint, unsourceable anxiety. As she reached the platform, she turned and held out her hand.

'Come on,' she said. 'It looks unsteady, but it's safe enough.'

'I'm not afraid of a fifteen-foot drop,' I said stiffly.

'What is it, then?'

I couldn't have explained it to myself, let alone to her. 'Nothing,' I answered, moving over to the ladder.

I'd imagined the loft very differently – hay bales, twine, dust and shadows; not that swept space, amply lit by the window and skylights and furnished like a nursery. Against one wall stood a low table, set as though for tea with a miniature porcelain service, sprigged with rosebuds; against the opposite wall, a small bench occupied by three exquisitely dressed china dolls. A blanket-chest, loosely draped with a fringed woollen shawl, had been positioned immediately beneath the skylight. Eleanor was looking at me, her head tilted a little to one side, evidently waiting for me to comment.

'I take it this used to be your playroom,' I said.

'In a manner of speaking. When I was sixteen my father told me I was to clear my bedroom of the trappings of childhood. That was the phrase he used. I said I wouldn't – told him I saw no reason to – but he wouldn't drop the matter. He quoted scripture at me – as if St Paul would have cared whether or not a young girl kept her dolls by her bedside – but I raged and cried, biting my wrists and knuckles until they bled, making him frightened I might do myself worse harm. In the end we agreed that I should be allowed a few keepsakes, so long as I removed them from the house. That was when I began to make a place for myself out here – a place where I can be as I am, not as he'd have me.'

Her voice, I noticed, had hardened as she was speaking; her expression was cold and distant. It seemed sensible to shift ground. 'You told me you had something to show me,' I said. 'Did you mean . . . ?'

'No, not these things. Something more important.' She stepped over to the blanket-chest, removed its covering and eased back the lid. Peering over her shoulder, I saw a neat bundle – a thick cylinder of tightly wrapped burlap about two feet long, tied at each end with a length of grubby cream ribbon – lying diagonally across the top of a disorderly heap of books. She removed the bundle, placing it carefully on the floor beside her, and rummaged through the books until she found the volume she was looking for.

'Do you know,' she said, quickly scanning the pages, 'I think no-one else has ever described things the way Milton does. Listen to this.' She settled back on her heels, angled the book towards the skylight and began to read.

And higher than that wall a circling row
Of goodliest trees loaden with fairest fruit,
Blossoms and fruits at once of golden hue
Appeared, with gay enamelled colours mixed:
On which the sun more glad impressed his beams
Than in fair evening cloud or humid bow,
When God hath showered the earth; so lovely seemed
That landscape: and of pure now purer air
Meets his approach, and to the heart inspires

Vernal delight and joy, able to drive
All sadness but despair: now gentle gales
Fanning their odoriferous wings dispense
Native perfumes and whisper whence they stole
Those balmy spoils.

She sighed and gently closed the book. 'Fanning their odoriferous wings,' she breathed, lifting her eyes to mine. 'Can you imagine?'

If, as I suspected, she had brought me to her hideaway in order to impress me with her little library and her modicum of learning, her rapture was no less genuine for that. I smiled, touched and faintly excited by her wide-eyed gaze. 'They're glorious lines,' I said.

'Yes, and frightening too.'

'Frightening? Why?'

'Because,' she said, and her mouth twitched uneasily, 'he's already there.'

'Who?'

'Satan. It's Satan approaching the garden. Prowling around, looking for a way in, plotting mischief. We've waited for our glimpse of paradise, and here it is at last, but he's there with us. And when we enter, we enter with him. Or he enters with us – I don't know exactly how it is. I want to see the garden pure and clear, and I can't. Milton won't let us. It's as if he's telling us the evil's deep in our own hearts and can't be rinsed out.'

'The gospels tell us otherwise. And Milton himself knew that the loss of paradise was only part of the story. It might be said that our fall can only be understood in relation to the act of redemption that follows it.'

'Are you a believer, Mr Redbourne? I mean, do you believe we can all be saved? Supposing someone sins – I mean a sin so terrible she can't speak of it, though it's not her fault – and goes on sinning because she has no choice. Might she still find her way back to paradise?'

'Everyone has a choice,' I said. 'That's the point. Sin is a choice, and so is repentance.'

There was a long silence before she spoke again. 'I don't believe that,' she said at last. 'It's too simple.' She turned away with an odd grimace and began to fumble nervously among the books in the chest. It struck me that I had not given her the answer she wanted.

'I'm no theologian,' I said gently. 'I may be wrong.'

She appeared not to have heard. 'Cowper,' she said, tugging a worn clothbound volume from the heap and handing it to me. 'All of Cowper's poems. And Crabbe's. Some of Byron's too. Bumped and battered, but that's all I can afford.'

'Don't you have access to your father's library?'

She gave an ugly, mirthless laugh. 'My father has no library,' she said. 'He thinks books are a waste of time and money. He'd be horrified if he knew of my own few shillingsworth.'

I opened the volume she'd handed me and made a show of examining the text, but found myself intrigued and vaguely distracted by the bundle on the floor. 'What's that?' I asked.

'I can show you,' she said, 'but you must promise not to say anything about it in my father's hearing.' Without waiting for a response, she lifted the bundle on to her lap, untied the fastening and began to unroll the cloth with quick, eager movements of her slender hands. I caught a glimpse of polished wood, a dusky gleam between the folds.

'Do you promise?' she asked, pausing suddenly in her task.

'I promise.'

She spread the cloth to reveal a carved figure lying on its back like a small brown baby, its stumpy legs slightly splayed and thrust a little forward from the hips. Neither the legs nor the skimpy arms suggested a great deal of care on the part of the carver, but the torso, though crudely modelled, was intricately decorated with tiny gouge-marks, and in the space where the thighs met under the rounded belly, the vulva was carefully delineated – a stylised leaf-shape bisected by a deep slit and fringed with finer incisions.

But it was, above all, the face that compelled attention: a polished oval, longitudinally ridged to form two distinct planes and dominated by the enormous, deeply sculpted eyes. I stared down at it, perplexed by its teasing inscrutability. It wasn't that the face was inexpressive, but that its expression was so deeply ambiguous as to engender a kind of confusion in my mind. Was the thing grieving, or were its features set, as the protruding tongue half suggested, in a mocking parody of grief? Was it angry? Lustful? Or had it perhaps withdrawn into some calm, contemplative space beyond the reach of passion? I stooped to examine it more closely and, as I did so, Eleanor smiled up at me.

'Don't you think she's beautiful?' she asked.

It wasn't the adjective I should have chosen. For as

long as I can remember, I have been fascinated by sculptural form, and I regard the sculptors of classical antiquity as having attained a level of artistic expression unmatched, in any medium, either before or since; among their productions are works of such refined and exquisite beauty that I have, on occasion, been moved to tears in their presence. In what sense, I asked myself, could this crudely worked totem be said to share their qualities?

'The piece has a certain power,' I said. 'I wouldn't call it beautiful.'

'The power and the beauty are the same thing. I came across her in a curiosity shop down by the harbour and the minute I saw her I began to shake, my whole body trembling so that I had to lean against the counter to steady myself. There was something about the way she stood, so sure of herself among all that dust and clutter. And something in the set of her face too – look at it – as though she were saying, very simply and firmly: this is what I am. There's beauty in that, Mr Redbourne – in the thing she's saying and in the manner of her saying it – and though it's a kind of beauty I hadn't met with before, I recognised it at once.'

'I'm not persuaded,' I said, running my fingers across the roughly tooled surface, 'but perhaps I'm missing something.'

'I'm not trying to persuade you. Either you see it or you don't. But I want you to understand that, for me, the world changed when I found her.'

I was taken aback by the extravagance of the claim, and my face must have betrayed my feelings.

'I mean it,' she said, looking hard at me. 'Nothing was ever the same again. When I came home that evening I leafed through some of my watercolours, and it seemed to me I was looking at a kind of trickery – all soft tones in those days, washes so delicate they barely tinged the paper – and seeing clean through it. I couldn't stop thinking about what I'd found. And it wasn't just regret at having had to leave her in the shop—'

'So you didn't buy the piece there and then?'

'I couldn't. The asking price was two guineas.'

'Not a vast sum.'

'An impossible sum at the time. My father keeps a tight grip on my allowance – wants me to account for everything I spend. Every so often the odd shilling might stick to my palm, but two guineas called for extreme measures. I waited my chance and filched a couple of sovereigns from his purse one evening after dinner.'

It was her matter-of-fact tone as much as the disclosure itself that shocked me. 'Surely you knew that was wrong,' I said.

'He owes me more than that.' She was repacking the books, but her hands fell suddenly still and she lifted her eyes to mine. 'You've promised, remember. You're to tell him nothing.'

I nodded. She leaned over the little totem and placed her hand gently against the curve of the brow, the way a mother might touch her child in greeting or fond goodnight; then she swaddled it again and carefully returned it to the chest.

9

I had deliberately put Bullen from my mind, but when I returned to the house for lunch he was there on the veranda, lounging in the shade with a glass in his hand. He rose to his feet as I approached and strolled down to greet me. He was a little more relaxed in his manner than on the previous evening, and considerably more casual in his attire, his shirt collarless and partially unbuttoned beneath a loose-fitting canvas jacket.

'I thought you might be game for an afternoon's shooting,' he said. 'If we set off directly after lunch we can ride down to the swamp, bag a few choice specimens and be back here in time for dinner.'

As I considered my reply, I saw Vane emerge through the french windows and step to the edge of the veranda. He raised his hand in salutation and rested his elbows on the rail, smiling in our direction. It seemed, in the circumstances, almost impossible to decline Bullen's invitation: the itinerary had clearly been arranged between the two of them, and a refusal might well be interpreted as doubly insulting, as much a gesture of disrespect towards my host as towards Bullen himself. I gave as warm a smile as I could summon up.

'Thank you,' I said. 'I should be glad to join you.'

I was not particularly hungry and Bullen, though apparently ravenous, showed no desire to linger over his lunch, so that by the time the groom appeared in the drive with our mounts we were ready to leave. Vane had provided me with a chestnut pony, rather short in the leg for a man of my height but sturdy and sure-footed, and we kept a steady pace for an hour or so, side by side at first and then, as the track narrowed, with Bullen leading the way. Eventually, as the track became too rocky for them to negotiate, we tethered the ponies and continued on foot.

It was hard going, and became even harder as we struck off at an oblique angle to the ridge and began to pick our way down the slope between the sandstone outcrops. The eucalypts here were stunted grotesques, their limbs twisted and their red boles pocked and rippled like diseased flesh.

'There,' said Bullen after a few moments. 'Do you

see?' I caught the glint of sunlit water between the trees and eagerly quickened my pace, but Bullen reached out and grasped my sleeve, holding me back. 'Easy now,' he said. 'Easy and quiet.' I slowed obediently and we moved cautiously forwards until we stood on the edge of a worn lip of stone, gazing out over the swamp.

What was it, the sick tremor that afflicted me at that moment? In part, I suppose, it was a product of the heat, beating down remorselessly from the open sky but at the same time fanning upward from the hot rock like the blast from an opened furnace. There was the smell too, a soft odour of ooze and rot; and as I stood there, the shrilling of the cicadas seemed to swell around me and resonate through the bones of my skull with an insinuating force that made me think of madness. But above all, I think, I was disturbed by something in the look of the landscape – not pitilessness exactly, since the term implies the possibility of pity, but a blank imperviousness to our presence. In the gleaming foliage of the waterline mangroves, in the lazy flow of the inlet and the flat shine of its silted banks, I read nothing that seemed intended for my eyes, or for those of any intruder in that heartless, unblemished wilderness.

I heard the click of Bullen's safety-bolt and turned to see him braced against a eucalyptus bole, his rifle trained on the swamp below. I followed the slant of the barrel but could see nothing for the shine and dazzle of silt and water.

'What is it?' I whispered.

'You'll see.'

A pale form lifted from the water's edge, rising on

broad wings in the instant before the shot sang out. I had a fleeting sense – seeing the wings at full stretch, the long legs just beginning to tread air – of explosive energy; then the bird crumpled and dropped back into the slime.

'Yes,' breathed Bullen, his face flushed, his eyes fixed on the spot. But the bird wasn't finished. It struggled to its feet and made for firmer ground, head and neck held low, its left wing trailing. Bullen slung his rifle back over his shoulder and began to scramble down the slope, his boots throwing up showers of dust and leaves. I followed at a slower pace.

I thought our quarry might have eluded us but its painful progress was clearly inscribed on the soft silt, and by the time I drew level with him Bullen was on his knees where scrub and swampland met, reaching into a thick clump of brushwood. He was breathless, agitated, his eyes glazed in an ecstasy of vicious excitement as he fumbled among the crackling stems.

'It's in here. Cover the other side in case it makes a break for it.'

I moved round obediently. He set down his rifle and kicked vigorously at the clump, breaking down the scrub and trampling it beneath his boot soles. Something stirred in the shadows. I caught sight of a glittering eye, a long, heavy bill; then Bullen lunged forward.

'Hah!' His cry of triumph was so wild and strident that I took it at first to have been uttered by the bird. There was a flapping and scrabbling, the snapping of dry brushwood.

'Over here, Redbourne. He'll not run now.'

Rejoining him, I found that he had one leg of the bird – which I now saw to be a squat, thickset heron – clamped in his right hand, and was groping with the other for a firmer hold on his prize. The heron was frantically resisting the manoeuvre, weaving its head from side to side and gripping the brushwood tightly with its free foot. I knelt to help, but as I did so, Bullen drew in his breath with a sharp hiss and jerked back his left arm.

'What's the matter?'

'Damn the brute,' he said. He extended his hand towards me, palm upward, and I saw the blood welling from a broad gash just below the ball of the thumb. 'Damn it to hell.' He yanked roughly at the bird's leg, bringing its breast hard against the enclosing lattice of twigs. It cried out, a single grating note.

'Careful, Bullen. The creature's in pain.'

He tugged again. The head lunged towards us, a string of mucus trailing from the corner of the bill. A stink of fish; the air electric with cruelty and terror. A spasm of revulsion went through me, and I rose to my feet and unslung my rifle.

'Stand aside, Bullen. I'll finish it off.'

He stared up at me, his eyes flashing. 'Damned if I will,' he said. 'This skin's almost unmarked. D'you think I'm going to indulge your finer feelings by standing back and letting you blast it to shreds?'

'It's the bird's feelings I have in mind.'

'It amounts to the same thing. Listen, Redbourne, these creatures don't suffer the way you or I would. Science tells us as much. A creature with a brain the size of a walnut – look, just cut this stem here, would you?

Here, below the foot. We'll have the brute out in half a minute.'

It was clearly not the moment for debate. I set down my rifle, took the clasp-knife from my pocket and began to saw at the woody stem, the dull blade squeaking as I worked.

Bullen gave a snort of impatience. 'Take mine.' He indicated with a glance the bone-handled hunting-knife hanging at his belt. I slipped it from its sheath and set to again. The steel was sharp and clean, and I worked with greater ease now, cutting away until something gave and Bullen hauled the bird clear of the tangled brush. He moved awkwardly, his bleeding hand held well away from the delicate plumage. The bird lunged again.

'The neck, man – get hold of its neck.'

I leaned forward and seized the extended throat, feeling with a subtle shock the hard, sinewy strength of the thing. Bullen breathed heavily at my ear. 'Flip it over,' he said.

Once the bird was on its back, it stopped struggling, though its eyes continued to move wildly in its angular head. Bullen edged forward, pinning the belly beneath his leg before setting the heel of his right hand firmly against the base of the throat and bearing down with the full weight of his shoulders. The bird quivered violently and beat the earth with its good wing in a pitiful travesty of flight; then it lay still.

Bullen rose stiffly to his feet, swinging the carcass up by the neck so that I saw the pinkish flush of the mud-stained breast-feathers, the slack line of the throat. 'This one's mine,' he said, his voice harsh and a little aggressive, as though I had laid claim to the bird. He picked up his rifle and we retreated to the shade of the eucalyptus trees.

We had a good afternoon of it, all told, bagging between us several duck, a species of rail, an elegant blue and white kingfisher and a pair of small doves, modestly coloured but strikingly marked. I should have been delighted but my mood, as we rode back, was sombre. The stink of silt and fish hung heavily about us and my mind reverted continually to the same disquieting cluster of images: the sun hammering down mercilessly from the wide blue sky, light glinting off slime and water, the heron on its back in the dirt, and the two of us leaning above the bewildered creature like the fiends I once saw in a painting of the last judgement, meting out their dark, incomprehensible punishment to one of the damned.

10

Bullen returned to the villa several times during the
following week, on each occasion taking me out for
a day or half-day of shooting. I wouldn't go so far as
to say that I was warming towards the man but I was
learning to tolerate his company, and our excursions were
proving so productive that I was increasingly inclined to
overlook his intellectual shortcomings. Indeed, we were
so successful that I was having difficulty in coping with the
influx of specimens: by the end of the week such time as
was not taken up with hunting the birds was almost
entirely given over to preparing their skins.

'How many honey-eaters do you need?' asked Eleanor one morning, coming up behind me and surveying the heap of little corpses at the edge of my table.

I set down my scalpel, not entirely sorry to be interrupted. 'It's not a question of the number,' I explained. 'The thing is that slight variations between individuals – variations that might be overlooked in the field – could turn out to be important from a scientific viewpoint. At best, close examination might show one of these birds to be a new species. At the very least the group provides a valuable record, a basis for future research.'

'Give me one,' she said. 'That one, there.'

'What do you want with it?'

'I'm going to paint it.'

I handed her the bird. She held it in the cupped palm of her hand, scrutinising it intently before returning with it to her table. 'I want to paint it the way it is,' she said. 'Stiff and still.'

I caught the note of reproach in her voice and responded with a touch of irritation. 'Listen, Eleanor, you mustn't imagine—'

'Nell. I'd like you to call me Nell. Everyone does, except him.'

'Your father?'

'Yes. We argue about it. It isn't appropriate, he says.'

'He may have a point. It's not unreasonable for a father to want his daughter's name to reflect her station in life.'

'I have no station in life,' she said, spitting my own phrase back at me as though it disgusted her, 'but I have a right to be called by the name I choose.' She returned to her seat, laid the bird on the table in front of her and began to pin a fresh sheet of paper to her drawing-board. 'And you, Mr Redbourne,' she continued: 'What name do you want me to call you by?'

There was a hint of insolence in the question, but a kind of bashfulness too: I saw the colour rise to her cheeks as she fumbled with the pin. 'If you wish,' I said, 'you may call me Charles.' And then, after a moment, regretting the stiffness of my initial response: 'I should like that, Nell.' She glanced up with a quick, brittle smile and reached for her paintbrush.

We worked for some considerable time without speaking, separately absorbed in our tasks. I had made a good job of the specimen in hand, and was just cutting the neck free at the base of the skull when I heard Eleanor sigh and set down her drawing-board. 'What do you think happens to them?' she asked.

'Wait a moment,' I said, working my scalpel-blade upward from beneath the vertebrae. 'There.' I lifted the body clear and dropped it to the floor beside my chair. 'Happens to what?'

'The birds. Once they're dead. Do you suppose they have any kind of after-life?'

I smiled at the fancy. 'A heaven for birds?' I asked.

'I don't know about heaven. Perhaps they just go on with their lives in some other form. Or in the same form but more shadowy, so we can't quite make them out.'

'Perhaps,' I said noncommittally. I turned back to my specimen and began to chip gently at the underside of the skull. When she spoke again, it was with an odd, compelling urgency that made me look up at once.

'Would you stop for a while?' she asked. 'Stop working, I mean. Just for a few minutes. I want to tell you about my brother.'

I laid down my scalpel and swung my chair round so that I faced her directly. 'Do you have brothers?' she asked.

'No,' I said. 'No brothers, no sisters.'

'Did you never feel the lack of company when you were growing up?'

'Not that I can remember. I'm not at all sure that I should have welcomed an addition to the family.'

'Well, when I was small I used to pray to be given a brother. And for a while I'd pester my mother about it, in a way that it shames me to think of now. Later, as I grew to understand such things a little more clearly, I began to realise that I was likely to be disappointed, and by the time she broke the news to me, I'd almost given up hoping. I can still remember my feelings – a kind of astonishment at first, and then joy, joy taking hold in me like a flame in dry tinder – when she told me she'd been blessed. That was how she phrased it, and I remember the look on her face too, a look of such sweetness that, even now, I find it hard to say that it was anything less than a blessing.

'We were both certain that the baby was a boy, and we talked of him so often that he became part of the family long before he was due to be born. I knew the places he'd want to go, and all my walks were taken with him in mind. And I'd talk to him as I went, as though he were really there, showing him the things I loved, and loving them all the more for being able to share them with him.

I always imagined him slung on my hip, not heavy at all, moving so easily with my own movements that he might have been part of me.'

She stopped abruptly, half turning in her chair, twisting away from the light. Something in her face – some clouding or agitation of her features – made me uneasy. 'Maybe you should get on with your painting,' I said. 'Tell me about your brother some other time.'

'I've finished the picture. And maybe there won't be another time. Not for this. I want to tell you now.' She edged her chair clear of the table and leaned towards me, her forearms resting on her knees. 'He was to be called Edward,' she said. 'Like my father. I used to make believe I was looking into his eyes and seeing something of my father reflected there, and I'd tell him how like he was, the very image of his papa. And sometimes I'd call him by his name, very softly, and I'd teach him to say mine, pretending to myself . . . pretending—' She broke off again and began to rock gently back and forth, rubbing the palms of her hands against the rough fabric of her skirt.

'So your brother—'

'No,' she said sharply. 'I want to tell this the way it happened. The way it seemed to happen, anyway. One morning I woke early – I mean I was woken, woken by footsteps clattering through the hall downstairs, someone running helter-skelter, not at all the way the servants would normally have gone about their work. And it wasn't just that. All the other sounds were different too, as though I'd woken in someone else's house. And my heart was beating very fast and hard, though at that point I couldn't really have known—'

'Don't do that, Nell.'

'What?'

'That rocking. It disturbs me.'

She glowered at me, but sat back in her chair and composed herself a little before continuing.

'I ran out on to the landing, calling for my mother. But it was my father who appeared, banging back the dining-room door as he rushed out into the hallway. I can see him now, the way he looked that morning, staring up at me as I leaned over the stair-rail, his face grey like dirty pastry and his mouth twisted as though he were trying to smile and couldn't. "Get dressed," he said, "and stay in your room until I come up." Then he turned to go back into the dining-room, and at that moment I heard a cry – not a loud cry, but a kind of sobbing moan. I knew for sure then that something was amiss and I pelted down the stairs and caught up with him in the doorway. "I want to see Mama," I said, and made to squeeze past him into the room, but he moved to block my way, grabbing at my arm and knocking me sideways so that my head struck the door-frame. Not hard, but I fell to my knees; and as I tried to scramble out of his reach, I saw her lying there.'

'Your mother?'

'Yes, stretched out on the floor with the top of her dress unbuttoned and Mrs Denman kneeling over her, smoothing the hair back from her forehead. I must have stopped short at the sight of her – her face drawn with pain and the skin white and shining with sweat – because next thing I knew my father was bundling me back through the door and up the stairs. "Do as you're told," he said. "Stay in your room and I'll come up when I can." He was trying to soften his voice, I could tell, but it came out wrong, and his fingers were gripping my shoulder so tight you could see the bruising for weeks after.' She put her hand up to the place, rubbing it gently as if it were still tender.

There was a long silence.

'And when your father came back?'

'He didn't. When I was dressed I sat on my bed for an age, and at last Sally – the maid we had then – came up and told me I was to go out and play, and wait for the baby to arrive. So I put on my shoes and my sun-hat and – have you been down to the creek?'

'Not yet.'

'Well, when you go, leave the main path at the fork and take the narrower track through the trees. After about half a mile you'll come to a small patch of rough grazing. Cross that and you'll find yourself at the edge of the most beautiful stretch of the creek. There's a bend where the water slows and deepens, and a stillness all around that frightens people who aren't used to it. That's where I go when I need to think. It's where I went that morning.

'I walked slowly along the bank, talking to my brother as I'd grown used to doing, pointing out the things he liked – dragonflies, spiders' webs, the swallows dipping over the water. But it seemed to me that he wasn't quite with me – drifting away as I tried to interest him in this thing or that, his attention wavering and fading like a dying candle-flame. Or perhaps it was me – my own attention somewhere else so I couldn't see him clearly or hear what he was thinking. After a while it became so difficult that I stopped trying and let him go. And that's when I saw Mama, standing at the edge of the grassland, her dress as pale as the silver stringybarks she stood against, so that I could hardly make her out at first. But as I looked, she seemed to come into focus – to sharpen somehow, I can't say how it was – and then I saw she was bareheaded, her hair unpinned and tumbling loose about her shoulders. And that was strange because I'd never seen her take a step beyond the garden gate without first putting her hat on; but it wasn't as strange as what happened after.'

She had begun to rock again, the chair creaking softly with her movements. 'I can't help it,' she said, catching my glance. 'When I think about these things—'

'There's no need to go on if it distresses you.'

'But it's important to tell you. I've never told anyone before – never met anyone I thought would understand.'

I was surprised to find myself blushing, flattered no doubt by her implied regard for my perspicacity, but stirred too, as I was later to acknowledge to myself, by the subtle suggestion of intimacy. I don't believe she noticed my discomfiture; at all events, she took up the thread again, moving smoothly on as though there had been no interruption.

'No, the really strange thing was this: one moment she was out there by the trees, and the next – I don't know how it happened because there's some gap, a blank space where something must have gone on that I didn't see or can't lay hold of – she was with me on the bank, almost as close as you are now. I remember thinking how young she looked, her features fine and her skin soft, but very pale, and her gaze so mournful I can still make myself cry by thinking about it.

'I'd thought when I first caught sight of her that she must have come to show me my brother, but now I saw that her arms were empty. "Where is he?" I asked. And then, because she appeared not to understand, I said his name, "Edward," very softly like that, the way I liked to whisper it to him on our walks together. That seemed to rouse her in some way, and she fixed her eyes on mine and held me with her gaze. Her lips didn't move, but I knew then, as surely as if she'd spoken, that she'd come to let me know that my brother was dead – that he wasn't coming to join me and I shouldn't wait any more.' She leaned forward again, cupping her chin in her hand, and I saw that her eyes were bright with unspilled tears.

'And your mother?'

'Not there, though I saw her clearly enough. She couldn't have been.'

'Couldn't have been? Is this a ghost story, Nell?'

'Not a story, but the plain truth. And my mother couldn't have been a ghost either, not in the way people usually think of ghosts. She didn't die until late that evening. But I suppose some part of her must have broken free before the end and wandered out to find me.'

I regarded myself at the time as a thoroughgoing sceptic in such matters, but there was something in her words – or perhaps simply in her guilelessly expressive features – that set my skin prickling.

'I think we should take a stroll outside in the sunlight,' I said.

'Let me finish.' She brushed angrily at her eyes with the back of her hand and stared hard at me as though daring me to move. 'I began crying then, whimpering like a hurt puppy, wanting it not to be true but knowing beyond all doubt that it was. But she reached out and took me up – I don't mean in her arms, and I can't say exactly what I do mean, but I felt myself gathered and raised, riding upward the way a boat lifts at its moorings as the tide turns in. And after she'd gone – and she seemed to slip away without my noticing – I was still held there, very quiet and still, sensing myself a little apart from the world but seeing it all so clearly – the ripples and creases on the surface of the water, the play of light on the eucalyptus leaves, the shadows sliding across the grass as the day wore on. And even that night, lying in bed, listening to my father sobbing and moaning in the next room, I could still feel myself supported, as if she were trying to . . .' She trailed off, lifting her eyes to the cavernous roof as though she might find among its shadows the words she was searching for.

'To console you?'

She seemed to consider this. 'Well,' she said at last, 'I suppose it was something of the kind. I felt she was offering me her protection, though I think in the end she wasn't strong enough to shield me from the worst. If she'd been able to give me everything she seemed to promise, the past ten years would have been very different. We'd have kept that gentleness about the household, the gentleness I remember touching us all – myself, my father, the servants – as she moved among us in life.

And certainly my father would never have mistreated me as he does.'

'Come now, Nell. I can see that you and your father have your differences, but you're hardly—'

'You can see nothing,' she cut in angrily, starting to her feet. 'Nothing at all.' The colour was up in her cheeks again, her breathing fast and shallow. She leaned over her drawing-board and began to unpin the paper. 'I did this for you,' she said, 'but I might have saved myself the trouble.'

'Nell,' I said, moving towards her, 'you're not to talk like that. Do you hear me? Let me look.' She glared but made way for me, stepping back from the table so that I could see the painting more clearly.

What is it in art that opens our eyes and hearts to truths barely glimpsed in life? I had spent the best part of a morning staring at a succession of small corpses without registering what I was dealing with. Now, bending above Eleanor's painting – nothing, on the face of it, but streaks and clots of pigment on a cockled sheet of paper – I was jolted into awareness like a man roused suddenly from a profound sleep. The bird had been represented in profile and at such an angle in relation to the paper that, with bill slightly parted and neck extended, it seemed at first glance to be singing in blind ecstasy. Even the stiff left wing, held just wide of the body, might have been taken to indicate a taut vitality; but then the eye travelled to the dull badge of blood on the breast, to the legs, folded too close against the belly, and to the cramped grip of the feet on thin air. It was a remarkable achievement. By some expressive sleight of hand, Eleanor had contrived to suggest, more or less simultaneously, both the brute fact of death and the vibrant life from which the creature had been plucked; and it was in that poignant double focus that I discovered a truth which none of the morning's cutting and probing had succeeded in laying bare.

It was undoubtedly the image itself that moved me in the first instance, but it may be that what tipped the balance was Eleanor's giving of it – half sullen, half eager, her eyes lifted to mine as she handed me the sheet. At all events, my voice cracked as I thanked her, and I found myself, quite unexpectedly and with some embarrassment, on the verge of tears.

II

'You'll be pleased to know,' said Vane as we sat at lunch that afternoon, 'that Bullen has made arrangements for your expedition to the mountains.'

'He was here this morning?'

'He called by on his way to the store. You'll be starting out on Thursday, first thing. I suggested he join us for dinner this evening to discuss details with you.'

Bullen and I had, it was true, worked our way round, after a little unpleasantness and a certain amount of further haggling, to a broad agreement on the matter but

I found myself vaguely disconcerted, not only by the fellow's high-handed assumption that he might plan our itinerary without further consultation with me, but also by the news that we were to leave so soon. I was debating the wisdom of saying anything on the subject when Eleanor spoke up.

'Mr Redbourne has scarcely been here a week,' she said. 'You're bundling him off into the bush before he's had a chance to settle.'

'Mr Redbourne is here with a purpose,' said Vane with a flicker of irritation, 'and Mr Bullen has kindly agreed to help him. It's not for you to interfere in their business.' And then, turning to me before Eleanor had time to reply: 'There'll be four of us tonight – I've invited Merivale.'

'Five,' said Eleanor. 'Five of us.'

'Male company,' said Vane brusquely. 'I think you might prefer to take supper in the kitchen with Mrs Denham.'

'And then again,' she retorted, the colour rising to her cheeks, 'I might not.'

Vane gave her a long, hard stare. 'As you please,' he said, 'but I want no nonsense from you. You know what I mean. If you're addressed, you may speak. Otherwise, keep your thoughts to yourself.'

'Thank you, Father' – under her breath, the words themselves innocuous enough, but the insolence unmistakable. She laid her knife and fork carefully on the rim of her plate, rose to her feet and swept out of the room.

*　　*　　*

From the moment we sat down at the table that evening it was clear to me how profoundly Eleanor had subverted her father's plans: seating herself at Vane's side with Merivale to the left of her, she effectively isolated the young man from our company. I could see, glancing across as he bent smiling towards her, that he himself was by no means dissatisfied with the arrangement, but Eleanor's apparent determination to engage him in private conversation was plainly an irritant to her father. At intervals during the main course Vane would attempt to draw Merivale away, seeking his opinion on this or that matter of concern, but on each occasion Eleanor drew the young man back again, reeling him in as an angler plays a hooked fish, and Vane eventually abandoned him to her.

'The thing is,' said Bullen, glancing up as the maid-servant reached over to set the fruit bowl on the table, 'that we'll have more equipment than we can carry. The train journey poses no problem, of course, but once we're out there we shall need assistance. I've made arrangements for one of the local guides to go out with us – fellow by the name of Billy Preece, highly recommended by one of my contacts in the area. More than willing to shoulder his share, I'm told, and knows the region like the back of his hand.'

I have a naturally romantic outlook, and Bullen's reference to the railway gave me a moment's pause. I had imagined us setting out from the villa on horseback, and plunging almost at once into the unknown: a train journey seemed altogether too mundane.

'Oh, you'll get your fill of the wilderness,' said Bullen,

when I touched on the matter, 'once we're in the mountains. On ponyback first, and then on foot. By the time we return to civilisation you'll be more than ready to take advantage of its comforts.'

'No doubt,' I answered, 'but sometimes I think how the face of England has changed since my childhood – the railways reaching into all those quiet corners, the cities spreading outward like dirty stains – and I find myself wondering whether we may not be paying too high a price for the comforts of civilisation. Out here, with so much splendid scenery still unspoiled—'

'That's precisely the point,' interrupted Vane. 'There's so much of it that our own petty activities – railway construction, tree clearance, mining – make scarcely any impression. If I were to return to England now, I might well share some of your anxieties, but Australia's a different matter. You can't imagine it, Redbourne – the sheer immensity of the land, the resources we've scarcely begun to draw upon.'

'Besides,' said Bullen, 'there's nothing wrong with taking Nature in hand and letting her know we mean business. As a culture we possess certain skills, certain powers. They're the reason we're here – I mean, they're the reason we own the country and the blackfellow doesn't.'

'Well,' I said, 'we own it at the moment, but who's to say we won't be dislodged a century or two from now?'

Bullen shook his head. 'If we are,' he said, 'it won't be by a race of barefoot dreamers but by a civilisation even more forceful in its dealings with the world than we are.'

'True enough,' said Vane, selecting a ripe peach from

the fruit bowl. 'I'm with Darwin there – it's the strong who inherit the earth. That's the way things work. And there's no doubt that the native tribes here have had their day.'

I sensed, rather than saw, that Eleanor had turned to look in our direction. 'Forgive me if I'm wrong, Father,' she said, cutting in with chilly precision, 'but isn't it the meek who are to inherit the earth? Or has that text had its day too?'

Vane ran his knife round the soft flesh of the peach, twisted the halves apart and set them carefully on his plate. 'I wasn't aware,' he said, 'that meekness was a quality you held in particularly high esteem, Eleanor.' He leaned forward and took up the decanter. 'More wine, gentlemen?'

As he reached across to fill Merivale's glass, Eleanor interposed her own. 'Thank you,' she said. I saw Vane hesitate.

Eleanor looked around the table. 'My father believes that good wine is wasted on young ladies,' she said.

'Your father believes,' said Vane, gruffly, 'that one glass is ample for any young lady worthy of the name.'

'But not,' Eleanor persisted, 'for a young gentleman.' She turned to Merivale. 'Do you think that's fair, William?'

The young man's confusion was almost comical. Undoubtedly flattered by her appeal, yet clearly conscious of his obligation to his host, he stuttered and goggled until Vane, perhaps out of pity for his predicament or perhaps simply in hope of restoring order to the proceedings, replenished Eleanor's glass.

'I don't think,' said Eleanor, picking up her thread as deftly as if the interruption had not taken place, 'that meekness means letting other people have their way at your expense, or being silent when you've a right or a duty to speak. I think it means being humble in the face of a universe we can hardly begin to understand. I think it means knowing when we should stop trying to set our stamp on everything we see – knowing when to stand back and admire the world instead of forcing ourselves on it.'

She took a gulp of wine and set her glass back on the table with clumsy emphasis. 'Mr Bullen seems to imagine,' she continued, 'that our culture will have fulfilled its destiny once it has taken everything else – the wilderness, other cultures, life itself – by the scruff of the neck and shaken it into submission.' Merivale shifted uneasily at her side and leaned forward as though to intervene, but if she saw the movement she chose to ignore it. 'We're cut out for better things, Mr Bullen – for higher things – but we live blindly, striking out at whatever displeases us, gathering up whatever takes our fancy. We don't see the damage we're doing or the suffering we cause. And until we do—'

'Whoa there, young lady,' cried Bullen, good-humouredly enough, I thought, given the circumstances. 'You can't hold me responsible for all the ills of the world.'

'I don't. Of course not. But when I hear you talk, I know where you stand not in the clear light I want to stand in, but in some dark place, among all the other lost souls who've confused power with progress.'

Vane made a little lunge across the table, rapping

lightly on the cloth with his knuckles. 'It seems to me,' he said with forced playfulness, 'that the ladies might reasonably retire now.'

Eleanor glanced at her father with an expression of such undisguised contempt that I felt myself wince on his behalf. 'I'll retire when I'm ready,' she said.

'In that case,' said Vane, reddening slightly but without faltering for a second, 'may I suggest that the gentlemen retire.' He drained his glass and rose unsteadily to his feet. 'If you'd care to join me on the terrace . . .'

Bullen and I fell in behind him but, looking round as I stepped out on to the veranda, I saw that Merivale was still in his seat. With one hand gripping his sleeve, Eleanor was literally holding him there, addressing him in low, urgent tones, her eyes fixed on his as though defying him to move. It crossed my mind that he might welcome my intervention but I couldn't be sure, and after a moment's hesitation I followed Vane and Bullen out into the darkness.

'. . . a mind of her own,' Vane was saying as I rejoined them, 'and I accepted that long ago. What I won't tolerate is being made a fool of at my own table, or having my guests insulted.' He turned as though to include me in the conversation, but seemed to think better of continuing. He felt in his breast pocket and withdrew his cigarette case.

'I believe Merivale will be with us directly,' I said after a moment, anxious to break the awkward silence. In the flare of his match I saw Vane's eyes lift towards the house. 'He's been detained by Eleanor,' I added.

'Detained at Her Majesty's pleasure,' said Vane sardonically. 'After an evening of my daughter's nonsense, I should think you'll be only too glad to get out into the bush for a couple of weeks.'

'It was an excellent evening,' I said.

Vane grunted and turned away, staring into the night. 'Fatherhood,' he said bitterly, 'is a mixed blessing.' And then, shifting his shoulders like a man easing away the afterweight of a slipped burden: 'You'll need the buggy early on Thursday, Bullen. What time shall we say?'

As they talked, I saw Merivale emerge on to the veranda, closely followed by Eleanor. The young man set his back against the rail and stood, starkly silhouetted against the french windows, his face turned towards his companion. As Eleanor closed in I lost sight of her behind his bulky form, but it was clear that she had not yet done with him: I heard her voice – not the words but the soft, insistent murmur of it – drifting out on the warm air. Merivale seemed to have little to say but his stance suggested that the girl had his undivided attention, and I was surprised when she broke abruptly away and stepped back into the house. He started after her, stumbling on the threshold so that he had to put out his hand to support himself.

What was it I saw then? I was tired and my mind was faintly clouded by the wine, but I thought Merivale reached out and grasped Eleanor by the shoulder, swinging her round – but her slight frame was scarcely visible at that point – to face him. I scarcely had time to register the movement before they were gone, passing swiftly across the windows and out of sight.

Bullen and Vane were discussing train times. 'If you'll excuse me,' I said, 'I think I'll turn in for the night.' My voice was thick in my throat and I was shaking with passion, as though the gripped shoulder or the grasping hand had been my own, but Vane, barely glancing my way as he bade me goodnight, appeared to notice nothing.

There was no sign of the couple in the dining-room, but as I stepped into the hallway I saw them there, in the half-light at the foot of the stairs. Merivale had been speaking but fell silent as I approached, shrinking further into the shadows, while Eleanor came towards me with a faint smile on her lips. I don't know quite what I had expected, but something in the assurance of her movements surprised and disconcerted me.

'I'm on my way to bed,' I said awkwardly, as though it were my own actions that required an explanation.

'Goodnight, Charles.'

Just that. I stood for a moment with one hand on the stair-rail, scanning her face for whatever clue might be visible in the dim lamplight. Not a flicker as she returned my gaze.

'Goodnight, Eleanor. Goodnight, Merivale.' I climbed slowly, my whole body suddenly slack with fatigue. As I reached the turn of the stair I almost looked back, but thought better of it.

12

I stretched out in extreme weariness but was unable to sleep for thinking of Eleanor down there with Merivale in the shadowed hallway. I told myself firmly that the girl's conduct was no business of mine but I couldn't settle, and after twenty minutes or so I rose from bed and seated myself at my desk with the idea that a little writing might steady my restless mind.

My journal, begun on shipboard as a simple aidememoire, had become increasingly important to me as the voyage progressed, and since my arrival in Australia I had begun to consider my writing in a new light. The field notes I had taken throughout the years of my youth and early manhood had been exemplary in their attention to detail but now, I realised, I was looking for something more than scientific accuracy. I had been aware since childhood that the minutiae of the material world – the veining of a beech leaf, the whorl of a snail shell, a fox's pad-mark in the silt at the river's edge – were a kind of code, and I had sometimes had bewildering glimpses of the vast and infinitely complex truth they represented, but I had seldom attempted to find words to convey those insights. Now, as I wrote of the sheen on a beetle's carapace, for example, or the patterns scribbled on the pale bark of a eucalyptus tree, I found myself working with a new refinement, honing my phrases to an edge I hoped might be sharp enough to slip beneath the dazzling surfaces of things.

I was describing the clearing I had entered late that afternoon, and the subtle agitation set up by a pair of wrens as they foraged through the undergrowth in the softening light, when I was startled by a shrill cry. I set down my pen and listened. A brief pause and then a thud, followed by a second cry. I took up my lamp, opened the door and stepped out into the corridor.

It was Eleanor's voice, I knew, hearing it again as I approached her bedroom – a staccato phrase delivered in an intense undertone. I placed the lamp on the blanket-chest outside the room and rapped gently on the door.

'Eleanor?'

No answer. I called again and heard a voice rasp out, breathy and urgent: 'Tell him to go.'

I leaned against the door, my lips close to the keyhole. 'Merivale? Merivale, is that you?'

Dead silence, except for the slow ticking of the clock from the hallway below. And in that instant, driven not only by anxiety for Eleanor but also by an obscure sense of outrage, I turned the handle and threw back the door.

The scene presents itself to me now as a static tableau, its detail simultaneously vivid and equivocal. Vane stands beside the washstand, one hand resting on the marble surface, the other held to the side of his face. His jacket and waistcoat are draped over the back of the bedside chair; his pocket-watch, lapped in the gleaming coils of its chain, is on the seat. On the rug at his feet, in two almost equal pieces, lies a broken jug; water has soaked the fawn pile, forming a dark, irregular stain. Eleanor faces her father, backed up against the bed, but bolt upright. She is clutching the neck of her loose white nightdress, gathering the fabric at her throat. Her hair is unbound and dishevelled, her eyes fixed in a wild stare.

Is it just a trick of the memory, that impression of breathless stasis? Maybe so, but the impression is all I have: the two of them locked together in a world somewhere beyond the ordinary flow of things, utterly oblivious to my presence. The air seemed to have thickened around them, dense with undischarged energy and the coppery reek of sweat. And then, with a muffled grunt, like a man waking himself with effort from a disturbing dream, Vane swung round to confront me.

Never, before or since, have I experienced such acute embarrassment. Think of it: close on midnight, and a man of mature years and some social standing bursts into a young lady's bedroom in his nightshirt to find himself face to face with her father. It was the stuff of farce, without the leaven of humour. I gawped; I mumbled. 'I'm sorry. I thought I heard . . .'

'It's nothing.' Vane was breathing hard, his face and thick neck flushed, his brow gleaming with perspiration. 'Eleanor dropped the water-jug, that's all. There's no great harm done.' His face, I noticed as he lowered his hand, was marked, the cheekbone a darker, angrier red than the surrounding flesh. He squatted down on his heavy haunches and picked up the two pieces. Eleanor slumped on to the bed and sat there, shoulders hunched, hands thrust between her thighs, her face averted. She was trembling so violently that the bed-frame shook.

I leaned forward, trying to catch her eye. I was looking for a sign, for something that might tell me what kind of drama I had stumbled into, but her gaze was rigidly fixed on a point towards the far corner of the room and never so much as flickered in my direction. Awkward and uncertain, I turned back to her father.

Vane raised his arm and drew his shirt-sleeve across his forehead. 'I'm sorry you've been disturbed,' he said.

'Please don't concern yourself on my account. But Eleanor—'

'Eleanor has been a little over-excited by the events of the day. She needs to rest.' His breathing was returning to normal; his hand, cupping my elbow as he steered me round and guided me back to the door, conveyed nothing more than a host's natural solicitude for his guest's well-being. But as we reached the doorway, Eleanor cried out – a stifled yelp of pain or fury – and I turned to see her rise from the bed and launch herself towards us. Vane hustled me quickly into the corridor, slipping out with me and slamming the door behind him. An instant later she was there, rattling at the handle, but Vane was gripping it firmly from our side, and the door remained closed. I heard her strike the wood with the flat of her hand, just once; and then she called my name.

An expression of something like panic crossed Vane's face, passing almost before I had time to register it. He jerked his head in the direction of my room. 'I'd advise you to get to bed,' he said. 'You can leave this to me.'

Close up against the door, Eleanor drew a long, sobbing breath. I hesitated. 'Perhaps I might have a word with her,' I said.

'Believe me, it's better you don't.'

I shifted uneasily from one foot to the other. 'Forgive me,' I said, 'but I feel there may be some advantage in letting me speak with her. In my experience—'

'I think,' he interrupted coldly, 'that I can be relied upon to know what's best for my own daughter.' And then, a little more civilly: 'Take it from me, Redbourne, there's nothing you can do for her.'

There seemed no point in persisting. 'In that case,' I said, 'I'll wish you goodnight.' I stooped to pick up the lamp and, as I did so, the rattling began again, followed by a heavy drumming against the panels. Vane flinched and tightened his grip on the door-handle. 'Go on,' he whispered hoarsely as I stood dithering. 'Get to your room.'

I was half-way back when she cried out again, the words ringing down the corridor with a terrible shrill clarity: 'He knows. He knows.' I turned to see Vane gesticulating wildly with his free hand, flapping me back as though I were a hen strayed from the coop. And then, even more stridently but no less distinctly, her voice cracking on my name: 'You hear me, Charles? You're my witness.'

Vane's features convulsed suddenly: a wincing grin, lips drawn back from the teeth, the eyes narrowed to slits. And still that panicky flutter, the hand wafting me back down the corridor. The air seemed charged with a kind of madness, a jittery, disruptive energy threatening my own stability, and it was with a measure of relief that I finally withdrew and returned to my room.

I reseated myself at my desk, still listening to the sounds from the corridor: the thick murmur of Vane's voice punctuated at intervals by his daughter's lighter tones, pleading, perhaps, or remonstrating. After a few moments I heard Vane's heavy tread on the boards as he drew closer. Then the door of his room creaking open; shut. The click as the catch snapped home.

I took up my pen again and wiped the clogged nib. There was something I had wanted to say about that moment in the clearing – something about the shifting, intricate patterns of sound and light set up around me as the birds flicked and piped among the leaves. I dipped the pen and wrote:

> long-tailed and small-bodied, beautifully marked above. By good fortune, I was able to secure both with the same shot. The female died instantly but the male scurried across the dry litter and wedged itself tightly

among the basal shoots of a small shrub. I thought I should be obliged to dispatch it, but by the time I had extricated it from its niche, it was already dead.

Even as I wrote, I knew that the moment was lost. I read back over my words with growing disappointment, then struck out the reference to my good fortune and paused for a moment over 'beautifully marked' before deciding to let the bland phrase stand. I left a two-inch space and then wrote again, more slowly now, and with some hesitancy:

I have just come from Eleanor's room, where

I sat back and looked at the words for several minutes; then I took my ruler and drew two lines through them, rendering them illegible. Beneath these and extending across the full width of the page I drew a third, indicating in my usual fashion the conclusion of the day's entry. I blotted the page carefully before closing the journal and retiring to bed.

13

I had anticipated a restless night but in fact I slept
deeply, waking only at the sound of the breakfast-
gong. By the time I came down, Vane had already
served himself and was seated at the table cutting
vigorously at a thick wedge of gammon.

'Help yourself, Redbourne. This' – he held up a pink
sliver on the end of his fork – 'is excellent. We rear and
cure our own and, if I may say so, we do it rather better
than most.'

I chose the eggs and joined him at the table. 'About
last night—'

'Please,' he cut in briskly, his mouth full. 'Please don't apologise. You acted, I know, with the best of intentions and you've no reason to reproach yourself.' He swallowed hurriedly, dabbed at his mouth with his napkin and reached for the coffee-pot. 'May I?'

'Thank you.' I pushed my cup towards him. 'Where's Eleanor?'

'Still in bed, I imagine.' He gestured towards my plate. 'That's not much of a breakfast. Let me help you to a little more.'

I shook my head. 'It's not like her to lie in so late. I'm wondering whether last night's disturbance—'

'Don't concern yourself. Eleanor's an excitable girl – some taint on her mother's side – but she calms down quickly enough if left alone.'

'This has happened before, then?'

'Episodes of this kind, yes.' He sat back in his chair, slightly flushed, and took a deep breath. 'Listen, Redbourne, I must urge you not to involve yourself in any way. The worst thing we can do – I have this on sound medical advice – is to appear to sanction her follies or to give credence to her fantasies. Last night's display' – he gingerly fingered the bruise on his cheek – 'was an extreme form of the hysteria that has afflicted her periodically since her mother's death. No cause for alarm, you understand, but the situation requires careful handling. I hope I can rely on you.'

Something in his speech struck me as faintly artificial, as though he were delivering lines rehearsed in advance, and whether for this or some other reason, I was slow to respond to his implicit appeal.

He leaned forward again, jabbing at the air with his fork, his eyes fixed on mine. 'I said, I hope I can rely on you, Redbourne. The girl's health depends on it.'

'I can assure you,' I said, 'that I would do anything in my power to safeguard your daughter's well-being.'

He held me with his gaze a moment longer and then addressed himself once more to his breakfast, hacking at the gammon with renewed energy, chewing noisily on each mouthful. The conversation was clearly at an end, and as soon as I decently could I excused myself from the table and stepped out into the garden.

It was a morning of exquisite serenity, clear but not yet hot, the air rich with the scents of the warming earth. A small flock of finches moved erratically among the glossy leaves of the citrus trees, their white breasts gleaming as they caught the light. I watched the birds intently, hoping for that fleeting release I sometimes experience in such circumstances: the mind – or spirit if you like – vibrating for a moment in sympathy with the stir and shimmer of the natural world. But the events of the night were still with me, a dark, distracting undertone, and my concentration lapsed.

Although I considered returning to the house and knocking on the door of Eleanor's room, it seemed wiser, on reflection, to go down to the barn and await her arrival. But as I approached the building, I heard the clatter of something dropped or overset, and I knew she was already there. I hurried to the entrance and peered round the door.

I thought at first that she was praying, down on her

knees on the dirt floor, her head bent forward, her lips moving spasmodically, spitting out broken, unintelligible phrases. But both hands were at the back of her neck, and as my eyes grew accustomed to the gloom, I saw what she was up to – hacking with a pair of rusted sheepshears at her dishevelled hair. I stepped forward, crying out her name, but as she raised her head and looked towards me I saw that the tresses which should have mantled her right shoulder were already gone. She dropped her hands to her lap, sat back on her heels and stared up at me, her lips wet with spittle, her eyes lit with a terrible wildness. I thought of her father's injunction against involvement, but I could see that it would be a grave mistake to leave her, in such a state, to her own devices.

'What are you doing?' I asked, as calmly as I could.

'You can see what I'm doing.' She raised the shears to the back of her neck again. I knelt beside her and took up a loop of hair from the packed earth.

'Your father said—'

'What my father said' – I heard the blades clash and grind – 'won't have come within a country mile of the truth. Did he tell you about this?' She hauled sharply on the hair twisted in her left hand so that her head went back between her shoulders and her long pale throat lay exposed. Her teeth were bared in a fierce rictus, the breath hissing between them as she struggled, in grotesque pantomime, to free herself from her own unyielding grip. I leaned forward and took her gently by the shoulder.

'Don't,' I said. 'You'll harm yourself.'

'Not the way he's harmed me. But let him try it now.' She relinquished her hold and ran her hand with a vicious clawing or combing motion across the cropped side of her head. 'See? Try for yourself. Go on.' I could feel her trembling beneath my hand. 'I said, go on. Make to grab me by the hair as if—'

'Easy, Nell, easy,' I said, very softly but firmly, as though I were quietening a frightened animal. 'You're not to excite yourself.'

'Who says not?' She peered into my eyes, her face so close I could feel the warmth of her breath on my skin. 'I suppose my father's told you I'm brainsick, has he? A poor deluded child who doesn't know what day of the week it is?'

I lowered my eyes, unable to sustain the intensity of her stare. 'Not exactly. He told me that since your mother's death you've been prone to—'

'Damn him,' she cried, arching her body sideways and breaking my hold on her shoulder. 'Damn him and his lying tongue.' She set to once more with the shears, chopping and tearing frenziedly at the remaining hanks of hair. I snatched at her arm, a futile gesture in any event and, as it transpired, worse than futile. She gave a sharp cry and the shears clattered to the ground. I leaned behind her with the intention of retrieving them and saw the smooth skin of her neck broken, the blood seeping into the white collar of her blouse.

I remember the momentary silence, the acute and quite disproportionate spasm of anguish that went through me as I gazed at the nick below the ragged line of her hair. I reached into my breast pocket for my handkerchief.

'Bend your head forward,' I said. I folded the handkerchief into a thick pad and dabbed gently at the cut. 'It's hardly more than a scratch. Certainly nothing to worry about.'

'Oh, I'm not troubled. Believe me, I'd take the blades to my face if I thought there was no other way of getting clear of it all.'

'This is wild talk, Nell. You're to stop it, do you hear?' I picked up the shears and slipped them quickly, blades first, into my side pocket.

'I'll talk as I please,' she said sullenly. She half turned, groping behind her with her left hand, then swung back violently to face me. 'Where are they?'

'The shears?' I fingered the protruding grip, feeling her touch still there in the warm steel. 'I have them.'

'Give them to me.'

'They're safer with me, Nell.' I rose cautiously to my feet and stepped back a couple of paces. 'You don't need them.'

'Of course I need them. I can't go back to the house with my hair like this.'

'You should have thought of that before you started.'

'I mean' – she tugged irritably at the last strands of uncut hair – 'with the job unfinished. Let me have them.' She held out her hand and stared up at me, her eyes daring me to refuse.

'I'll finish the job for you,' I said, 'but not with a pair of blunt sheep-shears. What were you thinking of, Nell?'

'I wasn't thinking. Just feeling. The shears came to hand, that's all – the way things do when they're needed.'

I went to my table, unfastened my satchel and drew

out the case of instruments. I spread it flat and selected the larger of the two pairs of scissors.

'Come and sit here,' I said, pulling the chair away from the workbench and swivelling it round to face her.

'Just give me the scissors. I can do it myself.'

'You can have no idea,' I said, a little more brusquely than I'd intended, 'what kind of a mess you've made. Let me tidy it up for you.'

She stood still for a second or two, irresolute but visibly calmer now; then she stepped over and seated herself decorously in the chair. I pushed the door wide and the light came flooding in.

I trim my own hair as a matter of course and I had no scruples about dealing with Eleanor's, particularly since, as I was tactless enough to hint, her recent efforts had left so much scope for improvement. There's no great mystery to the craft: like the skinning of a bird, it requires a certain delicacy of touch but is otherwise largely a matter of patience and concentration. I worked with care, but with vigour and fluency too, running my hand smoothly upward from nape to crown through the thick curls, lifting and cutting, lifting and cutting, absorbed in the easy, repetitive movement. And it wasn't until the job was almost done that I was struck – feeling with a queasy tenderness the contours of her skull beneath my fingertips – by the strange intimacy of the whole business, and by some attendant notion of its impropriety. I withdrew my hand and straightened up.

'Have you finished?'

'Very nearly.'

'What does it look like?'

'A good deal better than it did ten minutes ago, but – hold still now.' I leaned over her again and snipped away a stray wisp of hair.

'But what?'

I snipped again. 'You'd better go in and see for yourself,' I said. 'I've done what I can.' I shook out the folded handkerchief and flapped the cut hair from the back of her neck.

'You're angry with me, aren't you?' She tilted back her head, staring up into my face.

'Angry at what you've done, yes. Angry at this wilful violation of your own beauty.'

'If my beauty's my own,' she said, colouring, 'I can do what I like with it.'

'That's not true, Nell. Your beauty is valued by others. This isn't simply an outrage against yourself, but against those who care for you.'

I saw her shoulders stiffen and go back. 'Outrage?' she said quietly. 'Violation?' Her voice was very clear and cold. 'You don't know the meaning of the words. I'll show you outrage. I'll show you violation. I'll show you how he cares for me.'

She rose to her feet and turned to face me, both hands at her throat. I had no sense at first of what she was up to; then the hands slipped an inch or two lower, and I saw that she was unbuttoning herself.

'What is this, Nell? What are you doing?'

She made no answer but continued, with deft, economical movements of her thin fingers, to unfasten her blouse. It wasn't the action alone that alarmed me but the terrible fixity of her gaze, her eyes trained on mine but seeming to look clean through me to the shadows at my back. I stepped forward to restrain her.

'No,' she said sharply. And then, as I hesitated, she put her right hand to the collar of her blouse and tugged it down over her shoulder so that her left breast lay exposed.

You have to bear in mind that, since the death of my mother, all my dealings with women had been of an essentially impersonal nature, and certainly nothing in my experience had prepared me for this – an act of unsettling complexity, simultaneously suggestive of licentiousness and trusting innocence, of vulnerability and barely suppressed fury. And if I was unsettled by the act itself, I was horrified by the damage it disclosed: what I was looking at was not the smooth pallor familiar to me from my days in the art galleries of France and Italy, but a blotched patchwork of scabs and bruises.

What should I have said? I felt the need of words, but for a long moment could only stare in appalled fascination at what I took to be a bite-mark, a ragged oval, visibly infected, an inch or so above the nipple; and when words came they were, as I knew at once, the wrong ones. 'That needs attention,' I said, gesturing awkwardly at the inflamed area.

'I am attending to it,' she said quietly. 'I always do.' She turned away as though belatedly registering the impropriety of the situation, and began to refasten her buttons.

'If there's anything I can do . . .'

She raised her head and glanced back at me over her shoulder. 'I told you,' she said. 'You're my witness.'

Then she stepped out into the sunlight. I hurried after her as she strode purposefully up the path towards the house, her cropped head held high and her skirts swaying. It seemed to me that there was more to be said, but she never once slowed her pace or looked back.

Vane was leaning on the rail of the veranda, smoking. I saw his head jerk up as we approached; then he stubbed out his cheroot and struck diagonally across the lawn towards us, stumbling a little as he came, his eyes fixed on his daughter's face. As Eleanor drew level with him, he stretched out his arm, meaning, I supposed, to detain or embrace her; but she brushed past him as though he were an importunate street-beggar and swept into the house. As he gazed after her, I caught in his eye the most extraordinary expression of anguished entreaty, and I imagined that he would follow her; but he drew himself up sharply, rammed his hands into his jacket pockets and veered off towards the gates without so much as a glance in my direction.

I was seized by a longing for space and solitude. I left word with the servants that I should be away for the remainder of the day, then collected my net and killing-bottle from the barn and set out for the creek.

Dinner that evening was a miserable occasion. Whether as a result of the turmoil of the preceding twenty-four hours or because I had spent too long in the full glare of the afternoon sun, I was oppressed throughout the meal by a sick headache that deprived me both of my spirits and my appetite. And Vane, too, seemed distinctly out of sorts: moodily preoccupied, he scarcely troubled to acknowledge my presence until we were half-way through the main course.

'I've come to realise,' he said at last, 'that I should have been more explicit about my daughter's condition. What I described this morning as hysteria might more appropriately be characterised as a form of mania. To put it bluntly, Eleanor suffers from delusions. I don't mean the fantasies natural to impressionable girls of her age, but ideas – usually of persecution or assault – that invade her mind and grow there until they become indistinguishable from the reality around her. It's a vile business, Redbourne, hard for her, and harder still on those who care for her. And of course' – he shot me a sharp glance – 'it makes her entirely unmarriageable. That's a heavy burden for a father to bear.'

I said nothing. Whatever I thought I had seen – up in Eleanor's room, out there in the shadowed barn – seemed to melt and blur, equivocal as the broken images of a midnight dream.

Vane picked up his napkin-ring and studied it carefully, as though it bore some arcane inscription. 'There's something else I have to say, Redbourne. I believe that your presence in the household may have contributed in some measure to these recent outbursts. Please don't misunderstand me – there's no personal criticism implied – but the coincidence is suggestive. I'm no expert in such matters myself, and I make no judgement, but the plain fact is that until last night she was showing every sign of having outgrown the more extreme manifestations of her illness.'

'If you're asking me to leave—'

'Please, Redbourne.' He reached out and gripped my sleeve with awkward familiarity. 'I wouldn't dream of it. You'll be gone by Thursday in any case, and that's all too soon for me. But I suggest that you avoid Eleanor's company in the interim – avoid it entirely. For your own good as well as hers.'

He placed the napkin-ring carefully beside the meat-dish and glanced across at my plate. 'You're not eating,' he said.

I shook my head and felt a spasm of pain pass like fire from the back of my skull to my left temple. 'I seem to have lost my appetite,' I said. 'Do you mind if I retire?'

He leaned forward, scrutinising my face. 'You look flushed,' he said. 'Are you unwell?'

'A little. A touch of the sun, perhaps.' I rose unsteadily to my feet and made for the door.

'You'll bear in mind what I've told you, Redbourne?'

The words were clear as crystal but seemed to come to me from an enormous distance. I inclined my head vaguely in their direction, let myself out into the hallway and slowly climbed the stairs to my room.

I had made a vow to myself on leaving England that my opium-taking would in future be restricted to cases of medical necessity and, despite moments of temptation during the voyage, the bottle of tincture I had brought with me was still unbroached. I cracked the seal with my pocket-knife and eased out the cork. I took the tumbler from the washstand and poured into it a finger of brandy from my hip-flask. Then I added a few drops of the tincture, knocked back the mixture and eased myself, still half clothed, between the sheets.

It was a night of dreams, all forgotten now except the last. I was back in the swamplands where we had killed the heron, up to my calves in the silt at the water's edge. And she was there too, kneeling or squatting beside me, though in the half-dark – some dullness or misting of the air around us – I didn't recognise her until she spoke. Not in words, I think; but I knew clearly enough what she wanted and why she had joined me there, and I slipped the blouse back from her shoulders and began to wash the lacerated skin, scooping up the water in cupped hands and letting it fall from above so that it ran in rivulets down her throat and breasts. Swamp water, yes, but shining as it fell; and her skin taking on the shine, the scars and bruises fading as I worked. And then, because I knew that this, too, was what she wanted, I knelt and placed the tips of my fingers lightly against the healed flesh.

I can't get back to it now – not to the charged heart of the dream. But I remember that, lying there in its thrilling afterglow, I conceived the notion that the waking world and the world of the dream were one and the same; and in my confused or exalted state I imagined myself padding down the corridor to Eleanor's room and gently rousing her from sleep to ask whether she knew in what miraculous fashion we had both been blessed.

14

Eleanor wasn't at breakfast the next morning, and Vane seemed scarcely able to acknowledge my presence, let alone to maintain a civilised conversation. He ate with nervous, preoccupied haste, and only when he had cleared his plate and poured himself a second cup of coffee did he raise his eyes to mine.

'I've sent for Bullen,' he said. 'I thought you'd want another day out before you leave.'

'Thank you, Vane, but I'd prefer to stay here. I've two skins to prepare, and I shall need time to pack for tomorrow's journey.'

'Bullen won't be here until eleven. I imagine that will give you time enough.'

His anxiety to have me off the premises was so painfully evident that I decided not to argue the point. 'I'll set to work now,' I said. 'No doubt I can arrange my affairs around the excursion.'

'Thank you, Redbourne.' His features softened into a weak smile. 'I know you appreciate the delicacy of the situation.'

'Is Eleanor any better this morning?'

'It's hard to say. She's quieter, as she generally is after one of these episodes, but she's still far from well.'

'Has the doctor examined her?'

'There's no need.' Vane drained his coffee-cup and set it carefully back in its saucer. 'He'd prescribe complete rest as usual. If she keeps to her room for the next few days, she'll gradually return to a more orderly state of mind.'

'I hope I shall be able to see her before I leave.'

'I'm afraid that won't be possible,' he said, rising abruptly to his feet. 'But I should be glad to pass on any message you may have for her.'

I was quite unprepared for the wave of desolation that swept over me at that moment, and it took me a second or two to recover my equilibrium. 'Thank you,' I said. 'You might just tell her that I look forward to seeing her fully restored to health on my return.'

It was barely a flicker, but the expression that crossed Vane's face told me as clearly as words could have done that I shouldn't presume on boundless hospitality on any future visit to the villa. 'I mean,' I added hastily, 'when I call by to collect my trunk.'

'Of course,' he murmured, but even as he spoke I could see from his expression that something – perhaps some small sound from beyond the door – had distracted him. He stood alert for a moment, head lifted like that of an animal scenting danger, and then, scarcely troubling to excuse himself, strode swiftly past me and out of the room.

I was glad at first to get out to the barn but I found it difficult to concentrate and I made a poor job of the first specimen, tearing the delicate skin in several places. The second bird fared even worse, its pale breast-feathers stained with bile as a result of my carelessness and, on a sudden nauseous impulse, I disposed of the entire mess in the scrub outside the door. It was Eleanor, I realised, as I wiped my instruments and returned them to their case, who had distracted me, her presence so deeply engrained in the place – or perhaps simply in my receptive mind – that it was impossible to be there without thinking of her.

I made my way back to the house in a state of subdued agitation, and as I rounded the shrubbery and looked up I saw her at the window of her room, her face close against the glass. I was unable to interpret either the words she mouthed at me or the fluttering action of her raised right hand but I judged it best, in the first instance at least, to remain where I was. I ducked back out of sight of the house and waited.

I heard the rustle of her skirts as she approached, and knew from the sound that she was moving fast, half running towards me across the open lawn. As she drew level with the end of the shrubbery she caught sight of me and veered round with a movement so impetuous as to bring her within an ace of falling into my arms. And seeing her standing there, her face lifted to mine and her hand flat against the base of her throat as though to steady her own quick breathing, I was struck by the thought that a man differently reared or constituted – a man, in short, of less ambiguous temperament than myself – would hardly have let such an opportunity slip for want of a welcoming gesture.

She was flustered and dishevelled, her eyes hollow in her pale face and her hair standing out from her head in absurd tufts and spikes, yet her beauty remained somehow inviolate, too deeply seated, it seemed to me, to be dislodged by the accidents of life.

'I wanted to see you before you left,' she said. 'To say goodbye. I couldn't bear not to.'

I should have liked to tell her of my own desolation, earlier that morning, at the thought of leaving without sight of her, but the words wouldn't come. 'Your father told me you were keeping to your room,' I said. 'I'm glad to see you up and about.'

'Keeping to or kept to?' she snapped, her eyes flashing anger. 'There's a difference.' And then, more mildly: 'I'm sorry you've been witness to so much disturbance over the past few days, Charles. It must have been distressing for you.'

'I suppose it has been. Listen, Nell, I need to understand this clearly. Your father—'

'Not now.' She drew back with a little shake of her head. 'One day, perhaps. In any case, it's all done with.'

'And Merivale? What was I witnessing there the other night, at the foot of the stairs?'

'Oh, that.' She shrugged. 'William has been stealing kisses from me since we were children. He knows it's not appropriate any longer, but that doesn't stop him trying. I was telling him it's high time he went out and found himself a wife.'

'And he, I imagine, was telling you – maybe not for the first time – that he's already found what he wants, here on his doorstep.'

I saw from her expression that I had hit the mark, but there was no embarrassment in her reply. 'He needs to look further afield,' she said. 'It would be better for him.'

'And you?'

'I've never entertained the idea of marrying William. Even if my heart had been in it, it wouldn't have done. He sees his future here, in the valley. I can't tell him why that's impossible for me.'

I felt a faint exhilaration, a lightening of my breath as though some weight, far down, had eased or shifted, and at that moment I heard Bullen calling out to me from the terrace.

'You may have to go down and fetch him' – Vane's voice, curt and clear on the still air.

Eleanor pressed herself back against the dense mass of the shrubbery and gripped my sleeve. 'Go,' she said, tugging feverishly at the fabric. 'Quickly.' I brushed her fingers gently with my own, just once, and then stepped out to meet Bullen.

15

I had told Bullen that, short of coming across a significant rarity, I wasn't anxious to add to my collection that afternoon, and we set off on foot without any particular destination in view. I had in mind a few hours' gentle rambling in the immediate vicinity, allowing us to arrive back in good form for our departure on the following morning, but Bullen seemed to find the idea unappealing, and we were soon striding along with our customary briskness, though rather more convivially than usual.

Bullen deflected my questions about Eleanor's illness

but offered instead, with uncharacteristic frankness, a series of glimpses into his own life. I learned for the first time of the disciplinarian father who had bought himself out of his Lancashire regiment in order to begin a new life in Queensland, only to succumb to fever within a year of his arrival; the haphazard upbringing by a mother whose beauty was once a local legend but whose fondness for drink had drawn her progressively deeper into an underworld that had eventually destroyed her; the unfinished education provided at the expense of one of his mother's admirers and the hunger for success in a world that seemed repeatedly to balk his best efforts. It was a tendentious and sometimes disjointed account but I felt, by the time we turned and began to head back towards the villa, that I had gained a considerably fuller picture of the man fate had chosen for me as my travelling companion.

We had walked considerably further than I had intended, threading the narrow paths into the heart of the valley, and the afternoon was well advanced by the time we re-emerged on to the main track. As we crested the rise the breeze hit us, not cool exactly, but a welcome relief after the heavy stillness among the trees below. Bullen set his hat to the back of his head and wiped his sleeve across his brow.

'Best foot forward,' he said, 'and we'll be back in time for dinner.'

I think I was the first to see them, just off the track a couple of hundred yards ahead of us, three figures squatting in the shadow of a sandstone outcrop, their heads turned in our direction. As we drew near they rose to their feet, and the tallest of the three stepped out on to the track and hailed us.

'It's all right,' said Bullen, perhaps misreading my excitement at finding myself, for the first time, face to face with one of the indigenous inhabitants of the country. 'I know this fellow.'

The man appeared old, his beard and hair almost completely grey, but his body was spare and upright and his movements easy. He was barefoot and bareheaded but dressed in European clothes: a pair of flannel trousers, rolled up at the ankles and tied at the waist with a length of cord; and a threadbare black jacket, patched at the elbows with a lighter cloth. He wore no shirt; the jacket flapped open to reveal an almost fleshless torso, the collarbones prominent and the ribs individually visible.

'You keeping well, Mr Bullen?'

'Well enough, Amos.' Bullen gave a curt nod in the man's direction but didn't slacken his pace; barely looked at him. The encounter might have passed without incident if I hadn't lagged a little, curious to see the man's companions, who hovered a few paces behind him. They stood shoulder to shoulder, brother and sister, I thought, or perhaps a young couple. Their features were strong and handsome, but their eyes were uneasy, reluctant to meet mine. The youth wore a cotton shirt, loosely tucked into the waistband of his grey breeches; the girl was dressed in a cream blouse, far too large for her slender frame, and a print skirt, evidently home-made, which barely reached her calves.

Her hands were clasped in front of her and I saw, around her thin wrist, a bracelet of reddish spines punctuated at intervals by small bunches of bright yellow feathers.

As Bullen slowed, half turning as though to urge me on, the old man thrust his hand into his jacket pocket and tugged out a short-stemmed briar. 'You'll take a smoke with me?' he asked.

Bullen's face darkened. 'You mean you want me to fill your pipe for you?'

The old man shrugged his shoulders and held out the briar.

'If that's what you want,' said Bullen aggressively, 'then why not say so?'

The man took a pace backward, his eyes wary. 'You have tobacco?' he asked.

'I can sell you some.' Bullen extended his hand, rubbing together his thumb and forefinger. 'Do you have money?'

A shake of the head. Bullen turned away. 'No money,' he said, 'no tobacco.'

I saw the old man's face fall. 'Give him a pipeful,' I said.

'I give nothing for nothing,' said Bullen grimly. 'It's a simple policy and a sound one.'

'The girl's bracelet,' I said. 'Will they let us have that?'

Bullen leaned close, sly, conspiratorial. 'If we lay out enough tobacco,' he murmured, 'you can probably have the girl as well.'

I ignored the remark. 'Ask him,' I said. 'Will they trade the bracelet?'

Bullen peered at the object. 'It's made of thorns,' he said. 'Thorns and feathers. Completely worthless.'

I could see that the materials were of no intrinsic value, but I liked the brilliance of the little yellow tufts and the way the thorns fanned out against the girl's dark skin. 'Items like this have a certain cultural significance,' I said defensively.

'Some do. This looks to me like something she's made herself. These people here' – he lowered his voice – 'aren't the certified goods, if you take my meaning. Neither one thing nor the other.'

'Even so,' I said, 'I should like the bracelet.' Bullen shrugged and turned back to the old man.

'You hear? My friend wants the bracelet.' He leaned forward and grabbed at the girl's wrist, but she flinched and stepped back out of reach. Bullen tapped his own wrist. 'Bracelet,' he said. 'She gives us the bracelet, you get tobacco. Understand?'

The old man stared up at him from beneath his matted fringe. 'How much tobacco?' he asked.

Bullen held up his left hand, fingers extended. 'Five,' he said. He reached into an inner pocket and drew out a large wash-leather pouch. 'Look.' He loosened the drawstring and removed five small plugs of tobacco, placing them in a neat row on the gritty surface of the rock. The old man considered them for a moment, then shook his head vigorously. He held up both hands.

'Ten,' he said.

Bullen glanced sideways at me. 'Are you sure you want the thing?' he asked.

The question irked me and, at the same time, hardened

my resolve. 'Of course I'm sure,' I said. 'Give him the tobacco. You can trust me to pay you back in full.'

'No doubt, but there's an issue of principle involved. It doesn't do to let these people think they can get the best of a deal.' He took two more plugs from his pouch and laid them on the rock with the others. 'Seven,' he said. 'No more.'

The old man reached out and gathered up the dark oblongs. He slipped them into the pocket of his tattered jacket and turned to address the girl, speaking in his own tongue.

I could see at once that the transaction wasn't going to be straightforward. The girl muttered under her breath and backed away, covering the bracelet with her right hand. As the old man stepped towards her, one arm raised, she dodged behind the youth, who half turned to address her. It wasn't necessary to understand the language: it was clear enough what was going on. I glanced at Bullen.

'Let's leave it,' I said. 'She doesn't want to part with it.'

'Leave it be damned. They've got my tobacco.'

'Ask him to return it.'

Bullen grimaced. 'The deal's been done,' he said, 'and no one's going back on it.' He unslung his rifle and let it hang, lightly balanced, in the crook of his arm. The action seemed casual enough, but something in his expression alarmed me. And then I heard the dull click of the safety-bolt.

The others heard it too. They fell silent and turned towards us again. They might have been waiting for

Bullen to speak, but he said nothing. He just stared, gazing into each of the three faces in turn. As he fixed his eyes on the girl, she lowered her head and removed the bracelet; then she placed it on her palm, stepped over and held it out to me.

I am embarrassed to recall the scene. The girl – hardly more than a child, I thought, looking closely at her downturned face – stood before me, hand outstretched, like a schoolboy malefactor awaiting the sting of the master's cane. I remember the smallest details – the spring and twist of her thick hair, the quick pulse at the side of her neck, her bare foot scuffing the dust. Her expression was unreadable but her arm, I noticed, was trembling.

'For God's sake, Redbourne, take the thing.'

I reached out and picked the bracelet gently from her palm. 'Thank you,' I said, as though it had been a gift offered in love or friendship. 'Thank you very much.'

I wanted to catch her eye, wanted to tell her with a glance or a smile that I had meant no harm, but she didn't look up. Bullen slung his rifle back over his shoulder and turned away.

'Let's go,' he said. 'It's getting late.'

After dinner that evening I laid the bracelet on my writing-desk and examined it closely. Out there in the light of the afternoon sun, vivid and changeable against the skin of the girl's wrist, it had seemed a prize worth having; now, staring at the object stretched out in the lamplight against the polished wood of the desk, I wondered what I could have been thinking of. I opened my journal, dipped my pen and wrote, beneath the date:

> First encounter with indigenous people. Purchased a bracelet, an unsophisticated affair of red-brown thorns strung on a stout thread and interspersed with tightly bound tufts of yellow feathers. The girl who sold it to me

I set my pen back on the inkstand and took up the bracelet again, letting it swing from my fingers for a moment; then I opened the top drawer of the desk and dropped it in. No point in brooding on the matter, I told myself, ramming the drawer home again, but I was unable to obliterate the after-image of my last view of the group: the two men retreating together to the shade of the outcrop, leaving the girl gazing after us from the middle of the track, her legs a little apart and her arms folded across her chest, her print skirt lifted and ruffled by the stiffening breeze.

III

16

My first sight of the mountains was something of a disappointment. The modest ridge that rose up ahead of us as we crossed the plain bore no relation to the towering crags and pinnacles created by my imagination on the basis of an earlier conversation with Vane, and I couldn't help remarking on the fact.

Bullen turned from the window with a thin smile. 'Just wait,' he said. 'I've no doubt we shall be able to impress you soon enough.'

He was right, of course. As the train climbed steadily

higher, the grandeur of our surroundings became apparent. Where the land fell away from the track I was able to look out across the treetops and see how the forest stretched to the horizon under a soft bluish haze, while sporadic outcrops of grey and ochre sandstone hinted at sterner beauties to come. The occasional farmsteads and trackside settlements served only to emphasise the scale of the surrounding wilderness: watching a flock of cockatoos lift and wheel against that astonishing backdrop, I remembered Vane's assertion that the country's vastness made it almost impervious to human activity, and I wondered fleetingly whether I might have been too quick to dismiss the idea.

On alighting at the station we arranged temporary storage of our luggage before setting off on foot. Bullen had been given to understand that Billy Preece lived in a hut just beyond the edge of town, but we had been walking for upward of half an hour, and had left most signs of civilisation some distance behind us, by the time we reached our destination. We heard the cluck and cackle of barnyard fowl and then, rounding a bend in the track, found what we were looking for.

Built almost entirely of overlapping boards, rough-sawn and untrimmed, the hut was of a design too primitive to be entirely prepossessing, but I could see at once that it had been soundly constructed and well maintained. The threshold was a good two feet above ground level, and the low doorway was served by a little run of three wooden steps. To left and right of the building, an untidy fence of stakes, branches and brushwood marked what I took to be the front boundary of the property.

'Holloa!' shouted Bullen. 'Is anyone at home?' The sound of slow, uneven footsteps across bare boards, and then the door swung open.

The man was not above middling height and his body, as he stood there in the doorway, was twisted noticeably out of true, but something in his demeanour suggested power and presence. His hair and beard were grey, but vigorous in their growth, his face thin but strong-featured. He seemed in no hurry to come forward, addressing us from the threshold with an easy familiarity. 'You'll be the gentlemen from Sydney.'

Bullen advanced towards him. 'Billy Preece?'

'I'm Owen Preece. My son's round the back.' He stepped down and approached us with a stiff, lopsided gait, his right hand extended. 'I'm pleased to meet you, gentlemen.' His handshake was firm and his gaze, as he looked into my eyes, was clear and direct. He indicated a gateway in the fence and bowed us through with an odd, old-fashioned courtesy. 'This,' he said, touching the barrier as he followed us in, 'is meant to keep out the wallabies. I can't claim that it's entirely successful, but at least' – he turned to me, his tanned face creasing into a smile – 'it makes them stop and think.'

'There's only one way to stop a wallaby,' said Bullen. He slapped his ammunition-belt twice with the flat of his hand. 'Ask any grazier.'

There was a moment of strained silence before Preece brought us to a halt. We were looking down a long, gently sloping strip of land, so completely unlike the

165

surrounding bush that we might have stepped into a different country. Close at hand, vines ran riot over a rough trellis, their arching stems festooned with clusters of small purplish grapes, while further down I could see staked rows of beans, the brighter greens of assorted leaf-crops and the gleam of melons and pumpkins lying in the shadow of their own broad leaves. Half-way down, a boy, barefoot and stripped to the waist, his brown skin glistening, was bending over a patch of freshly dug earth.

It was an extraordinary sight, that rectangle of lush colour laid down among the subtler shades of the bush. I brushed my hand across the vine-leaves, as though I might apprehend their soft lustre through the skin of my palm. Preece glanced sideways at us, waiting, I thought, for our response.

'It's a veritable paradise,' I said. 'I can't imagine how you maintain such a fertile garden out here.'

'Oh, it's simple enough, but not easy. Half a dozen cartloads of dung each winter and bucket after bucket of water raised from the gully throughout the summer. In this weather you might be at it from dawn till dusk. I'd be down there now, only my leg's been giving me trouble all day.'

'At least you have assistance,' I said, glancing down the slope just as the boy turned to look at us.

'Yes, in that respect I count myself fortunate. I've only been blessed with one son, but I couldn't wish for a better helpmate than he's turned out to be.' He threw back his head and called out, 'Billy! Come up and meet the gentlemen.'

I had assumed, seeing the half-naked brown body stooping above the turned soil, that the boy was a hired hand, one of the aboriginals of the neighbourhood, and I was glad to have recognised my error without having revealed it. Billy straightened up and wiped his palms on the seat of his ragged breeches before starting up the slope towards us.

He moved lightly and with a dancer's grace, his slender arms held out a little from his body, his feet sure and nimble. As he drew level with us, he swept the tangle of black curls back from his forehead and flashed me a smile of such unguarded warmth that my own more formal greeting died on my lips. Bullen gave the boy a curt nod and turned aside.

'You're Mr Redbourne, aren't you?' said Billy, looking into my face with undisguised curiosity. 'Da says you've come from England.' His voice was deeper than his childlike manner and physical slightness had led me to expect, and I saw, examining his features more closely, that his cheeks and chin were lightly downed with dark hair.

'Yes,' I said, 'that's where I live. Very far away, Billy, on the other side of the world.'

Even before he replied, I could see from the change in his expression that I had struck the wrong note. 'I know where England is,' he said stiffly. 'I've not had much schooling but I'm no dunce, and we're not short of books and maps. You'll see when you step inside.'

'If you gentlemen are agreeable,' said Preece, cutting in quickly, 'we'll have a bite to eat now. Billy will take the ponies down to the station and collect your luggage.'

167

Bullen gave a grunt, which I took to signify assent. Preece indicated a low bench in the shade of the vines. 'If you'd like to sit there for a moment,' he said, 'I'll call you in when it's ready.' And then, turning to Billy, who was showing signs of wanting to resume his discussion with me: 'Go on now – the sooner you're off, the sooner you'll be back.' The boy flitted away towards the gate with Preece following on at his own slow pace.

I sank gratefully on to the bench. Bullen made no move to join me there but stood looking down the garden, tugging irritably at his beard.

'What is it?' I asked. 'Is anything wrong?'

He swung round savagely. 'For God's sake, Red-bourne, you can see what's wrong. We've been palmed off with shoddy goods. As scrawny a runt as I've ever clapped eyes on, and a bloody half-and-half into the bargain. If I'd known—'

'Quietly, Bullen. Preece will hear you. And in any case, I don't see any great difficulty. Assuming Billy's up to the job—'

'How could he be up to the job? I'm prepared to believe that he knows the territory – these people always do – but how's he going to cope with his share of the baggage? We need a man with the strength of a mule, and we're lumbered with a skinny boy.'

'Appearances can be deceptive. And no one in his senses would set himself up with a job he knew to be beyond his capabilities.'

'These are poor people, Redbourne, scratching a living from the dirt. You can see how it is. I send word that we're willing to pay good money for certain services, and of course they'll come forward claiming to be able to provide those services. Whether they can be relied upon to do so is another matter.'

What little I had seen of our hosts inclined me to give them the benefit of the doubt, but all my attempts to reason Bullen into a more charitable frame of mind proved futile. I was relieved when Preece appeared at the window and called us in to eat.

It took me some moments to adjust to the gloom of the interior but there wasn't, in truth, a great deal to see. Bare walls and floor, the sleeping area curtained off from the living room with a length of plain burlap; four shelves supported on iron brackets, three lined with books and one piled untidily with cooking utensils; a small blackleaded stove, a sturdy pine table set for our meal and four wicker-seated chairs that had evidently seen better days. There was only one item of any distinction: against the side wall stood a dresser of dark oak, beautifully crafted and speaking with mute eloquence of another time and place.

'It's not what you're used to, perhaps,' said Preece, catching my glance, 'but you'll get used to worse once you're out in the bush. And I'll guarantee,' he added, motioning us to our seats, 'you'll not taste food as good as this again before your return.' He leaned over the stove and began to ladle thick orange-brown stew into an earthenware bowl.

At certain junctures in my privileged but not entirely happy life, I had found solace in contemplating the pleasures of a simpler existence. Imaginary pleasures, I would tell myself, returning obediently on each occasion to the cares and duties I was born to; but sitting at my meal with Preece that afternoon, listening as he discoursed with quiet passion on his own experience of simple living, I was seized again by the old longings, and forcefully struck by the notion that a man might take more pleasure in a single well-managed acre than in a neglected estate.

Bullen was clearly less favourably impressed than I was. I could see him out of the corner of my eye, shifting and fidgeting as Preece veered from agricultural matters to philosophical speculation, and at last he set down his spoon, scraped back his chair and rose to his feet. 'I'm going for a stroll,' he said. 'Do you want to join me, Redbourne?'

'No,' I answered, irritated by the interruption and scarcely troubling to glance up. 'I'll stay here.'

'As you please.' Bullen picked up his rifle and strode to the door. 'Call me when the boy arrives with the luggage.' I heard the rap of his boot heels on the steps, and then he was gone.

17

I was, to tell the truth, glad to be rid of Bullen for a while, and I sensed that Preece felt much the same. His manner became more confiding, his matter more directly personal, and I, for my part, was sufficiently intrigued to encourage his disclosures. I don't mean to imply that there was anything culpably indiscreet about his conversation, but it seemed to me that I was being offered privileged access to his life, and I was flattered by the thought. His childhood, I gathered, had been a happy one, and he had been considered something of a scholar in the small-town school he had attended, but he had chosen to follow his father into the mines, moving westward in his early twenties as the industry expanded.

'It wasn't what my parents had wanted for me, but I was doing well for myself, earning good wages. My lodgings were cheap and I'd no family to support, nor any vices to speak of, so I was able to put something by. I'd had it in mind from the time I started at the mine that I should work there until I was thirty and then get out and buy myself some property – a few acres, a small herd of cattle. I'd even chosen the spot. There's a stretch of land along the Hawkesbury river, a little beyond Wiseman's Ferry, that I used to visit with my parents when I was a child – meadows so fresh and green they seemed to glow with their own light. That was where I thought I'd fetch up, though as you see . . .' He leaned back in his chair and spread his calloused hands palm upward.

'It seems to me, Preece, that you're very well placed here.'

'Oh, don't mistake me. I'm where I belong, and glad of it. But in those days I thought a man – any strong-willed man – could choose his path through life, and I had to learn through suffering that that's not so. I had a notion that by bending my body to my will I could bend the world, and the closer I drew to my thirtieth birthday, the harder I drove myself. In the end I was working all the hours I could keep myself upright, sometimes two shifts back to back. I won't say no one questioned it, but no one stopped me. There was an understanding: they needed the labour – and when I was whole there wasn't a man in the company could match me load for load – and I wanted the money. And though I'd begun by

172

imagining a small-holding, I came to think – well, it was a kind of madness, Mr Redbourne, dreaming of myself as a big landowner in a fancy house. Thoroughbred, servants, society wife, the lot. I'd got it all mapped out in my head, that other life, so different from the one I was leading. And though I knew it for a dream, I couldn't rid myself of it.'

'Young men are bound to dream,' I said. 'It's natural. And there's no telling how their visions may inform the pattern of their future lives.' I was thinking, in fact, of my own case, of the strange, late flowering of my youthful ambitions in a land as extraordinary as any I had ever dared to imagine.

'True enough. But I think this was a dream gone wrong, like clear spring water souring where it pools. And what I was about to tell you is that it came near to destroying me. It was a sweltering evening in early January, and I rolled up for the night shift half dead on my feet with weariness. My mates could see at once that I wasn't fit for work. "You go home," they said, "go home and get some sleep." It was good advice, but I wouldn't heed it. And that was the night the dream came to an end.'

There was a crash from outside, the echoing report of a rifle-shot. Preece eased himself to his feet and stepped over to the doorway, squinting into the sunlight. 'It sounds as though your friend is starting as he means to go on,' he said drily. There was, I thought, a hint of reproof in the observation, but I didn't respond. After a moment, he returned to his chair and picked up the thread of his tale.

173

'I was working, I remember, in a kind of daze, keeping at it by sheer force of will. I was hunkered down when it happened, reaching for my pick, my cheek up close against the coalface so I couldn't see clearly. I heard it all right, though – a hard, tearing sound as the lump split from the seam – and if I'd had my wits about me I might have got clear in time, but I was slow on the uptake and slow on my feet. I remember one of my mates crying out, but I think I was already under it by then, pinned by the legs and twisting from side to side like a crushed snake.

'I was lucky to be alive, I see that now, but that's not the way it seemed then. I was screaming fit to wake the dead as they lifted the fallen coal, moaning and crying out as they stretchered me down to my lodgings. When Dr Milner told me the left leg would be fine, I knew at once what he was going to tell me about the other, and I began to blubber like a baby. He'd have had it off there and then, but I wouldn't let him. "You think it over," he said at last, "and I'll call by again first thing." I let him dress it as best he could, but I wouldn't take the morphine he gave me, for fear of weakening my resolve.

'When he arrived next morning, I told him I wanted more time. "More time for what?" he said angrily, and then, a little more gently: "You must believe me, Owen, the leg's too badly smashed to mend." There were moments I thought so myself, but there was a kind of stubbornness in me kept me going, though the pain gave me no rest. "You're putting your life in danger", Dr Milner told me when he called again that evening. "If you won't let me amputate, I'll take no further responsibility for you." Even then I wouldn't let him. I was waiting. I can see that now.'

'Waiting? For what?'

'For her. The third morning after the accident she turned up at the door. Let herself in as though she'd been summoned, though I know for a fact that no one had sent for her. I'd had a terrible night, I remember, the pain a little dulled by that time but lodged close, if you take my meaning, as if it had moved deeper into my body and meant to stay. And I can see it now, how she steps in – yes, with the shine from outside making a path from the doorway to the foot of my bed so that she seems to be walking on light – and unslings a small basket from her shoulder. And though she comes towards me so softly—'

'Who is this, Preece? Who are you talking about?'

'My wife. I mean the woman who was to bear my child, though at the time I'm speaking of, I'd no more idea of that than – but that's not quite right. Because what I was going to say was that as she approached the bed, I began to tremble, and my heart banged away at my ribcage like a steam-hammer.'

'Love at first sight,' I suggested, smiling.

There was no answering smile. He was staring out through the open door, his eyes glittering in his thin face.

'Love didn't come into it,' he said. 'Not then. Just the certainty that she was there by way of answer to some cry or prayer I'd been too proud to utter. And it was fear I felt – no doubt of it – but something else too: a sense of being visited by a power that wasn't my own. Not hers either – not exactly – but streaming from her like sunlight off a looking-glass. I'd been a chapel-goer all my life and I'd often thought about those early Methodists, the way they'd known the call when it came. Well, this was my call, Mr Redbourne, only it came from a quarter I'd no knowledge of – had barely thought about. And perhaps that's the nub of the matter: we know it's the real thing because it's like nothing we could ever have invented for ourselves.'

'So this was some kind of religious conversion?'

He seemed to consider the phrase. 'I don't know what you'd call it,' he said at last. 'What I do know is that from the moment she walked through the door I understood that my life was set to change, bottom to top.'

'And your leg?'

'I was coming to that. She set her basket on the floor and pulled the coverings down to the bed-end. And it might have been because of the pain and fever, but I felt no shame at that, nor when she lifted my nightshirt and pushed it back. And she, for her part, didn't flinch, though knee to ankle looked like something you'd find on a butcher's slab. Everything was strange, yet nothing seemed out of place, if you see what I mean. I remember her holding the leg, just above the damage – her hands very cool against my skin. And with that, the pain drew off, and the fear with it, and I found myself watching her with a kind of curiosity, as though her actions had nothing to do with me. She reached down and took a little knife from the basket – not a steel knife, but one of the chipped stone blades they make. And even though I thought at first she was going to cut me, I wasn't remotely troubled by the idea.'

'But she didn't?'

'Cut me? No. She stretched out her arm and rolled up the sleeve of her blouse. Then she nicked the flesh' – he tapped the spot on his own arm – 'just here, on the inside of her elbow, and began sucking at it.'

I said nothing, but my expression must have given me away. 'Maybe we're the unnatural ones,' he said, looking hard at me. 'Anyhow, you can't judge this until you've heard the upshot. After a while she spat the blood into her palms and rubbed it over the upper part of my leg, very gently at first and then with firmer movements. And as she worked – I can't explain this, Mr Redbourne, I can only tell you what happened – as she ran her hands back and forth, my leg began to throb and twitch, and the life flooded back into it like water through a lifted sluice-gate. I don't want to call it a miracle – it was weeks before I was able to walk again and, as you see, I'm still slow on my feet – but the point is, the leg was saved. And that's not the whole of it, either, because whatever happened on that morning set my mind off in new directions. I had plenty of time for reflection in the days that followed, of course, and little by little I came to see what a fool I'd been, reaching out for a dream while the life I'd been given slipped by without my noticing. She showed me what I'd almost lost, and made it all real to me again. Just ordinary things, you might say – the sound of rain beating on the panes or the doorsill, the smell of hot bread, her footfall as she crossed the floor to tend to me – but coming at me so sharp and sweet they brought the tears to my eyes . . . Does this make sense to you, Mr Redbourne?'

I nodded. It crossed my mind that I might tell him

something about Eleanor, but before I could speak, he rose stiffly to his feet and pulled open one of the drawers of the dresser. 'I'd like you to see this,' he said, handing me a photograph mounted on a dog-eared rectangle of green card. 'It doesn't do her justice, but it catches something of the look of her.'

The photograph itself was scarcely larger than a postcard and I had some difficulty in making out the detail, but it seemed at first sight to be a rather conventional studio portrait. Preece's tale had led me to expect a figure altogether more dramatic than this full-featured housewife, a little beyond the first flush of youth, her hair pulled back from her face in the European fashion and her dark skin set off by a plain white blouse. But peering more closely, I was struck by something in her gaze, some quality of abstraction or inward concentration, as though she'd taken the measure of it all – the photographer and his paraphernalia, the absurd painted backdrop she'd been posed against – and decided that it didn't concern her. It wasn't haughtiness exactly, and certainly not contempt, but she had the look of a woman whose mind was on higher or deeper things. I handed back the photograph. 'Mrs Preece was evidently a woman of character,' I said.

'She never took my name. To tell you the truth, we didn't marry, though that wasn't for want of asking on my part. "We have what we have," she used to say. Sometimes I wondered whether she'd already given herself – to one of her own people, I mean – before she came to me, but she never said, and it didn't seem right to question her. I didn't even know where she came from – she certainly wasn't from the mountains – but after a while there seemed no need for questions. She was right: we had what we had, and though I wish she'd been with us for longer, you'll not hear me complain.'

I sat very still, waiting, watching his face. He seemed to have withdrawn into a state of quiet meditation, and after a while it occurred to me that he had said all he wished to say, and that I should leave him to his thoughts. But as I made to rise, he looked up sharply, as though at some unwarranted interruption, and I realised that there was more to come.

'They were the best years of my life, no doubt of it, the years I spent with her. Once she had me back on my feet again I found work in the company office, but I knew that wasn't for me. I was biding my time, Mr Redbourne, waiting for the next thing. Not fretting, just waiting. And one day she looked across at me as we sat at breakfast – and I remember her having to raise her voice a little against the rattle and clank of the freight-wagons going by on the track beyond the back yard – and she said, very simply and firmly, "I don't want the child to grow up here." That was how she broke the news to me, and it was the sign I'd been waiting for. Within a fortnight I'd found this plot, and by the time Billy was born the hut was built and furnished, and I'd started to clear the scrub out back. And as I worked, the strength returned to my arms and shoulders, and the hope to my heart – not the mad hope of wealth and power that had led me astray, but a sweet and steady sense of the worth of what I was doing.

'We weren't well off – I'd left my job as soon as I was

sure that the plot was mine – but I was never worried on that score. And Billy – well, the child was a revelation to me. I mean, I hadn't known I could feel such tenderness, such patient tenderness. He was just a scrap of a thing at first, so small the midwife doubted he'd survive, but when I cradled him for the first time in the crook of my arm and felt the softness of his skin against mine – do you have children, Mr Redbourne?'

I shook my head. 'I'm not married,' I said. 'I've only recently begun to consider what I might have missed.'

'Well,' he said, manoeuvring with a tact and delicacy that took me by surprise, 'a child's no guarantee of happiness, nor a wife neither. But speaking for myself, I felt truly blessed. It was a kind of heaven we lived in then – she and I grown so close for all our differences, and the child drawing us closer still. I remember sitting with them one day in the shade of the back wall, looking down over the ripening crops. And I thought, I want nothing more than this. If that wasn't heaven, Mr Redbourne, I don't know what is. And heavenly too because, strange as it sounds, I had no thought of it coming to an end, no thought at all.'

He faltered and broke off, evidently caught off guard by his emotions. I should have liked to be able to respond with greater compassion, but I knew too little about the man and his sorrows, and I simply sat back in respectful silence until he resumed.

'It was like a bolt of thunder from a cloudless sky. I'd been out until dusk, splitting wood for the stove, and I came in to find her in her chair, exactly where you're sitting now, with her head in her hands. And that was strange because there was no food on the table and she wasn't one for sitting around when there was work to be done. She raised her head as I came close, but slowly, as though it were weighed down in some way, and I could sense then that something was amiss. I dropped the firewood I was carrying and knelt beside her there, reaching for her hand. And as soon as I touched her skin, I felt the chill of it, a chill from somewhere far down in her body. "What is it?" I asked her, and my heart was banging already as though it knew something my head didn't. "What is it?"

'It was a gift she had, to be able to tell me what was in her mind without putting it into words – with a look, it might be, or with something less than a look. She just lowered her eyes, and something in the manner of her doing it frightened me horribly – as if she were saying, *Enough* or *It's over*. "I'll fetch the doctor," I said, knowing full well she'd no more want to see one of our doctors than plunge her arm in scalding water, but I was in a panic, d'you see, not knowing what to do, and that was all I could think of. Anyway, she shook her head, very slow and sad, and placed her hand over mine, and we just sat there watching as night came on and the stars brightened in the sky. After some time she told me I should go to bed – insisted on it, with a kind of anger I'd not seen in her before, though I sorely wanted to stay – and I left her there, her arms folded across her breast, her body hunched and twisted a little to one side, leaning out into the darkness.

'It was just getting light when I woke to see her over by the window, kneeling beside the dilly-bag she'd brought with her when she first moved in with me. When I saw that – saw her packing a spare skirt and blouse, her ebony hairbrush, a velvet ribbon – I thought perhaps I'd misunderstood, and that she'd simply decided to go away for a while. But there was something in the set of her face that told me otherwise, and at last she straightened up and said very quietly, "I'm going home." "This is your home," I said, and with that I hauled myself out of bed and stepped towards her. But she backed away as though she didn't know me, as though I might harm her. "To my people's lands," she said, and then, very softly: "It's time."

'Of course I was in a terrible state – you can imagine – but not wanting to let on, not wanting to hinder her. "What shall I tell Billy?" I asked. "I've spoken to Billy," she said. Then she picked up her bag and walked out, quite slowly and carefully, the way people do when they're in pain, but not hesitating at all. I wanted to hurry after her and catch her in my arms, but I could see that wouldn't be the right thing. She stepped away down the track, very clear at first in the early sunlight, then half lost against the shine and shadow of the trees. I watched her out of sight, but she didn't once look back.'

He leaned forward in his chair and stared out through the doorway, his mouth clamped tight and his eyes glistening.

'And you had no word from her?'

'Never. Nor expected it. But for weeks after she'd gone I dreamed of her, night in, night out. Always in the same flat landscape – very harsh and dry, scattered with boulders. No shadow, the sun beating down on her. I can't tell you what it was like to see her out there time after time, very small and lost, with the desert stretching as far as you could see on every side. And she was searching, it seemed to me, always searching, so that I found myself desperate to help, but because I wasn't allowed to be with her – I can't say exactly how it was, but that much was plain – there was nothing I could do. There was a time I thought it would go on like that for the rest of my life and maybe beyond, the same vision over and over; but one night, a couple of months after she'd left, I saw her walking along very fast, her head up and all her movements firm and certain. No searching now, and her step so light that her feet barely touched the sand. There was no change in the landscape – none that I could see – but I knew she'd found what she was after. And as I looked, her form thinned and dwindled like a scarf of mist when the sun breaks through, and I woke with a cry of joy on my lips or in my ears – her cry or mine, it wasn't clear, and it didn't matter – and hurried to the doorway. It was still dark, but with that faint stirring or softening that you sometimes feel in the few moments before dawn. And as I looked out, I knew there was no call to fret about her any more, and my heart – well, I was weeping like a child, but there was no bitterness in the tears. After that—'

He stopped and raised his head. I had heard it too, an inarticulate shout ending on a rising note, half roar, half yelp. A second or two of blank silence followed, and then a string of sharply delivered expletives. 'Something's got Mr Bullen's dander up,' said Preece grimly, levering himself to his feet. He limped over to the doorway

183

and peered about, one hand lifted to shade his eyes, then stumped down the steps and out on to the track.

It was Billy, I saw, as I followed Preece out, who had aroused Bullen's wrath. The boy stood between the two ponies, his head thrown back in sulky defiance, while Bullen berated him in a vicious undertone. '*Damned fool of a boy*', I heard as we approached. '*Cack-handed incompetent*'. The reaction might have been excessive and the language uncalled-for, but the reason for Bullen's rage was immediately apparent: the ground was strewn with cartridges, evidently spilled from the open ammunition box that Billy was clutching in his left hand.

'What's going on?' asked Preece.

'You can see what's going on. The lad's been scattering our ammunition about like seed-corn.'

'I've done nothing wrong,' said Billy. 'The box fell open as I was unloading it. Look.' He held up the object and shook it, making the hinged lid clack and swing. 'If it had been properly fastened—'

'That's enough, Billy,' said Preece, leaning forward and laying a hand on the boy's arm. 'There's stew for you in the pot. You go on in and leave us to attend to the baggage.' He eased the box from the boy's hand, dropped awkwardly to one knee and began to gather up the spilled ammunition.

'It's as well I arrived back when I did,' said Bullen, turning to me as Billy stalked off. 'There's no knowing what damage he might have done.'

Preece looked up over his shoulder. 'It was an accident, Mr Bullen,' he said. 'Just an accident.' Bullen opened his mouth as though to reply, but seemed to think better of it. He stepped over to the nearer of the two ponies and began to unfasten the luggage-straps.

By the time we had the luggage indoors the sun had sunk behind the trees, and the sky outside was fading to a softer blue. I should have liked to sit and rest, but with Preece wordlessly tidying the room around us and Billy huddled over a book in the corner, pointedly refusing to acknowledge our presence, it seemed sensible to get out of the hut and to take Bullen with me.

A light breeze was springing up as we left, stirring the eucalyptus leaves into whispering life. Bullen strode off at an unnecessarily brisk pace, still visibly angry and showing no sign of wanting either my company or my conversation. We had travelled a good half-mile along the track before he slowed and turned to address me. 'What a pair of fools we've been landed with,' he said. 'I've been badly let down over this business, Redbourne, I don't mind telling you.'

'It's too early to make a judgement. Give the boy a chance to prove his mettle.'

'And each as bad as the other,' he went on, ignoring my intervention. 'The son incapable of carrying out the simplest task and the father a fount of nonsense. And you should know better, Redbourne – it's no kindness to encourage a man of his sort by listening to his ramblings.'

'It seemed to me,' I said cautiously, 'that some of his views were worthy of serious consideration.'

'Preece is a fool and his views are balderdash. What kind of progress do you think we'd have made in a country like this if we'd been guided by such views?

Make no mistake about it, Redbourne, the wilderness doesn't want us here. We're engaged in a war, an unending battle with a heartless enemy, and men like Preece, with their crackbrain dreams of harmony, are a menace to us all.'

'Yet there's something persuasive in his arguments. Listening to him, I had some notion of a better future – for myself certainly, maybe for all of us.'

'But look at the man, Redbourne, look at the way he's living. He's a throwback, barely one rung up from the savages he evidently consorts with. If I believed that the future of humankind rested in the hands of men like that, I'd cut my throat.'

I wasn't inclined to let him have the last word on the subject, but as I meditated my reply I became aware of a clamour in the air overhead. I looked up. 'Ravens,' said Bullen, lifting an imaginary rifle and drawing a bead on the flock. They were calling as they flew, not in the guttural tones of our own ravens, but high and clear, a disconsolate wailing sound. I watched them cross the pale strip of sky above us, drifting over like flakes of soot, and as I stood gazing, something in their sombre progress and the melancholy music of their cries stirred me so deeply that, just for the barest instant, I imagined myself in uncorrupted communion with the wilderness and the luminous skies above it.

Perhaps Bullen felt something too. As the cries died away, I saw him shiver and clutch his jacket more tightly about his body. Then we turned, moving in unison as though at some inaudible word of command, and made our way slowly back to the hut.

18

It was still dark when we rose the next morning, but by the time the ponies had been watered and loaded up the light was beginning to filter through the mist. Billy appeared to have dressed up for the occasion, in a pair of fawn-coloured breeches, frayed but neatly pressed, and a startlingly white shirt or blouse of unconventional cut, loose-fitting and wide open at the neck. Flitting ahead of us as we set off down the track, he seemed to shimmer and dance on the air, more spirit than substance.

The mist drew off with remarkable suddenness, exposing a serene sky, clear blue overhead but stained towards the west by a long, flattened band of mauve cloud. The sun was still low but it touched the tops of the eucalyptus trees, making the red tips of the leaves glow like fire. Preece and Bullen appeared to be in sombre mood, but I was in a state of strange excitement, my mind alert and all my senses heightened. Everything delighted me – the beaded threads of gossamer strung among the shrubs, the drone of a passing insect, the wet shine of the fern-leaves, the fragrance exhaled from the freshened earth. Every so often I would stop to examine the plants growing beside the track, not with a botanist's interest but with the curiosity of a child. Running my hand lightly across a cluster of vivid blue florets, I was struck by the thought that I had no name for the plant that bore them, nor for any of the other small plants whose flowers glowed in the muted light beneath the trees. In normal circumstances my ignorance would have irked me, but that morning I took a deep pleasure in the very namelessness of the things around me and I remember wondering, not entirely playfully, whether Adam's fall might have begun not with the eating of a fruit but earlier, with the arising of the desire to catalogue the animals and plants in his teeming paradise.

The air quickly grew hot but we pressed on without stopping, and a little before midday we emerged on to a tract of more open land, a long slope of grass and low brush punctuated at intervals by small sandstone outcrops. From somewhere higher up, I heard the mellow warbling of an unseen bird and, closer at hand, the faint trickle of water. Preece led the ponies a little uphill, hugging the shade, before bringing them to a halt and beginning to disburden them.

'Is this it?' asked Bullen.

Preece gestured obliquely across the slope below us. 'A couple of hundred yards on, where the scrub thickens again, you'll start to take a line along the cliff face. It's not as dangerous as it sounds, but it's no route for a pony, laden or unladen. Nor,' he added with a wry smile, 'for a man with a gammy leg.' He tugged a bundle clear of its fastenings and handed it to Billy. 'We'll just get this done, and then we'll see about lunch.'

Looking back, I invest that meal with a significance it could hardly have held for me at the time. The sweet-fleshed fowl we shared, the bread we broke, the clear water lifted in cupped hands from the trickling rill, all appear now as emblems of untainted wholeness, and our eating and drinking as a valedictory ritual. But then? I was, quite simply, impatient to get on. I remember moving away from my companions as the meal drew to a close and gazing down at the faint line of the track ahead, eagerly tracing its meandering course, its sudden drop and disappearance into the scrub.

'A word with you, Redbourne,' said Bullen, stepping up alongside me.

'What is it?'

'The boy's fee. Preece is asking for payment now.'

'Of course.' I fumbled in my pocket for my purse but Bullen drew close and gripped me by the arm. 'Offer him half now and half on our return,' he whispered into my ear. 'That way we'll be sure of the pair of them.'

Something in his words, in his absurd conspiratorial

189

posture, filled me with disgust. 'For God's sake,' I said, shaking myself impatiently free of him. 'If we can't trust people like Preece and Billy, who can we trust?'

'For my part,' he said coldly, 'I trust no one. You may do as you like.' He turned on his heel and stalked off.

I called Preece over and paid him the modest fee he requested. He resisted my attempt to give him an additional sum for our food and lodging, observing, with a turn of phrase that would have done credit to a man of a far higher station in life, that he had been amply rewarded by the pleasure of my company and required no other recompense for his hospitality. 'And this,' he said, shifting ground before I had time to pursue the matter, 'is where it begins in earnest. You've a testing time ahead, no doubt of it.'

'You seemed earlier to be making light of the dangers.'

'I said that the route's not as dangerous as you might imagine, but it's no Sunday stroll either, and you've more baggage than I'd recommend for the journey. Go carefully. And please', he added, glancing up anxiously, 'look after Billy.'

I smiled. 'I thought Billy was here to look after us.'

'Oh, he knows the land well enough – I'm not troubled about him on that score. But he's had very little experience of dealing with people, and Mr Bullen' – he hesitated, lowered his voice – 'Mr Bullen is a difficult man.'

'I give you my word,' I said. 'Billy will come to no harm.'

'Thank you, Mr Redbourne. I'll be waiting here with the ponies five days from now, Wednesday midday. Billy can time it right, just so long as he's not hindered. Would you see to it that Mr Bullen doesn't interfere with his planning?'

I looked up to where Bullen and Billy were stooping together over our kit, their heads almost touching. 'You've no cause for concern,' I said. 'Mr Bullen will be as keen as any of us to ensure that everything runs according to plan.' Preece was silent. I had the distinct impression that he was waiting for me to continue, but there seemed nothing more to say, and after a moment we moved slowly back up the slope to rejoin the others.

Preece was not, it struck me as he took his leave of us, a man given to dissembling his feelings: the perfunctoriness of his farewell to Bullen was in marked contrast to the warmth with which he shook me by the hand. 'I'll wish you a safe journey, gentlemen,' he said. And then, without any of the awkwardness or embarrassment I remember my own father displaying on similar occasions, he took his son in his arms and held him close. 'And you, too, Billy,' he whispered, releasing the boy at last and turning quickly away. He mounted the taller of the two ponies and, with the other falling into step behind, rode off the way we had come.

I have to confess to being gripped, as I watched him disappear from view among the trees, by a spasm of something close to panic. With Preece at our side, I had barely given a thought all morning to the wide and increasing distance between us and the civilised world, but in that instant I saw with disquieting clarity just where I stood. I mean, literally so: out on that open slope, surrounded by the bush and its wild denizens, under the blank glare of a cloudless sky. I felt my legs trembling beneath me, and it was a moment or two before I felt able to join Bullen and Billy at their work.

They had divided our baggage into three units, two of which had been bound with leather strapping and thick twine to form bulky packs. Bullen was working on the third, while Billy was attaching an array of smaller items to the other two – a kerosene lamp, a cooking-pan, an iron ladle, a length of coiled rope. What had seemed a modest enough load when conveyed by other means now appeared intimidatingly large and cumbersome.

'Do we really need all this?' I asked.

Bullen raised his head and fixed me with a cold stare. 'If we didn't,' he said, 'we wouldn't have brought it. Give me a hand with this strap.'

Once the packs were ready, Bullen sent Billy to fill the water-canteen. 'Your pack,' he murmured, leaning in close as the boy moved away, 'isn't as heavy as it looks. I've taken care to distribute the items appropriately.'

'Appropriately?'

'You'll be carrying less weight. There's no point in wearing you out.'

'Then your own pack—'

'Billy's pack, Redbourne. Billy will take up the slack.'

'You mean he'll carry the heaviest load?'

'Exactly. It's what we're paying him for.'

'He's here as our guide, not as a beast of burden.'

'Guide and porter, Redbourne. That's what he signed on for.'

'Even so, he's a young lad, and not strongly built.'

'The very point I was making yesterday. "Give him a

chance to prove his mettle," you said. Well, he has his chance, and we'll see what he makes of it.' He glanced up as Billy began to walk back towards us. 'Best to say no more about this,' he whispered. 'With any luck, he won't even realise.'

Billy lashed the canteen to one of the packs and tugged tentatively at the straps. 'Not that one, Billy,' said Bullen. 'This is yours.'

It crossed my mind that I might, by a sleight Bullen would be obliged to ignore, exchange my pack for Billy's, but the boy was already squatting down, wrestling his burden on to his narrow shoulders. I saw him stagger as he rose, his thin frame taut with strain, and I stepped forward to steady him.

'It's all right, Mr Redbourne. I'm stronger than I look.' He straightened his back a little and took a few careful steps. 'I've carried heavier loads.'

'You're to tell me if it becomes too much for you. Do you hear me, Billy?'

He glared up at me from beneath his dark fringe. 'I'm not a child,' he said. 'There's no call to fuss over me.' It seemed best to drop the matter. Bullen and I shouldered our own packs, and the three of us set off, moving cautiously down the slope towards the shadowy edge of the scrub below.

19

Bullen seemed particularly ill-humoured that afternoon, and I quickly tired of his company. Wherever the track narrowed I would drop back and
slow down, hoping that he would press ahead, but on
each occasion he simply matched his pace to mine while
Billy, trailing some twenty or thirty yards behind us, did
the same. From time to time, guiltily conscious of the
weight the boy was carrying, I would turn to make sure
that he was bearing up. He would nod or raise his hand
in casual acknowledgement, but he made no attempt to
close the gap.

Late in the afternoon we reached an open space, a small clearing where the wall of rock above us curved away from the path in a wide, irregular arc to create a flat arena of rough grassland. Bullen stopped and looked around. 'Perfect,' he said. 'We'll set up our base here.'

I stepped off the path and immediately found myself ankle-deep in soft ooze. 'We can't camp here,' I said. 'Look at this.' I stood on one leg, extending my muddied boot towards him.

Bullen gave me a patronising smile. 'Not in the swamp,' he said carefully, as though speaking to an obtuse child. 'I meant over there.' He indicated a point a little further on, where the curve of the cliff wall brought it back to the edge of the track.

As we advanced, I realised what had attracted his attention. The section of the cliff he had pointed out to me was extensively eroded, undercut from a height of about ten feet to form a shallow recess. I could see at once that the protection afforded by the overhang, though limited, would be useful. Moreover, I noticed as we reached the spot that the sandstone floor of the recess projected forward from the line of the cliff, a platform of firm, dry ground raised a little above the level of the swampland. There was no sign of running water in the vicinity but, that apart, the site seemed ideal.

Bullen slipped the straps from his shoulders and eased his pack to the ground. 'We'll set up a lean-to against the rock,' he said. 'Just there, where the undercut's deepest.' He turned to Billy who was labouring up the path towards us. 'You hear that, Billy?'

The boy dropped his burden and squinted up at the

rock face; then, without a word, he was off, picking his way along the margin of the swamp until he reached the platform of solid rock that fronted the recess. Bullen shot me an irritable glance.

'It's not intentional,' I said. 'He's tired. You can see it in his face.'

'What I see in his face,' said Bullen sharply, 'is insolence. Sheer insolence. What's he up to now?'

Billy was standing beneath the overhang, peering from side to side, his face close up against the sandstone wall. I saw him reach up and place his palm against the hollowed surface, then step away and stumble wearily back to rejoin us.

'Good enough for you?' asked Bullen sardonically. 'Do you think you'll be comfortable?'

'Not here,' said Billy. 'I'll find us a better place.'

'Better than this? Where?'

'A little further down the track.'

'How much further?'

The boy shrugged. 'About an hour,' he said vaguely. 'Maybe two.'

'It's getting late,' said Bullen, glancing up at the sky. 'We're staying.'

'Not here,' insisted Billy, stubbornly. 'We mustn't stay here.'

'Mustn't? What the devil do you mean by that?' Bullen swung round to face him, flushing with anger.

Billy shifted uncomfortably from foot to foot, his head averted. 'This place belongs to my mother's people,' he said quietly. 'It's a gathering place.'

Bullen looked up and down the track in exaggerated

dumbshow. 'I don't see any sign of a gathering,' he said. 'Do you?'

'They're here whether we see them or not. The ancestors, I mean. People from the faraway time. Except they're not people, not exactly. They're . . .' He faltered and turned towards me, holding out his arms in silent appeal, as if he thought I might be able to explain or amplify his halting phrases for Bullen's benefit.

'Listen, Billy,' I said gently. 'Mr Bullen thinks this is a suitable place, and I have to say that I agree with him. The stories your mother told you when you were a child shouldn't be allowed to govern your life now that you're growing to manhood. When we're young we're entitled to indulge our fancies, but maturity entails a more stringent vision of the world.'

'But the stories are true stories. My mother said so.'

Bullen gave a snort of exasperation. 'We're stopping here,' he said, 'and that's the end of it. We need poles, Billy, a dozen strong poles. Ten of them about my height, and a couple of longer ones. Take this' – he tugged his hand-axe from his belt and held it out – 'and see what you can find.' Billy hesitated for a moment, standing stock still, his eyes fixed ferociously on the ground in front of him; then he reached out, snatched the axe and strode back down the track the way we had come.

'It seems to me,' I said, as soon as I judged the boy to be out of earshot, 'that the matter will require careful handling. Billy clearly believes—'

'I don't care what he believes, Redbourne. He's in our employ and he'll do as I tell him. It's as simple as that. You can see he's been indulged by his father – all these sulks and silences when he feels he's been thwarted or put upon – and it's about time someone took him in hand.' He drew out his knife and began hacking savagely at the scrub, cutting from the base of each plant and piling the stems and branches alongside the track. 'We'll need plenty of this,' he said. 'Perhaps you'd be good enough to help me?'

It was his tone, rather than the request itself, that irked me. 'In a moment,' I answered coolly, moving away. I was reminding him, of course, that whatever authority he had assumed in his dealings with Billy he exercised none over me; but I was also genuinely curious to see what had aroused the boy's interest. I made my way to the rock face and scanned the shadowed wall beneath the overhang.

It took me a little time, but once I realised what I was looking for, I saw them everywhere: delicate hand-shapes outlined with a haze of reddish pigment, the fingers spread wide. They were concentrated in a ragged band around chest height, but some could be seen as high as the curve of the overhang, and several within a couple of feet of the platform. Where, at one point, the rock had been differentially eroded in such a way as to form a narrow shelf just above ground level, I found two hands aligned as though stretching towards one another on its horizontal surface.

'Bullen,' I called. 'Come and look at this.'

He clearly shared none of my excitement. 'I've seen such things before,' he said brusquely, turning away without a second glance. 'It's their idea of art.'

I should have liked to know more, but it was apparent

that Bullen wasn't the man to ask. 'You wanted my help with the brushwood,' I said.

'If you can spare the time.'

The insult was delivered almost casually, and it seemed best to let it pass without comment. I took out my pocket knife and set to, working with a vicious energy that doubtless owed something to my resentment, and by the time Billy returned, trailing two slender saplings, topped and trimmed, I was drenched in perspiration and breathing hard. He dropped the saplings at the edge of the platform, and was moving off again, without a word, when Bullen called out to him: 'Billy, those aren't straight.'

Billy stopped in his tracks and turned back. 'The shorter ones are better than these,' he said, 'but nothing grows straight in this part of the forest. These are as good as you'll get if you want the length.'

'Those are the long ones? They'll need to be longer than that. The shelter has to be wide enough for the three of us.'

Billy shook his head. 'Just for you and Mr Redbourne,' he said. 'I'll not sleep here.'

Bullen shrugged and stooped to his task again but Billy, who had evidently been brooding on the matter, broke out in sudden fury: 'You think you know best, don't you? You think you can do what you like out here, trampling and cutting and breaking things down without thought of the spirits you're disturbing, without please or thank you or sorry. And you won't listen. You hire me as your guide but you won't be guided by me.'

I saw Bullen stiffen. He straightened up slowly and

wiped his knife-blade twice across the rough fabric of his breeches. His voice, when he eventually spoke, was thick with suppressed anger. 'I hired you to show us the way and carry our kit, not to instruct us in the superstitions of a dying race. If you know what's good for you, you'll do the job you're being paid to do and keep your opinions to yourself. Do you hear me?'

'You'll see I'm right, Mr Bullen. You'll find out.'

Bullen lurched towards him but I was there first, seizing the boy by the elbow and steering him back towards the track. 'I'll help you carry up the other poles,' I said quickly. And then, under my breath, feeling the resistance in his trembling arm: 'Don't argue, Billy.' Only when I felt him fall into step with me did I consider it safe to relax my grip. We walked on for a minute or two in uncomfortable silence.

'If my father had known Mr Bullen was going to treat me like this,' he said at last, 'he'd never have let me come.'

'I think,' I said judiciously, 'that Mr Bullen might have behaved better. But the same applies to you, Billy. You must to learn to curb your anger.'

'If I'm angry, it's his fault. And anyway, it's not just anger. I'm frightened too.'

'What are you afraid of?'

'The ancestors.' He came to a sudden halt and glanced nervously around as though expecting ambush. 'I'm afraid for you and Mr Bullen if you build the shelter where you shouldn't. I'm afraid for myself if they think I'm to blame for bringing you here.'

Now that we had stopped walking, the trembling of

his body was more noticeable and his face, as he turned towards me in the shade of the trees, looked drawn and grey. I reached out and gently touched his shoulder. 'There's nothing to worry about,' I said. 'The dead won't harm us.'

'Not if we treat them as we should, no. If you respect them, they'll look after you – keep you from danger, guide you home when you're lost. But if you anger them . . .' He paused, staring beyond me into the shadows, and I took advantage of the moment to shift ground.

'Those decorations on the rock face,' I said. 'The hands. When were they made?'

He shrugged his shoulders. 'A hundred years ago. A thousand. What does it matter?'

'I'm interested, that's all. It's natural to be curious about things we don't understand.'

'Maybe. But you might have to learn to understand them in a new way.' And then, his tone softening: 'You know how it's done?' He opened his mouth and mimed the placing of some object or substance on his extended tongue; then he held his left hand in front of his face, palm outward and fingers splayed, and blew softly against it. And just for a moment he seemed to draw away from me, his entire being concentrated in that mimic act, and I glimpsed fleetingly – a filigree of roots extending endlessly through subterranean channels – his dark, inexplicable connection with his mother's land.

I had imagined that I should have to spend the evening keeping Billy out of Bullen's reach, but the boy took matters into his own hands, slipping silently away as soon as he had brought up the last of the poles. Bullen, for his part, seemed barely to notice his absence, preoccupied as he was with the building of the shelter. He worked steadily and with uncharacteristic concentration, lashing the poles firmly together to form an irregular box and filling the sides and the sloping top with a taut lattice of twine before weaving in the strands and clumps of cut brushwood. He gave particular attention to the roof, selecting the densest vegetation and packing it as thickly as the slender framework allowed. At intervals he would rap out a curt instruction – 'Hold this', he'd say, or 'Tie that' – but he showed no sign of wanting to involve me more fully in the operation.

The finished structure, sited beneath the overhang but projecting a good three feet beyond it, looked neither neat nor entirely stable, but Bullen assured me that it would meet our needs for the next few days. 'Of course,' he added, stepping back to survey his handiwork, 'it may be more than we need, but up here the rain can sweep in so fast you hardly see it coming. It's as well to be prepared for the worst.'

'And Billy?' I asked. 'What protection will Billy have from the rain?'

'Billy has made his choice. If it proves to have been a foolish choice, that's not our fault. I want to make this clear, Redbourne: we've not brought the lad along for his benefit, but to make the journey easier for ourselves. And let me warn you now against taking his side against me. I've noticed it on more than one occasion, and you can bet your life he's noticed it too.'

I was stung by the accusation. 'I'm not taking sides,' I said heatedly. 'It's natural to have some concern for the boy's welfare.'

'He's a sly one, Redbourne. If it serves his turn, he won't hesitate to set us at loggerheads. Just bear that in mind next time you're tempted to stand up for him.' He broke away and strode over to the edge of the platform. 'Bedding,' he said tersely, squatting down above the ooze and hacking savagely at the marsh-grass with his knife. 'Give me a hand with this.'

By the time we had finished our task the light was fading. I was more tired than hungry, and I stretched out on my grass couch while Bullen lit a fire and boiled water for tea. I must have dozed off for a minute or two: I remember sitting up with a start, momentarily disorientated, then scrambling to the doorway and looking out.

I wonder now what it is about that scene that keeps it so vividly present in my mind: Bullen stooping red-faced over the flames while the eucalyptus twigs spit and crackle, his right arm extended as he tips tea-leaves carefully from a screw of white paper into the steaming pan; behind him, the looming mass of the bush and, above that, the deepening colours of the evening sky. It has something to do, I suppose, with the incongruity of that little ceremony out there in all that unimaginable vastness; but I think, too, that the scene offers me a way of rehabilitating Bullen – of visualising him not simply as an invasive presence in a world too subtle and delicate for his clouded understanding, but also as the improbable heir of those aboriginal rock-painters, a keeper of the human flame in a dark, inhuman wilderness.

He glanced up as I emerged. 'Tea, bread and jerked beef,' he said. 'Not on a par with Vane's dinners, but good enough for now. Given a reasonable day's hunting, we'll no doubt eat better tomorrow evening.'

'Any sign of Billy?'

He bent to lift the pan from the fire. 'I imagine he's still sulking. He'll be back when he gets hungry.'

I ate a few mouthfuls and sipped at the scalding tea, but absently, my thoughts running on the boy. 'We might have expected him to show up by now,' I said. I rose to my feet and called his name, but there was no response. 'I'd better go and look for him.'

Bullen paused in his chewing and stared up at me. 'I'd not advise it,' he said. 'The lad's not far away, depend upon it. And he'd be only too pleased to think he's got you running around after him. I say we leave him to his own devices.'

'I can't do that. I'll not sleep easily until I know he's safe.'

Bullen shrugged. 'I tell you,' he said, 'you're fretting for nothing. But you must do as you please. I'm turning in for the night.'

He was right, of course. I wasn't twenty yards down the track before I saw Billy moving towards me, the white cloth of his shirt glimmering in the dusk. As he drew close I could see or sense a kind of wariness in him, as though he were uncertain what kind of reception he might expect.

'Did you call me, Mr Redbourne?'

'I was concerned about you, Billy. I'd expected you to join us for supper. Will you come up now?'

He shook his head. 'It's not a place for everyday doings. Anyway, Mr Bullen doesn't want me there. I can tell.'

'But you must eat. Shall I bring you some food?'

'I'm not hungry tonight. You've no need to worry about me, Mr Redbourne. I can look after myself.'

'You've no shelter. If it rains—'

'If it rains, I shall build my own shelter. But it won't rain. Not over the next few days. I could have told Mr Bullen that if he'd asked me.'

'Even so, I don't like to think of you out there alone.'

'I'll be safer out there than you'll be in your bush-hut. At least I'm showing the ancestors the respect they deserve.' And then, more gently, as though to soften the implied reproach: 'Thank you for thinking about me, Mr Redbourne. And listen: if you see anything unusual, don't go near it. Leave the place as quickly as you can.'

'What kind of thing?'

'Maybe something like a human figure, or maybe some wild creature. But not an ordinary creature – you'll notice its strangeness as soon as you set eyes on it.'

I smiled. 'Billy,' I said, 'you have to remember that all the creatures here look strange to me.'

There was no answering smile. 'When people see them,' he continued, 'they know. Sometimes they can't even describe the thing they've seen, but they always know.' He gave a little shiver and drew the loose cloth of his shirt more closely around his shoulders.

'You'd better stop this talk, Billy. You're only frightening yourself.'

'I'm telling you things you need to understand. But I don't think you'll listen.' He turned and began to move off, slipping away from me into the darkness as Daniel had done that night at the Hall, and I cried out in sudden anguish: 'Billy!'

He stopped and looked back over his shoulder, his features invisible now. 'What is it, Mr Redbourne?'

'Nothing, Billy. Sleep well.' He turned again, and I stood and watched until the pale gleam of his shirt was lost among the shadows.

20

I was roused at first light by the echoing crash of rifle-fire, two shots in quick succession. I turned stiffly on my grass couch to find Bullen gone, his blanket thrown untidily back against the side wall. I pulled on my boots, rinsed my mouth with water from the canteen and went out to investigate.

I found him a couple of hundred yards up the track, squatting beside the path in a haze of tobacco-smoke, his back against the cliff wall and his rifle propped against a projecting branch. As I approached, he took the pipe from his mouth and hailed me.

'You're up early,' I said.

'I had a restless night. Dreams, noises, night-sweats, heaven knows what.' He ran his hand wearily across his face and I saw that he was trembling.

'What noises? I heard nothing.'

'Murmurings. Breathings and groans. I might have imagined them but they seemed real enough at the time.' He thumbed out his pipe and rose heavily to his feet. 'I'm glad you're here, Redbourne. You can give me a hand with these.'

Until that moment I hadn't noticed the bodies. Two wallabies, huddled on their sides against the cliff wall, the brown fur of their flanks streaked with blood.

'Right and left.' Bullen mimed the two shots. 'One after the other, dropped as they broke cover. I tell you, Redbourne, I'm as sharp now as I was twenty years ago.' He stepped over to the bodies, motioning me to follow, and then, leaning above the nearer of the two, gripped it by the wrist and dragged it on to the track. The head lolled back as the upper part of the body twisted round and I saw, with a shock of grief and astonishment, the rich orange fur of the creature's chest and throat. I stooped to examine it more closely and, as I did so, the muscular hindlegs twitched and kicked. I started back.

'It's still alive.'

'Barely.' He flashed me a grim smile. 'I'm not expecting it to recover.'

'But you can't—'

'I'll handle it. You take the other.'

He grasped the base of the tail and swung the wallaby

208

over his shoulder, staggering a little under the weight. I found myself faintly unsettled by the rolling movement of the animal's slack mass against his back as he steadied himself and began to walk back down the track towards the camp, but I was relieved to see that there were no further signs of life. I bent down and tugged the second carcass clear of the cliff wall.

It was the weight, I suppose, of a young child – nothing unmanageable, but I had to brace my mind as well as my body before heaving it up, and I was glad to shrug myself free of it on reaching the platform. I had rather hoped that I might leave the skinning of both specimens to Bullen, but he ducked quickly into the shelter and re-emerged with a pair of skinning knives. 'You'll need this,' he said, handing me the smaller of the two.

'I prefer my own instruments.'

'They're too delicate for this job. Use the knife.' He straddled the larger carcass and heaved it on to its back. I remember the arms spread wide from the bright chest, the still eloquence of the small black hands; and then the knife moving slowly down from the throat to the genitals, fur and skin parting beneath the blade. I looked quickly away.

'I've not skinned anything like this before,' I said, turning over the second carcass.

'You've skinned a rabbit?'

I nodded.

'Think of it as a rabbit.' He gave a sharp bark of laughter. 'A bloody big rabbit. It's no different.'

It was, in fact, very different. In part, it was a question

of the creature's size – the sheer bulk and density of the dead flesh – but I was struck too, leaning above the body, by the refinement of the long features and by some quality of gentle resignation in their expression. I hesitated for a long moment before beginning the incision.

'You'll need to bear down more firmly,' said Bullen, glancing across at me. 'You're not skinning a fairywren.'

I was sweating in the strengthening sunlight. A thick, musky odour came off the dead animal, and I felt the bile rise in my throat. I straightened up and threw down my knife, surprised by my own distress.

'I can't do this,' I said.

Bullen stepped over and shouldered me aside. 'Firm and smooth,' he said, drawing his blade down the creature's vivid bib. 'It's not difficult.'

I saw it, I think, a little before he did, the quick movement of pink flesh squirming back from the light as the flap of the cut pouch fell aside. I had read, of course, of the remarkable breeding habits of the continent's marsupial fauna, but for a second or two I was unable to interpret what I had seen. Then Bullen fumbled in the soft belly-fur and drew out the naked, writhing scrap, and I realised, with a renewed pang of grief, that he had shot a nursing mother.

He made light of my concern. 'Kill a female wallaby,' he said, turning the tiny oddity about in the palm of his hand, 'and it's ten to one you'll find her nursing. And at this stage' – he prodded at the translucent skin with a bloodstained forefinger – 'it's barely an animal at all. It doesn't do to get dewy-eyed about such things.' And as if to reinforce his point, he dropped the hapless creature to the ground and crushed it beneath his heel.

If I were asked to provide a rational explanation for my apparently irrational behaviour, I should say that I was responding to the casual cruelty of Bullen's action, but there was more to it than that. As the nailed heel came down, I experienced its weight as though the crushed spark of life were my own, and I felt myself, for the briefest instant, lost in a smothering darkness. I struggled like a man in the grip of a nightmare; then, as the darkness cleared, I rounded on Bullen with vituperative passion, my voice harsh and my whole body trembling.

'The creature couldn't have survived,' he said, cutting in quickly as I paused for breath. 'Surely you can see that? What kindness do you think there'd be in leaving nature to take its course?'

I breathed deeply, steadied myself. 'In themselves,' I said carefully, 'actions are neither cruel nor kind. Kindness and cruelty are qualities of the human heart. I saw no sign that your action was informed by kindness.'

'And what's in your own heart when you lift your rifle and draw a bead on a choice specimen? Where's the kindness then?'

I was searching for an answer when I became aware of Billy standing motionless on the track below, looking towards us, one hand pushing his thick hair back from his forehead and the other shading his eyes. 'Let's drop the matter,' I said brusquely. And then, in a more conciliatory tone: 'I'm afraid I wasn't thinking very clearly.' Bullen grunted and turned back to his task while I, with an obscure feeling of failure, busied myself with preparations for the day's expedition.

Bullen was by no means happy about having to deal with both wallabies himself. He had wanted to make an early start but the morning was well advanced by the time we set out from the camp, and for the first mile or so he seemed to find it impossible to open his mouth without venting his displeasure. I was careful not to respond, while Billy, now burdened with nothing weightier than the day's provisions, strode purposefully ahead, just out of conversational range. As we pressed on, however, the mood lightened a little, and our spirits were further lifted by the discovery of fresh water running in a thin cascade down the rock face above the track. Bullen held the canteen to the warm trickle until it was full, and we drank by turns until our thirst was quenched.

It has often struck me that my approach to the natural world is imaginative rather than analytical, and it was borne home to me with increasing force, as we plunged deeper into the wilderness, that my expectations concerning this part of our journey had been tinged with fantasy. In particular, I had vaguely supposed that our travels would bring us progressively closer to some teeming source or centre of life, and it was only when I traced this notion back to its origin – a painting remembered from boyhood and depicting a patently implausible gathering of exotic mammals and birds massed rank on rank in a dark-tinted forest or jungle setting – that I saw clearly the childish extravagance of my imaginings.

Even so, there was birdlife in fair quantity, as well as evidence – odd scufflings in the undergrowth, a sloughed snakeskin by the side of the track – of other less visible lives, and we took a good number of specimens, including three brilliantly coloured parrots and several small passerines of quite remarkable beauty. 'Nothing of great rarity,' observed Bullen, taking them from his satchel and examining their vivid plumage as we rested at the side of the track in the noontide heat; but to me, encountering them for the first time, the birds were extraordinary, each bright body a minor revelation.

I had found myself unable to eat earlier in the day, but now I was hungry. I unpacked the remaining bread and a few strips of jerked beef from Billy's knapsack, and began to eat. Billy followed suit but Bullen rose impatiently to his feet and picked up his rifle. 'I may as well scout ahead,' he said, moving away down the track. 'Come and find me when you're ready.'

Conversation with Billy was appreciably easier in Bullen's absence and we were talking with some animation when the first shot rang out. A heartbeat's space, and then a second report. 'A couple more for the bag,' I said, looking casually over my shoulder as the echoes died away; but Billy rose to his feet and stood stiff as a ramrod, listening, his head cocked to one side.

'He's left the track,' he said. 'He's somewhere lower down.' He gathered up the debris of our lunch and crammed it into his knapsack before throwing back his head and calling out, his voice unnaturally high and clear: 'Mr Bull-en! Mr Bull-en!' There was no reply.

Billy slung the knapsack over his shoulder and stepped briskly forward, motioning me to follow.

The ground below the track fell away more gently here, a rocky slope patchily covered with tall scrub. 'He's down there,' said Billy, stopping suddenly. As he spoke, I saw the vegetation tremble and part some twenty feet below, and Bullen emerged and scrambled towards us, breathless and visibly excited.

'Did you see it?' he called.

I waited for him to rejoin us on the track. 'We've seen nothing out of the ordinary,' I said.

'Believe me, Redbourne, this was very much out of the ordinary.' His eyes, I noticed, were abnormally bright, his cheeks suffused with a hectic flush.

'A bird?'

'A dream of a bloody bird. I didn't get a clear sighting, let alone a good shot at it, but I know it's nothing I've ever come across before. The colours on it, Redbourne, the way it lifted as it flew off. And not a small bird either – hard to judge from the glimpse I had, but maybe a foot or more in length.'

'What kind of bird?'

He shrugged. 'Long-tailed, I think. Could have been a parrot. All I can tell you for certain is that I'm not budging from this place until I've had another crack at it.'

'You may be in for a long wait,' I said, scanning the expanse of scrub. 'It could be anywhere among that lot. And in any event it's not likely to return with the sound of rifle-fire fresh in its memory. I suggest we press on now and look for it again on our way back.'

'I'm not interested in your suggestions,' he said. 'I'm staying here. You do as you like.'

I was stung by the sharpness of his tone. 'In that case,' I said, with equal asperity, 'expect us back in three hours' time.' I made to move off but Billy edged forward, blocking my way, speaking urgently under his breath.

'Tell Mr Bullen he should come with us,' he said.

Bullen leaned towards him. 'What's that, boy?'

'I said you should come with us, Mr Bullen. You'll be safer.'

'I can't see any particular danger. Can you?'

'Nothing particular. Only—'

'I can do without your protection, thank you. You look after Mr Redbourne. I'll look after myself.' He turned abruptly and began to pick his way back down the slope. Billy hesitated, but I could see that any further intervention on his part would be a mistake.

'Three hours,' I called out, moving quickly away and signalling to Billy to follow. I remember Bullen raising his hand in acknowledgement before edging into the scrub and disappearing from view.

'Don't worry about Mr Bullen,' I said, as Billy fell into step beside me. 'There's no need.'

'More need than you'd think, Mr Redbourne.'

I stopped in my tracks. 'What do you mean by that, Billy?'

He stood in silence for a moment, fingering the strap of his knapsack, his eyes avoiding mine. When he spoke, his voice was hushed, so soft I had to strain to catch his words. 'I dreamed about Mr Bullen last night,' he said. 'I can't say exactly what was happening in the dream, but I know he was in danger.'

'We dream all sorts of things, Billy, but few of our dreams have much bearing on the events of our waking lives.'

'That's not what my mother told me. She said I was to pay attention to my dreams and to let them guide my life.'

'I think we should move on,' I said firmly. Billy glanced once over his shoulder but raised no objection, and we set off again at a gentle but reasonably steady pace. I was soon thoroughly absorbed in my quest for specimens, and it was only much later, when we sat down to rest, that Billy voiced his anxieties again.

'But you must realise, Billy, that Mr Bullen knows what he's doing.'

'Mr Bullen knows less than he thinks he does,' said Billy bluntly. 'And he sets himself at odds with the world. He damages the things he touches, and doesn't understand there's a price to be paid for the damage. If he'd heeded me when I told him about the ancestors, he wouldn't be sick now.'

'Whatever makes you think Mr Bullen's sick, Billy?'

He looked up sharply as though surprised by my question. 'You can see it,' he said. 'You can see it in his face.'

'He's a little out of sorts, perhaps. But he's a man of moods – up one minute and down the next. I can guarantee that if he's bagged the bird he's after we'll find him in excellent spirits on our return.'

Billy glanced away. 'I think,' he said slowly, 'that it

would be better for him if he didn't kill it. He doesn't know what it is.'

'That's exactly the point, Billy – that's why he's so excited about it. He believes he may have stumbled upon a rarity, or even an unrecorded species.'

He was silent for a moment, gazing out across the valley. 'I mean,' he said at last, 'that it mightn't be a bird at all.'

I laughed at that, but he turned to me with a look of such ferocious intensity that the laughter died in my throat. 'Mr Bullen knows it was a bird he saw,' I said. 'It's just that he doesn't know what kind.' The boy continued to stare at me, his expression gradually softening into what I took to be a kind of bewilderment. I remember thinking that he had failed to grasp some essential detail of my discourse; only later did it occur to me that the failure was my own, and that I had missed his meaning entirely.

21

Bullen was waiting for us. He was sitting beside the track with his elbows resting on his knees and his head bowed, the very picture of despondency.

'It's in there somewhere,' he said, rising to his feet as we drew level with him, 'but God knows where.' His voice was dull and his movements, I noticed, as he slung his rifle across his shoulder and stepped forward, were heavy and listless. 'I shall have to come back tomorrow.'

'I understood,' I said, 'that we had other plans for tomorrow.'

'I want that bird, Redbourne, and I'm damn well going to get it. The valley can wait.'

Our agreement had been vague, admittedly, but his words implied a thoroughly unacceptable interpretation of the arrangement between us. I was about to respond, and sharply too, when I caught the look in his eye. I don't want to overstate the case, but I had the fleeting impression of something crazed there; not much more than a glimmer, but sufficient to give me pause. I held my tongue and we moved off in strained silence, a silence not broken until we reached the cascade.

Billy was there first. He put his face to the rock and sucked up the water in long, noisy draughts while Bullen unstrapped the canteen and pulled out the cork.

'Let me in,' he said, elbowing Billy aside.

The boy gave ground, but with evident reluctance. 'There's enough for everyone,' he said. Bullen made no reply, but held the canteen in the wavering flow until it was full. I saw him lift it to his lips, then lower it suddenly, thrusting it at Billy, his eyes fixed fiercely on a point further along the track and a little above head height. 'Take it,' he muttered. And then, more urgently, still without looking at the boy: 'Take the bloody thing.'

Billy could have had no clearer understanding of the situation than I had, but he reached out and snatched the canteen from Bullen's outstretched hand. Bullen slipped his rifle from his shoulder and took aim, and it was only then, following the line of the barrel, that I became aware of the bird.

I could only just make it out, a wedge of fragmented colour half concealed among the leaves of an overhanging banksia, but I knew at once that this was Bullen's dream-bird, and that he had been given a second chance. I caught a glimpse of the long tail-feathers and, as the creature turned on its perch, a startling flash of red.

It could hardly have been an accident – Billy, usually so sure-footed and circumspect, stepping forward at that precise moment with a townsman's clumsiness, stirring the dry litter with his feet. The shot was snatched and an instant too late: the bird was already winging away low and fast under cover of the scrub. Bullen dropped his rifle, swung round and caught the boy by the shoulder, ramming him back against the blotched bole of a paperbark. I stepped in quickly, dragging at his outstretched arm. 'Let the lad alone, Bullen. You'll hurt him.'

He drew back his hand and whipped round to face me. 'That was deliberate,' he said hoarsely. 'Malicious sabotage.' And then, rounding once more on Billy: 'What in the devil's name do you think you're playing at?'

Billy looked up at him, his eyes sullen under his dark brows. 'You've ripped my shirt,' he said flatly. 'You shouldn't have done that.'

'Damn your shirt, boy – you can get yourself another.'

'There isn't another. Not like this.' He was probing the torn cloth, running his fingers over the exposed skin below his collarbone. 'My mother gave it to me,' he said, and with the words his face crumpled and he began to cry, quietly at first and then more wildly, his thin body racked by long, shuddering sobs. Bullen stared down at him for a moment, then turned on his heel and stalked off down the track.

I pulled a handkerchief from my jacket pocket and held it out. 'Here,' I said. 'Stop that and dry your eyes.'

He snatched the cloth and passed it quickly over his face, but the sobbing continued almost unabated. He struggled to speak, the words catching in his throat. 'She didn't want to leave' – he swallowed hard, dabbed at his eyes – 'but it was time. She folded it up . . .'

There was a long pause.

'The shirt? She folded the shirt?

He nodded, dumb with misery; the tears poured down his cheeks. He began to mime the act, moving with such poignant delicacy that I seemed to see the woman's dark hands passing across the white cotton, tucking, folding, smoothing. 'And then,' he said, 'she put one hand up like this' – he reached towards me, the gesture bringing her so close that I felt the brush of her fingertips on my own skin – 'and she told me . . .' He pressed his knuckles to his mouth and closed his eyes.

'Told you what?'

He turned away, shaking his head helplessly from side to side; and as I looked at his quaking shoulders, something of my old longing quickened and flared. It even occurred to me that I might take him in my arms and comfort him but Daniel was mixed up in it all too, that troubled soul whose unassuageable grief had shown me the inefficacy of my own confused love, and the impulse faltered and died. I glanced down the track to where Bullen brooded, still as a statue, above the valley rim.

'We need to get on,' I said, moving away. 'Dry your eyes now and join us when you're ready.'

Bullen turned as I approached, his face still dark with

anger. 'We should have known better,' he said savagely. 'I'd sooner have no guide at all than that misbegotten half-and-half.'

'Go easy on him, Bullen. He's not much more than a child.'

'Exactly. And we're not nursemaids. I tell you, we'd be a good deal better off without him.'

'Sssh. He'll hear you.' I glanced over my shoulder. Billy had evidently managed to stem his tears and was moving slowly down the track towards us.

'I don't give a damn whether he hears me or not. He's lost me a prize, Redbourne, a real prize, and I see no reason to spare his feelings.'

Billy had undoubtedly heard him. As he drew close to us he lifted his head, addressing himself pointedly to me. 'I can leave now if Mr Bullen wants me to,' he said.

'Mr Bullen is angry, Billy. He doesn't mean what he says. We're both grateful to you for accompanying us.'

The colour deepened in Bullen's hollow cheeks. 'I'll thank you to let me express my own opinions,' he said. 'I've a tongue of my own, and what I've said, I'll stand by.'

'This is absurd, Bullen. We need the boy's help. Besides, we have some responsibility for his welfare.'

'You've no call to worry on my account, Mr Redbourne. I'm as safe in these mountains as I am in my da's back yard.'

Bullen flung out his hand in a brusque gesture of dismissal. 'Let him go,' he said. 'I can find the way back.'

Was it some premonitory tremor that passed through me as he spoke? I was suddenly swept by an anxiety so intense that, just for a second or two, I felt myself on the brink of falling. I remember reaching out and grasping convulsively at Billy's arm. 'You're not to leave,' I said. 'Do you hear me? Don't listen to him.'

I can hardly blame the lad. He would have seen in my momentary panic an opportunity to hit back at his tormentor, and the temptation must have been irresistible. I saw his eyes narrow.

'I'll stay,' he said, 'if Mr Bullen tells me he's sorry.'

Bullen shot the boy a look of such undisguised malevolence that I wondered whether he might drop him on the spot. Then he turned abruptly and moved off down the track. I hoped that might be the end of the matter, but Billy sprang forward, tucking in behind him like a terrier at his master's heels.

'Come on,' he shouted excitably at Bullen's broad back, his brown feet dancing on the dry leaves. 'Say it. Sorry. Sorry. Like that. It's not so much to ask for, is it?'

Bullen spun round, his face contorted. 'What you're asking for,' he shouted, 'is a prime thrashing, and I've a good mind to give it to you.' I could see again the terrible wildness in his eyes, and it struck me with disquieting clarity that Billy was making a serious misjudgement. I stepped forward quickly. 'Billy,' I said, 'calm yourself. Let Mr Bullen alone. He'll apologise in his own good time.'

Bullen raised his head slowly, as though with difficulty, transferring his unsettling gaze to me. 'Apologise?' he spat. 'To this jumped-up by-blow? I'd as soon beat myself senseless with an iron bar.'

The boy muttered something under his breath, inaudible to me, I confess, but Bullen started forward and let fly at him. More a cuff than a punch, but delivered with vindictive force. Billy dodged back and the blow fell short. I thought at first that it was Bullen, teetering with his left hand extended at the edge of the drop, who was in danger; but in fact it was Billy who, stumbling sideways, lost his footing and was gone.

If he made any sound – any utterance, I mean, any cry of despair or alarm – I don't recall it. Only the rush of loosened debris slipping away down the cliff face and pattering through the canopy below; and, in the appalling hush that followed, the quick rasp of my own breath. I stepped to the edge and peered down into the gloom.

'Holloa!' I called, scanning the shadows for any sign of movement. 'Can you hear me, Billy?' My voice echoed briefly from the rocks around, but there was no answering shout.

'You heard him,' said Bullen, lurching towards me and laying hold of my arm. 'You heard what the pup said to me.'

'Never mind about that. Did we bring the rope with us?'

He was staring at me as though I had addressed him in a foreign language.

'The rope, Bullen. Where is it?'

'Back at the camp. Look, you saw how it was. I'd never knowingly—'

'We can discuss it later.' I broke his hold on my sleeve and hurried down the track as fast as the failing light and the dangerous terrain allowed.

The rope was coiled on the platform just outside the lean-to. Unnecessary weight, I had thought, watching Bullen lash it to Billy's pack the previous day, but now the coil struck me as regrettably insubstantial, a bare thirty feet, at a rough reckoning, of flimsy hemp. I seized it and stumbled back up the track.

Bullen was exactly where I had left him, but squatting on his haunches now, his shoulders bent forward and his head between his arms, as though he were trying to lose himself among the rocks and scrub. I was almost upon him before he looked up.

'What use do you imagine that will be?' he asked, eyeing the rope.

Darkness falling, the rock face dropping away below us to indeterminate depth, the rope itself not much above a tether's length. The question was, in its way, a good one, but I was finding in action some antidote to the panic at my heart. I hitched one end of the rope to the base of a sturdy sapling and tugged the knot tight.

'The lad's dead,' Bullen continued. 'Dead or dying. If he weren't we'd have heard him call out by now.'

I passed the free end of the rope once round the base of a second tree, looped it beneath my arms and tied it securely. 'Let it run as I need it,' I said. 'No slack. I'll give a shout when I'm ready to come up again.'

'It's a pointless risk. Leave it until daylight, at least.'

I positioned myself above the drop. 'I'm going down,' I said. 'With or without your assistance.'

'You're a fool, Redbourne. Take it from me, there's nothing to be gained by a display of schoolboy heroics.'

I was stung by the remark, but not deflected. 'Are you going to help?' I asked.

'You've no experience in these matters,' he said. 'You'd do well to defer to mine.'

It was, given the circumstances of the accident, an astonishing remark, and I think Bullen himself recognised as much. At all events, he stepped abruptly forward and took up the rope, bracing his left hip and shoulder against the sapling it was tied to. I leaned back gently, gauging resistance; then I dropped to my knees and eased myself over the edge.

The face was steep but not quite vertical, and though I could see very little, I found no great difficulty in feeling my way down. I went cautiously at first, testing each hold offered by the sandstone or the stunted scrub, acutely aware of the slenderness of the rope that half supported me; but as I continued my descent I began to move more freely, with a confidence – no, more than that, with an exhilaration generated, I think, by the very precariousness of my situation. I had a fleeting recollection of my childhood dreams of power – the delirious fluency of the body's progress across landscapes strewn with irrelevant obstacles – and then my right foot, feeling for the next toehold, found nothing but air. Hopelessly unbalanced, I slid sideways, scrabbling at the rock, and fell into space.

The shock of my fall and the jolt as the rope arrested it were almost simultaneous. For a long moment I hung inert, turning and swaying with the movement of my fragile lifeline, staring down into the shadows under my feet; then I raised my head and looked around.

I could see at once how matters stood. I was suspended immediately beneath an outcrop of rock, an irregular protrusion heavily undercut from below. It was on the overhang, I realised, that I had lost my balance, feeling for a foothold that simply wasn't there. I knew that, provided the rope held, I was in no immediate danger; my task now was to bring my feet back into contact with the cliff-face.

'Bullen! I shouted. 'Haul me up. Easy as you go.'

His answer came back, but very faintly, the words lost on the breeze. I hung there, listening, waiting, alert to every tremor of the rope. I had my eye on a tuft of scrub a few feet above my head. When I draw level with that, I said to myself, I shall be back in control. I watched intently for a minute or more, and with each lapsing second I felt my terror mounting, blind and ungovernable as a rising tide.

'Bullen!' I yelled again, my voice shrill now, and horribly raw. 'Bullen! Pull me up!'

There are, I imagine, few circumstances so terrible that the imagination cannot make them more so. As I hung there, revolving slowly in my flimsy harness above that inscrutable vacancy, it came to me that Bullen must have decided to do away with me. Later, reflecting on the moment, I would discover or invent reason enough for having entertained such an idea, but what flashed through my mind at the time had nothing to do with reason. It was an image, shadowy but compelling: Bullen's tall figure stooping beside the sapling at the far end of the rope, his long fingers fumbling at the knot.

I kicked out in panicky spasm and strained upward,

gripping the rope as high above my head as I could reach. The lack of any purchase for my feet made the action peculiarly difficult and, as I jerked and twisted in the void like a hooked fish, it occurred to me that my struggles might be futile. But fear lent me strength: little by little, hand over hand, I drew myself upward until I felt my boot soles strike rock.

'Praise,' I remember my mother saying, 'must be heartfelt or it is nothing.' As I established my footing more securely, wedging my boots firmly against cleft stone and knotted scrub, it seemed to me that I knew for the first time what heartfelt praise might be. In other circumstances, I might have dropped to my knees and raised my voice to the heavens; as it was, I set my lips against the dry sandstone, feeling with a giddy exultation the day's heat still contained in it, and breathed thanks for my deliverance.

The line went taut: Bullen taking up the slack, hauling me in. It was easy now, my body held and steadied, my feet and hands clever in the deepening gloom. As I drew level with the top, Bullen knelt and took hold of my collar, but I had no need of his assistance. I remember crying out, with a mixture of relief and triumph, as I breasted the lip and threw myself face down on the track; and I recall, too, the pungent scent of some herb or shrub coming off the stained sleeves of my shirt, sharp as smelling salts. I lay still, breathing deeply, feeling my heart hammering against the packed earth.

When I raised my head I found Bullen still kneeling close at my side, watching me intently. 'Well?' he asked. 'Did you find him?'

I have to confess that Billy's plight had been thrust to the back of my mind by my own trials. I must have hesitated, because Bullen found it necessary to prompt me. 'The boy,' he said. 'Is there any sign of him?'

'I've found nothing, but that doesn't mean there's nothing to find.'

He opened his mouth as though to reply, but swayed suddenly from the waist and lurched sideways. He put one hand to the ground to steady himself and I saw, in the violent trembling of his extended arm, how deeply the fever had taken hold. I recognised then the preposterousness of my earlier expectation: in health Bullen might conceivably have hauled my dead weight up from beneath the overhang, but his sickness had made him as weak as a baby. I scrambled to my feet, slipping free of the rope.

'Come on,' I said firmly. 'I'll help you back.'

He rose with difficulty, moving as though dazed. 'I don't say there's nothing to find,' he said slowly, 'but I can tell you there'll be nothing worth the finding.' He shuffled over to the sapling and bent stiffly to unfasten the rope.

'Leave it,' I said, more sharply than I had intended. 'We'll come back at first light and try again.'

He shook his head wearily but said nothing. I gathered the rope in loose coils and dropped it at the side of the track. 'We must do everything we can,' I said. 'We certainly can't leave the area without making a more thorough search.' I took up his satchel, feeling the meaty weight of the birds' bodies as it swung from my hand, and we moved on.

I must have appeared rather brutal, urging him on over that rough terrain when it was clear that each step drew heavily on his diminishing reserves of strength. Every so often I would grip him by the elbow, trying to support and steer him where the track seemed most uneven, but each time he shook me off. After a while he stopped and lowered himself unsteadily to the ground.

'I'm dead-beat,' he said. 'You go on. I'll rest here for a moment.' He leaned back against a spur of sandstone and closed his eyes.

'We can't be more than a couple of hundred yards from the shelter now. You'll rest more easily there.' I stretched out my hand, but he ignored it.

'Water,' he said dully. 'Where's the canteen?'

'I thought you were carrying it.'

His hand went up to his shoulder and fumbled the crumpled fabric of his shirt where the canteen-strap should have been; dropped to his lap again. 'Billy,' he whispered. 'Billy had it.'

'I believe we may have a little water in the shelter,' I said. I knew for certain that we had none, but I wanted Bullen on his feet and walking.

'Bring it here.'

I stood silent, embarrassed by the exposure of my childish stratagem. He leaned forward, suddenly animated, prodding the air with his forefinger in a febrile show of anger.

'Don't play games with me, Redbourne. Do you hear? I'll get down to the camp in my own good time.'

'Please yourself.' I turned and walked away, but I hadn't gone twenty paces when I heard the clump and shuffle of his boots on the track behind me. He called out once, his voice thin and tremulous, but I judged it expedient to ignore him and I didn't slacken my step until I reached the shelter.

I had already lit the lamp by the time he joined me. His face, as he ducked under the flimsy lintel, was blank with fatigue, and he barely glanced my way before lowering himself to his couch. I removed his boots and drew the blanket over his shivering body, and after a few moments his eyelids flickered and closed.

Once I was sure he was asleep I unfastened the satchel and laid our specimens on the ground beside the lamp, the three parrots a little apart from the smaller birds. In the cold yellow shine their colours seemed oddly lustreless, and such small pleasure as I was able to derive from close examination of their plumage was quickly stifled by darker emotions. He's out there, I thought, imagining Billy's slender form spreadeagled on the valley floor, the white cloth of his shirt stained and tattered, his thick hair matted with blood and dust; out in the dark alone. I bowed my head, meaning to pray for him, but no words came.

I gathered up the stiffening bodies and dumped them in the corner, beside the wallaby skins. Then I eased off my own boots, doused the lamp and curled up on my spartan bed, tugging the blanket tightly around me.

22

It was still dark when I woke, roused by a soft scrabbling, the rustle of shaken vegetation. Some small marsupial, perhaps, moving through the brush outside? But the sounds continued, and as I listened, I was able to locate them more precisely: not outside, I realised, but within the walls of our flimsy shelter.

Lying in bed as a small child, I would shiver as the owls called from the beechwood or feel the hairs on my neck prickle at the vixen's scream as she quartered the dark fields in search of a mate. 'There's nothing to be afraid of out there,' my mother would say, leaning over me with a candle in her hand, her fine features irradiated like those of the angel in the east window of the church; and when I was a little older, no less fearful but ashamed to call out, I would repeat her words like a charm as I lay listening to the stir of nocturnal life in the darkness outside. Now, in a wilderness shared with blacksnakes and death-adders, I was learning a fear scarcely less intense than my childhood terrors, and altogether more rational. I felt my arm trembling beneath me as I eased myself forward and fumbled for the lamp and matches.

But it was Bullen, I saw, as the flame steadied on the wick, who had disturbed me. He was lying on his back, arms raised, groping blindly to and fro across the ferny ledge behind his head. I threw back my blanket and scrambled towards him.

'What's the matter?'

'My pillow.' His voice was hoarse and plaintive, like a troubled child's. 'I can't find my pillow.'

'You have no pillow,' I said. 'Lie still now and rest.'

He screwed up his eyes as though he were about to cry. In the dull lamplight his brow and neck glistened with perspiration; his shirt was drenched.

'My mother's gone for water,' he said, 'but she'll be back soon. She knows where my pillow is.'

I pulled a shirt from my pack, folded it neatly and slipped it beneath his head. He lay quiet for a moment, then rose awkwardly on one elbow, leaning towards me but with his gaze fixed fiercely on the shadows at my back. His tongue moved restlessly between his cracked lips.

233

'What is it?' I seized him by the shoulder, leaning close, trying to intercept his crazed stare.

'I thought she'd be back by now,' he said. And then, with sudden, startling vehemence: 'Damn the bitch. Out dancing while her own son dies of thirst.' His head drooped and he began to rock back and forth, whimpering softly to himself.

'Sssh,' I said, as soothingly as my own unease allowed, 'lie back now.' I patted the folded shirt with the flat of my hand. 'There's your pillow.'

'But no water.' He seemed to reflect for a moment. 'Are we in hell?'

'No. Not in hell.'

'Then there must be water.'

The logic was wild but the fact was indisputable. 'Yes,' I said, 'there's water.' I picked up the lamp and took the pan and ladle from the rock-shelf. I could feel his eyes on me, anxiously following my movements.

'Don't worry,' I said. 'I shall be back in a few minutes.' I ducked outside and made my way to the far edge of the platform.

I knew, of course, that it would have been safer to walk back up the track at first light to collect fresh water from the cascade. But think about it: a three-mile trek with no better container than a couple of chipped mugs and a lidless cooking-pan, Bullen helpless with fever and racked by thirst, Billy perhaps waiting for rescue . . . My reasoning, I would maintain even now, was essentially sound; but if my experience out there taught me anything at all, it was that we live in a world that cares nothing for reason.

The wallabies' carcasses, I noticed, had been disturbed by scavengers, the soft flesh of their bellies torn open. I raised the lamp. A slick shine off the spilled entrails, off the pooled water around them; a whiff of staling blood. I skirted the remains and picked my way across the plashy ground until I judged myself well clear of their taint; then I squatted down and began to fill the pan, dipping the ladle where the water lay deepest, careful to avoid stirring the sediment below.

As I worked, I became aware of Bullen's voice drifting out to me on the quiet air, the words incomprehensible but edged with anger or desperation. I finished my task as quickly as I could and hurried back to the shelter.

He was staring up at the roof but turned his face to the light as I entered, scarcely pausing in his monologue, his eyes wide and vacant. I spoke his name softly, but he gave no sign of having heard. 'Bullen,' I said again. 'It's Redbourne.'

His gaze flickered. 'I know who you are,' he said aggressively. 'What do you want?'

'Nothing. You were talking to yourself.'

'Not to myself. To my mother. She's come back without. Says I can get my own damned water. Her very words. That's not natural, now, is it?'

'Your mother's not here, Bullen. Only me.' I set the lamp and the pan of water on the ground beside him.

'And Billy?'

'Sit up now.'

He eased himself laboriously on to his left side and propped himself on his elbow again. 'I dreamed I'd killed him,' he whispered.

235

'Drink this.' I dipped the ladle and held it to his lips.

He drew back, averting his face. 'Poisoned,' he said. 'I can smell it.'

'Come on, now. You'll feel better for it.'

'Poisoned,' he insisted. 'Smell for yourself.' He pushed the ladle away and slumped sideways to the ground.

I bent forward and sniffed at the water. The faintest tang of iron and rot; nothing to speak of. 'It's not as fresh as it might be,' I admitted, 'but we've no choice at present.'

'There's running water somewhere. Listen.'

I could hear nothing but the dry whisper of the breeze in the eucalyptus leaves and the monotonous croaking of the frogs. 'I'll get you fresh water when I can,' I said, 'but you'll have to make do with this in the meantime.' I slid my right hand beneath his head and tried to raise him, but he twisted away.

'I can't drink that filth,' he said.

'Then you must go without.' I banged the ladle angrily back into the pan, but he reached out and gripped me by the wrist. 'Give me the water,' he said, bearing down on my arm as he raised himself again. 'I shall have to drink something.'

He grimaced as he swallowed, like a child taking medicine; then he snatched the ladle from my hand, refilled it and drank more greedily, the water spilling in a small clear runnel from the corner of his mouth. He wiped his forearm across his chin and lay back, letting the ladle drop.

His breathing was quick and his colour high, but the

agitation was gone from his face and his movements seemed calmer. After a moment his eyes closed and, judging that he had no further need of me, I extinguished the lamp again and returned to my couch.

23

On the edge, legs braced against the gritty sand-stone, my back and shoulders quivering as I pull on the rope. The body bumps slowly up the rock face, the white shirt snagging and tearing on scrub. The head lolls sideways, the arms hang limp. I haul my burden level with the cliff-top, hitch the rope around a broken branch and lean over. The rope twists as I draw it towards me; the face turns, staring into mine. *Daniel?* My mouth is dry, my whole body shaking. The loop is tight around his neck and I realise, with a spasm of guilty terror, that I have made a terrible misjudgement. *Daniel?*

What's happening? The boy's lips move in response, but silently. In the instant before I wake, it occurs to me that I know what he has to tell me, but as I open my eyes the unvoiced message fades from my mind.

'Billy!' I sat up, kicking myself free of my rucked blanket, and hurriedly pulled on my boots. Bullen was stirring, moaning softly and stretching one hand towards me. As I made for the doorway, I heard him whisper my name.

'I'll be back shortly,' I said.

'I need a drink.'

I took the pan from the shelf and helped him to a ladleful of water. He drank slowly, with evident distaste or discomfort. I dipped the ladle again. 'Do you want more?' He grimaced and shook his head. I lifted the ladle to my own lips and drained it. A little like blood, I thought, running my tongue over the roof of my mouth; the same metallic aftertaste. 'It's not so bad,' I said.

He had begun to moan again, burrowing back down among the tangled folds of his blanket, but my mind was on Billy. I scrambled out of the shelter and ran up the track in the early light. The air was cool and moist, but by the time I reached the spot I was sweating profusely, my shirt cleaving to my back.

Apart from a slight roughening of the surface a few feet above the loop, the rope showed no sign of damage. The sun was still far too low in the sky to illuminate the cliff face directly but, peering down, I was able to make out the bulge of the outcrop I'd hung beneath on the previous evening; and then, a few yards below that – I craned downward, suddenly alert, staring into the shadows – the outside edge of a second projection, a flat ledge fringed with scrub.

I had no doubt that I should have to go down again, and less fear than you might imagine about making the descent alone. I retied the knot around the sapling, shortening the rope by a good six feet; then I slipped the loop under my arms and let myself over. This time I could see what I was about, and within a couple of minutes I was braced just above the overhang, the rope at full stretch and my body canted backward from the rock face. I turned my head and looked down over my right shoulder.

The floor of the valley was carpeted with mist but the air around me was brightening by the second, and I was able to see clearly the line of the ledge below. Not an isolated projection, I realised, but a trackway as broad as the one we had been travelling on, running as far in both directions as the crowding undergrowth allowed me to see.

'Billy!' I shouted. 'Billy! Can you hear me?'

My voice reverberated among the rocks and died away. I listened, straining into space, but there was no answering cry.

I twisted round in my harness, leaning out sideways above the ledge now, desperate for a sign. Was that faint localised darkening of the track's surface a disturbance of the leaf-litter? Even if it were, my reason told me, I could hardly read it as evidence of Billy's survival. It might denote almost anything: a wallaby startled into sudden activity, a lyrebird scratching for food, the boy's body – and I felt my own body tighten in sympathetic spasm – striking the shelf before continuing its headlong descent to the valley floor.

It was difficult to see what more I could do. I climbed back to the top, untied the rope and coiled it loosely about my arm before making my way back to camp.

I thought at first that Bullen must be on the mend. He had left the shelter and was kneeling at the edge of the platform, staring out across the swamp. Then his body convulsed and he pitched forward on to his hands, retching violently. His breeches, I noticed as I approached, were unbuttoned and gaping wide, his shirt-front stained. He wiped his mouth and glanced up at me. 'The water,' he said. 'You wouldn't listen, would you?' His face was white, his whole frame quaking. I could tell that the fever had abated, but his extraordinary pallor made him appear sicker than ever.

'That's nonsense, Bullen. You were already ill when you drank the water.'

He screwed up his face as though he were struggling with a complex idea. 'The fever's one thing,' he said slowly. 'This is another.' He eased his body wearily to the ground and lay with his knees drawn up, his hands clutching at belly and groin. He glanced briefly up at me; then his eyes closed.

'You can't sleep here,' I said. 'Not in full sunlight.'

He let me help him back to the rock face and huddled in the shade of the overhang, a few yards from the shelter. I was about to turn away when he stretched his arm weakly towards me, palm upward, like a beggar asking for alms. 'I need water,' he whispered. 'Fresh

241

water. And' – I leaned down to catch his words – 'opium for this damned flux.'

'I'll try to find water,' I said, moving away.

'And opium? Do you have any?'

I hesitated, not turning back but feeling or imagining his gaze fixed on the space between my shoulder-blades. 'Yes,' I said at last. 'I have a little tincture in my pack.'

I ducked into the shelter and fumbled among my belongings for the bottle. I removed the cork and sniffed it, the smell taking me back, as it invariably did, to my childhood: my mother stooping above my bed, administering comfort from a tiny silver beaker.

Bullen appeared to be drifting off again, but he roused himself at my approach and leaned forward on one elbow.

'Open your mouth,' I said, kneeling at his side.

'I can dose myself without your help. Give me the bottle.'

He reached out and, as he did so, I caught the stink coming off his body, and felt my gorge rise. I struggled for control. 'You're very ill, Bullen. You'd do better to let me attend to your medication.'

He was clearly in no state to prolong the debate. He opened his mouth wide and I sprinkled a few drops of the paregoric on to his discoloured tongue. He swallowed hard. 'Is that all?' he asked, eyeing me as I recorked the bottle.

'For the moment, yes. I'll give you more later.'

He sighed, letting his head sink back to the ground. 'And you'll fetch fresh water?' he asked.

I nodded. 'I shall be gone for an hour or two. Try to rest while I'm away.'

I returned the tincture to my pack, collected the pan from the shelf and set out in the direction of the cascade. The smell of Bullen's sickness seemed to hang about me like a poisonous fog as I walked, and by the time I reached the site of Billy's accident, I knew beyond doubt that the sickness was also my own. I squatted at the side of the track and voided myself in long, racking spasms.

To continue would have been out of the question: it was as much as I could do to drag myself back down the track to the camp. I made straight for the shelter, dropped to my knees and rummaged frantically through my pack for the tincture, persisting until it became apparent that the bottle simply wasn't there.

'Bullen,' I shouted, giddy with rage and nausea. 'Where's the paregoric?'

No reply. I stumbled back into the sunlight. Bullen was lying, sound asleep, more or less where I had left him, but he had clearly found sufficient strength to make the short journey to the shelter and back in my absence: the bottle stood on a low ridge of stone a couple of feet in front of him. I snatched it up and held it to the light.

He had evidently dosed himself generously, but the situation might, I reflected, have been worse: he had, at least, left more than enough for my immediate needs. I put the bottle to my lips and sipped, feeling the familiar restorative warmth like a golden wafer on my tongue; and then, for good measure, I sipped again.

*　　*　　*

I should like it to be understood that I tended Bullen throughout the course of that long, bewildering day as conscientiously as my own condition allowed. I assisted him to the edge of the platform as his needs dictated, even, on one occasion, helping him to clean himself – though the fact is that my own needs were almost equally pressing. At intervals I administered small quantities of paregoric. I took no more myself: I was rationing the supply, intending to take a powerful dose immediately before turning in for the night.

Despite the medication, Bullen grew increasingly restless as the day wore on, shifting and turning irritably on the platform's uneven surface. Some time late in the afternoon, as the sun began to sink behind the trees, he lifted himself on one elbow and called out: 'I need more medicine.'

I fingered the fluted surface of the bottle in my pocket. 'There's none left,' I said. 'We've finished it.'

If he recognised the falsehood, he gave no sign of it. He raised his head for a moment and stared out across the swamp at the encroaching shadows; then he slumped back with his arm angled across his face, like a man who has seen more than he can bear.

By nightfall he was delirious again, moaning and gabbling, his fever rising as the air around us cooled. I roused myself and helped him back to the shelter, coaxing and tugging as he crawled painfully over the unforgiving sandstone. I guided him to his makeshift bed and pulled the blanket over his trembling body.

I had some compunction about taking the opium in his presence, but no serious fear of discovery. Kneeling in the darkness beside my bedding like a man at prayer, I silently eased out the cork; then I raised the bottle to my parched lips and took what I thought I needed to see me through the night.

I dreamed vividly and confusedly, and the shout that woke me may well have belonged to that strange interior world of luminous streetscapes and predatory figures, though at the time I assumed that Bullen had cried out. I lit the lamp and held it up.

Bullen had thrown off his blanket and was lying on his back, his eyes wide open and rolled slightly upward. He was whispering to himself, but the words made no sense. I remember thinking, carefully isolating the ideas from the haze that surrounded them, that he must be talking in code to avoid detection, and that unless I could persuade him to speak in English, his secret would be lost for ever.

'Bullen,' I said, 'what is it?'

His lips stopped moving but there was no change in his expression.

'Bullen?'

He turned towards me; his gaze wavered and came to rest on the lamp. 'Thank heaven,' he said. 'I thought the night would never end.'

I set the lamp on the ground and moved to his side. I had some sense of his delusional state and a fainter if more unsettling awareness of my own, but I was unable to dispel the notion that he had something of the most immense importance to tell me. I leaned over him and placed one hand on his shoulder, and at that moment the flame guttered on the wick, burned suddenly low and went out.

Bullen whimpered in the darkness. 'I can't see,' he said. 'I'm dying, aren't I?'

My tongue moved clumsily in my mouth, searching its dry recesses for the words I needed. 'The lamp's gone out,' I said.

A long pause, and then: 'Can't you light it?'

'We've no oil.'

'They'll have plenty next door,' he murmured. 'I'd go myself, only . . .'

I sat back on my heels and felt his misery flood the little space between us, unignorable as a child's cry. I fumbled for his blanket and tried to draw it over him, but he reached out convulsively and grasped my forearm. 'Please,' he breathed. 'I must have light.'

I gently loosened his hold. 'Sssh,' I said, and the sound shivered and broke far down in my body like a spent wave lapsing on the shore. 'We need to rest.' I crawled back to my own side of the shelter and took a quick pull at the paregoric. Then I sank down and lay on my back listening to the deep, unhurried breathing of the wilderness.

24

The sky was just beginning to lighten when I opened my eyes to see her crouching at the entrance, her back towards me and her head bowed.

'Nell?'

She swivelled round to face me and I saw the baby cradled in her skirts. It was swathed in a filthy shawl, its head hidden deep in the folds, but its smooth brown legs stuck out beyond the hem, kicking stiffly to the jittery rhythms of my pulse.

'Where did you find it?' I asked.

She looked at me with a strange, sly smile. 'I thought you knew,' she said. 'The child's ours.' She loosened the shawl around the baby's head and tilted the face towards me. 'Can't you tell?'

I strained forward, trying to make out the features, but could see only the sheen of the brown skin. Then Eleanor slid her hand beneath the folds and slipped the shawl right back to the shoulders so that the wicked little face came clear, its glittering eyes staring back at me from beneath the high, domed brow. I knew then that it wasn't a baby at all, and wanted to tell Eleanor so, but she was gazing down at it with such rapt adoration that I hadn't the heart to say anything.

After a while she raised her head again. 'Would you like to hold her?' she asked.

I drew back, feeling the bile rise in my throat, but she thrust the bundle towards me. 'Go on,' she said. 'Take her.' It was impossible to refuse. I held out my arms and, as I did so, the thing lunged at me. I felt its wet mouth clamp on the flesh at the base of my thumb, and its tongue, rough as a cat's, begin to rasp the skin. 'Little mischief,' said Eleanor softly, 'she's hungry.' She tugged the creature away and returned it, kicking and squirming, to her lap; then she undid the buttons of her blouse and laid bare her left breast.

'Look at her face,' she said. 'She knows what she wants.' She lifted the creature and settled its head in the crook of her arm. I saw its mouth widen to receive the nipple, and I cried out a warning, starting forward and scrambling across the sandy floor; but Eleanor twisted quickly round and, without a word or a backward glance, rose lightly to her feet and walked away.

'Bullen,' I whispered. 'Bullen, did you see her?' I knelt at his side and shook him gently by the shoulder.

It was the first time I had touched a corpse, but I could tell at once what I was dealing with. Bullen was lying on his side with his face turned away from me and half buried in the folds of his blanket. Sleeping peacefully, I might have said from the look of him, but my fingertips knew better, and my heart contracted in terror. I remember staggering from the lean-to and stumbling barefoot down the path, as though I might find help out there; then my guts clenched in spasm and before I could get my fingers to my belt, I had fouled myself.

We deceive ourselves constantly, in ways at once so subtle and so fundamental that only the sharpest of blows can bring us to our senses. Until that moment I had been a hero or, to put it more accurately, I had been playing the role of one of the heroes of my childhood reading, battling gamely against a dangerous but ultimately tameable universe. I don't mean that I hadn't been frightened, but my fear had been tempered by the unspoken assumption of my own invincibility. Now, weak and giddy, lost in that vast wilderness like a glass bead dropped in a cornfield, I felt myself jarred into some new and terrible understanding. Nothing clear, nothing readily explicable; not strictly an illumination, but a tremulous recognition of the darkness that lies concealed beneath our intricately woven fictions. I stood shivering in my soiled breeches and howled at the sky.

I must have cut an abject figure, yet I would have given anything just then, out there in that inhuman solitude, to have been gazed upon by human eyes. I don't know how long I stood there, but after a while it came to me that I should wash myself down. I made my way slowly to the edge of the swampland and stripped off my clothes; then I squatted above the stagnant seepage and cleaned the filth from my legs as best I could.

Each small action seemed to require an inordinate effort, and by the time I had ferreted out my spare clothes and put them on, the chill had gone from the morning. The still air in the lean-to was growing heavy: a sweetish smell of excrement, a darker undertone of decay. I dosed myself with the last of the paregoric, draining the bottle dry, and then turned my attention to Bullen.

Certain ideas are so firmly established in our minds that it is almost impossible to eradicate them. I realised at once that I possessed neither the tools nor the physical resources to bury the body, yet I found myself unable to dislodge the conviction that it was my duty to do so. After a moment or two of confused deliberation, I knelt at Bullen's side, gripping his shoulder with one hand and laying the other on his bony hip; and it was only when I felt the body's stiff resistance to my tentative coaxing that the sheer absurdity of the enterprise was borne home to me. I sat back on my heels and felt the heat rising through my own body, licking upward like an unguarded flame.

'Burn it,' she said.

I started and swung round, expecting to see her there

at the entrance again, but there was no sign of her. Yet the voice had been as clear as if she had been standing at my shoulder. I stumbled outside and looked up and down the track.

'Nell,' I called, and my voice came ringing back to me from the cliffs, mingled with hers. 'Now,' she said. 'Do it now.'

I ducked back into the lean-to and gathered up my belongings, stuffing them haphazard into my pack; then I spread my blanket and piled on to it the wallaby skins and bird carcasses, a foul jumble of sticky fur and dulled feathers. I folded the blanket over them and roped it up to form a loose bale. The effort left me trembling and breathless, and while I was resting she drew close again, so close that I could feel her voice resonating in the aching hollow of my own throat.

'You can't carry these things,' she said, and I felt her hand pass across my face, light as breath and moving with such expressive delicacy that the tears sprang to my eyes. 'You don't have the strength.'

'I'm only taking what needs to be taken.'

Some faint stir in the air around me signalled disapproval. 'Let it burn,' she said. 'Everything.'

I remember the anger rising in me then, anger at her persistence, at her unwanted interference in my affairs. 'It's not your business,' I shouted, tugging at the bale, manoeuvring it clumsily towards the entrance. But as I cried out, something flared and roared – whether within me or around I couldn't tell – and I staggered and fell heavily against the wall of the shelter. Then I knew that I should have to do as she said.

There was no shortage of tinder – the ground inside and around the shelter was littered with eucalyptus leaves – but in my weakened state I took some time to gather all I needed. Little by little I raised a small mound of the brittle debris at the entrance before transferring it, in rustling handfuls, to the space between Bullen's body and the brushwood wall.

I struck a match and leaned over and, as I did so, I was seized by anxiety. Was some ritual required? Some form of words? If you had asked me six months earlier, posing the question in theoretical form, I should doubtless have said that the freed soul has no need of ceremony and that – supposing such a place or state to exist – it will find its way to heaven unaided. Now, stooped above Bullen's earthly remains, I was tormented by the fancy that some omission on my part might doom his spirit to an eternity of aimless wandering among the trees and lowering crags. I blew out the match and began to pray, cobbling together such phrases as I could remember from the prayer book with others of my own invention. When I ran out of words, I took a handful of leaves and scattered them over the body.

Whether because of the trembling of my hands or the faint dampness still in the leaves at that early hour, I found it more difficult than I had anticipated to ignite the heap. The oils would flare and sputter at the touch of the match and then, almost as suddenly, the flame would die back along the blackened edges of the leaves. After the third attempt, I sat back on my heels and drew out my pocket-book. I tore half a dozen pages from the back and twisted them loosely, one by one, inserting them at intervals along the base of the heap. And as I did so, Daniel's mournful face slipped from between the pages and fluttered to the ground.

Nothing could have prepared me for the violence of her intervention, the terrible jolt of anger she sent through me as I stared down at the photograph. She said nothing, nothing at all, but her intention was as plain as if she had screamed the words in my ear. I picked up the little scrap and placed it on the pyre. Then I struck another match and set it to the twists of paper, coaxing each in turn into flickering life.

That did the trick. The flames licked up the heap and began to eat at the base of the wall so that the brushwood crackled and spat. I piled on more debris, but there was no need. I felt the heat strike upwards as the fire took hold, and I withdrew from the shelter and moved upwind of the blaze, my eyes smarting.

I might attribute my languor to sickness, or to the effects of the opium; or it may have been that the flames offered a spectacular and welcome diversion from darker thoughts. Whatever the reason, I stood gazing in a kind of trance as the blaze intensified, and it was only when the breeze stiffened and veered, scattering sparks and burning leaves in my direction, that I saw with any degree of clarity the implications of my action. 'Nell,' I whispered, thinking she might have further instructions for me, but I could hear nothing through the roar of the burning brushwood.

It was the smell of scorched flesh and feathers, reaching me as the wall lurched inward and the roof subsided, that spurred me into action. I stumbled to the track and set off in the direction of a civilisation whose very existence in this wild and remote corner of the earth seemed suddenly questionable.

25

I had no strategy; I was in no condition to formulate one. Weak and confused, I had only the vaguest notion of the distance I should have to travel or of the time it might take me to cover the ground. The nausea and cramps were less troublesome now, but I was afflicted by a raging thirst and so preoccupied by my immediate need for water that nothing else seemed important. Every so often I would stop and listen, and occasionally I would hear, or perhaps merely sense, what might have been a thin trickle through overgrown or subterranean channels; but each time, my investigations proved fruitless.

I'm not sure how long I had been walking when I came upon the gully, but the sun was high in the sky, filtering through the branches almost directly overhead. The terrain below the track was less precipitous here, a rocky slope falling away into densely wooded shadow. The gully cut through it at right angles to the track, its course marked by a lush growth of fern and sedge.

I leaned out cautiously and sniffed the air. Moist earth and leaves; a cleaner undertone I could only interpret as fresh water. I stepped gingerly on to the slope and began to follow the line of the gully down, hugging its edge. The shadows deepened around me and the air grew cooler.

I don't know whether it was the change of atmosphere, operating on a system sensitised by illness, that affected me at that moment, but I found myself suddenly struggling for breath and balance. My legs trembled violently and my vision dimmed. I sat down heavily among the tumbled rocks and, as I reached out to steady myself, the singing began.

I call it singing, but there was nothing melodic about the sound. A chant perhaps, a rhythmic, humming monotone swelling and diminishing among the trees, vocal rather than percussive, yet unlike any human voice I had ever heard. I listened for a minute or two, maybe longer, and little by little it dawned on me that the sound came from the gully. I scrambled to my feet and looked over.

The creature was only a few feet below the lip, crouching among the ferns, but I couldn't make it out at first. I mean, I could see the curve and pale sheen of the bowed back, a white heel braced against a fissure in the sandstone, but I couldn't make any sense of what I was looking at. I squatted down, angling for a better view, and as I did so, the thing raised its head and I saw that it was Daniel huddled there, stripped to his glistening skin and quivering like a trapped rabbit. His mouth was open but the singing, I realised in that instant of astonished recognition, had stopped.

He stared up at me, his eyes gleaming; his voice was as light as the breeze in the eucalyptus leaves. I leaned forward, straining to catch his words.

'I could have stayed,' he whispered, 'only you wouldn't have it. Sent me out into the dark alone.'

I said nothing, watching his eyes the way you'd watch the eyes of a wild animal. He ran his tongue along his upper lip. 'You could let me in now,' he said.

He raised his arms above his head like a small child asking to be picked up, but the opium had made me as cunning as he was, and I could see at once what he was after. I backed away from the edge and turned to run, but he hauled himself up the slope and lunged at me, clutching at my ankles so that I stumbled and went sprawling among the ferns. I felt his hands fumbling at my back – a soft fluttering, at once tender and malign. Then he began to test the space between my shoulder-blades, pressing insistently on the spine, and I braced myself and clenched my heart like a fist, knowing that if he were to find a way through to its warm chambers, I should be lost.

'Let me in,' he pleaded. I looked over my shoulder and saw his face hanging above me, but crumpled now and streaked with tears. I shook my head and his features seemed to shift and blur like the contours of a stone seen through running water. 'Daniel,' I said very gently, my fear subsiding as the pressure on my back diminished, 'you died. Last winter, in Jack Waller's barn.'

He bent close to my ear and spoke again, but there were no words any more, just the faint whisper of breath passing between his fading lips and out into the damp air. He brushed my face with his fingertips and I raised my arm to push him away, but he was already drawing off, dissolving among the trees like a scarf of mist.

I lay there for a moment, my cheek pressed to the ground, trying to bring my trembling limbs under control; then I rose clumsily to my feet and dusted the debris from my jacket. I was anxious to leave the shadows and rejoin the track, but it was obvious that I couldn't expect to travel much further without water. I listened again, holding my breath, staring into the gloom until something came clear: a curved ridge of stone overhung by ferns, black water brimming at the lip. Thinking about it later, I wondered how I could have seen the pool from where I stood, but I'm tolerably certain that, as I scrambled down the slope to the gully floor, I knew already what I should find and where I should find it. I pushed my hands in among the fronds until my palms touched water; then I crouched down, beastlike, and drank greedily, sucking cold mouthfuls from just beneath the oily surface.

The climb back to the track left me breathless, but I was eager to press on immediately. The water was seething and churning in my gut, but I had been refreshed by it, and for some time I tramped steadily without any particular thought of my situation. 'One foot in front of the other', my father would say, urging me on when, as a child, I trailed behind, complaining that I could go no further; one foot in front of the other.

It was a fallen branch, lying at an angle across the track, that checked me in my stride. Literally, yes, but I mean more than that. As I raised my right leg to step over it, the loose cloth of my breeches snagged on a projecting twig and I heard the dry wood snap, sharp as a pistol-shot. I staggered backward, physically unbalanced but startled, too, by a bewildering flash of recognition: I had stepped over the same branch earlier in the day.

My first thought was that I had turned the wrong way on rejoining the track and was now retracing my steps. But that explanation, I sensed darkly through a rising wave of panic, was at odds with the evidence. The memory triggered by the crack of the breaking twig was not a recollection of having approached the branch from the opposite direction, but one that conformed in every detail to the more recent event. Even the twig itself, hanging now by a thread of bark and swaying erratically to and fro, seemed obscurely familiar. I stared down at it, my mind reeling.

I stood for a long time, rigid in the middle of the track, not so much attempting to make sense of the aberration as waiting for some clue or signal that might make sense of it for me. The silence deepened around me; the twig stopped dancing on its thread and hung still.

I moved, in the end, simply because the alternative was unthinkable. I stepped over the branch and continued on my way, but more slowly now, dogged by uncertainty. I remember stopping at intervals and scanning the under-growth at the edge of the track, the way a traveller might search an English roadside for a milestone smothered by meadowsweet or dog-roses; but if I had been asked what I was looking for, I should have had no answer.

I had grown used to the dappled shade of the trees, and the full sunlight, when I emerged into it, hit me like a fist. Here the cliff plunged sheer below the track on one side; on the other a stand of stringybarks, monumental columns of solid white light, dazzled and perplexed me. My eyes watered and the sweat poured from my skin.

Surely I remembered this from our outward journey? Looking backward as we stepped into the shade, Bullen and I together, to see Billy toiling up the slope behind us in the punishing glare, bent under his burden. The sweep of the cliff-top behind him as he rounded the track's long curve. Or had that been somewhere else entirely? I struggled to hold and clarify the vision, but the equivocal fragments fused with the scene in front of me, and I gave up the attempt.

I edged back into the shade and sat down. My head throbbed, not painfully but heavily, and the landscape pulsed and shuddered. Like a living thing, I remember thinking queasily, squinting upward to where the stringy-barks stood in loose formation, their pale limbs lifted to the sky; and it was at that moment that I saw the lories.

A small flock of the elegant creatures perching among the twigs, the whole tableau seeming, at the precise instant of my glancing up, so unnaturally still that I might have been looking at an extravagant example of the taxidermist's art. Just for that instant; then a breeze lifted the loose strips of hanging bark, rattling them softly against the tree's white bole, and everything was in intricate motion – the twigs and leaves dancing and shimmering while the birds wove their elaborate patterns of sound and colour among them. And as I followed their movements, something stirred in the cramped recesses of my heart, forcing a cry from my lips, a cry of exultation that rose through the branches above me and was absorbed in the luminous air. Praise at its purest – wordless, impassioned praise, flying straight as an arrow to heaven. Yes, and the birds rising too, flashing crimson and azure against the softer blue of the sky, and some part of myself caught up in the winnowed air so that I had to place the flat of my hand against the hot earth to remind myself where I belonged.

It was love that had lifted me, I realised, whirling me up among the beating wings; and love, I thought, looking down the track and seeing him standing there in a blaze of light, his white shirt fluttering in the breeze, that had brought Billy back from the world of the dead to guide me home. He was looking in my direction, one hand sweeping the dark curls clear of his face in a gesture at once familiar and disquieting. I called out and scrambled to my feet, but he started like a frightened deer and began to run back the way he had come.

'Billy!' I staggered into the sunlight and picked my way clumsily down the slope, calling and waving, but he neither slackened his pace nor looked back and, as I gazed after him, he rounded the bend in the track and was lost to view. Dazed by the glare and trembling with weakness, I should have been glad to return to my seat in the shade; but it was in my mind that he intended me to follow, and I drew myself together and stumbled after him.

By the time I reached the bend myself, I knew that such strength as I had been able to summon was failing. I remember thinking, carefully if not quite lucidly: I'm coming to the end. Perhaps I articulated the thought; at all events, I have a vivid but confused recollection of the words echoing through or around me as I raised my head and looked up the track to see Billy walking back towards me, no longer alone but accompanied by a taller figure. I stood staring into the light in a perplexity of hope and doubt.

If I was slow to recognise Preece, that was doubtless due in part to my own confused state, but also to the fact that the man himself appeared transfigured. He was bearing down on me with a force that seemed to disguise his halting gait, his mouth set in a thin, hard line and his eyes burning. Like an Old Testament prophet, I thought, as he drew up in front of me with his staff held menacingly before him, a prophet fired with rage against sinful humanity. And it struck me as a little absurd to be extending my hand to such a figure in such a place, but the formal greeting was, at that moment, all I was capable of imagining. He seemed barely to notice me.

'Preece,' I murmured, and my voice rang in my skull like a cracked bell. 'I can't tell you—'

'It's not you I want,' he said curtly, glancing over my shoulder. 'Where's Bullen?'

I must have stood gawping like a fool. Preece leaned in

close. 'Bullen,' he repeated. 'Where is he? I tell you, Redbourne, I'll have the hide off his back for what he did to Billy.'

'Bullen's dead,' I said. I sank down at the side of the track, put my face between my hands and began to cry.

Water, I remember, fresh water from a tilted flask. And I remember them raising me to my feet, Preece on one side and Billy on the other, and helping me forward. I tried to keep step with them but my legs were weak and clumsy, and after a few paces my determination lapsed. We moved slowly. Sometimes the track narrowed, and one of my companions would drop behind; at one point I was obliged to negotiate a particularly difficult stretch unaided, and did so on my hands and knees. Billy spoke only to urge me on; Preece, as far as I can recollect, said nothing at all until we reached the upland clearing where the ponies were tethered. Then he turned to me, his gaze milder now and his voice soft. 'You'll take the lad's mount, Mr Redbourne. Billy's legs are good for a few miles yet.'

I wanted to thank them both, but the words wouldn't come. Billy helped me up and I sat slumped in the saddle like the proverbial sack of meal while Preece adjusted the stirrups. 'You're a lucky man,' he said. 'Lucky we found you. And lucky' – he straightened up and gestured back the way we had come – 'the wind's in the right quarter. If that bushfire had been moving in this direction it's ten to one you'd have been burned to a cinder.'

I twisted round and looked over my shoulder. The late sunlight was still bright on the nearer treetops, making them shine like polished copper, but out in the middle distance a long smudge of grey smoke hung above the forest, dulling the air for what must have been mile upon smothering mile. My head swam and I swayed forward, clutching at the pony's mane. Preece swung himself, stiff-legged, into his saddle. Then Billy clicked his tongue twice against his palate and we moved on.

26

I can't fault Preece's treatment of me. He took me back under his roof and surrendered his bed to me; he cooked the little portions of bland food my weakened body needed, and served them up at appropriate intervals; and when I woke crying and trembling in the dark, my skin slick with perspiration, he would rise from his mattress at the far end of the room, draw up a chair and sit at my side until I was able to sleep again. But there was a subtle constraint in his dealings with me now, a reticence that I interpreted as a form of reproach. I had the impression that he was waiting, courteously but with something less than complete equanimity, for the day I should be well enough to leave.

I can hardly blame him. Heaven knows, I've reproached myself often enough for what I've come to think of as culpable inertia. In the course of our brief, abortive journey Billy had been routinely mistreated, and finally assaulted, by a man ostensibly in my employ. Although I had spoken up once or twice in the boy's defence, I had done far too little for him: he owed his survival not to my half-hearted interventions but to a combination of good fortune and his own youthful agility. I was mortified to learn that he had been huddled on the ledge when I began my first descent of the rock face but had chosen to scurry away and conceal himself, judging me incapable – he said as much, and the accusation smarts even now – of protecting him from Bullen's vindictive anger. That he should have considered it safer to return home alone under cover of darkness than to make the journey in our company reflects almost as poorly on me as it does on Bullen.

There was no refuge. Catching Preece's eye for an instant as he stooped to tuck in my blanket, or hearing through the hot boards the lilt of a whistled tune as Billy went about his business in the garden, I would remember again, with undiminished shame, how I had failed the boy. And to make matters worse, the hatchet-faced constable who came to question me on the evening after my return seemed to be exercised at least as much by the attack on Billy as by Bullen's death. 'I've two of my own,' he said grimly, 'and heaven help anyone who laid a finger on either of them.' He leaned forward in his chair, bringing his face uncomfortably close to mine.

'Bullen was ill,' I said. 'I don't believe he knew exactly what he was doing.'

'Not so ill that he couldn't throw a punch at the lad.' I could see the sweat beading the man's brow and upper lip; his short hair stuck out from his scalp in damp spikes. I leaned back wearily against the iron bars of the bed-head.

'Mr Redbourne has been very sick himself,' said Preece, stepping forward protectively.

The constable nodded. 'I've almost done,' he said, rising to his feet. 'If we should need to find you once you've left the mountains, Mr Redbourne . . . ?'

I gave him Vane's address, spelling it out slowly for him as he bent over his pocket-book. 'And the dead man's family?' he asked.

'I'm fairly certain there were no close relatives. I shall make . . .' My head swam as I groped helplessly for the word. 'Enquiries,' I said at last. 'I'll let you know.'

'Thank you, Mr Redbourne.' The air around us seemed to flicker and dim; I could barely make him out as he stepped over the threshold and into the gathering dusk.

Just once, on the third morning of my enforced stay, the atmosphere lightened briefly. I was up and about for the first time since my return or, to put it more accurately, I was seated at the table with my pencil in my hand and my journal open in front of me, my mind as blank as the page I was staring at. Billy was sitting just inside the doorway with his shirt on his lap, carefully stitching the torn fabric, his eyes narrowed against the sunlight and his bare feet braced against the door-frame, while Preece busied himself with his broom, sweeping the dust into a small heap just in front of the boy's chair.

'It's a strange thing,' said Preece, straightening up with a smile, 'how some people have a knack of putting themselves in other people's way.' He was looking in my direction, but I saw from his expression that his words were intended for Billy's ears. Billy continued with his stitching, giving no sign of having heard.

'I said,' Preece persisted with humorous emphasis, leaning over the boy and ruffling his hair, 'it's a pity I can't get to the doorway for the great lummock skewed across it.' Billy let his needle fall and grasped his father's wrist with his left hand, at the same time aiming a gentle punch at his ribs with his right. The broom clattered to the floor as Preece moved in close and held him in a lock or embrace, the two of them laughing as they struggled together. Watching their good-natured scuffling from across the room, I should have liked to laugh with them, but found myself instead on the point of tears.

I can't say exactly what it was, the grief that welled up in me at that moment, but I know that I seemed to be standing at the boundary of some charmed enclosure, like a soul exiled from its true habitation, looking for a way in. And as Preece released Billy and turned back to his task, his face still creased with laughter and his eyes shining, I heard myself say, in a voice not quite my own, 'Give him his due, Preece, he's a fine young man,' and then, following through with feigned nonchalance: 'Cle-

268

ver, too. He might go far with a good education. If you wanted to send him to Sydney to continue his schooling, I've no doubt we could come to some arrangement.'

It was as though a cloud had passed across the sun. Preece's features stiffened, the laughter fading from his eyes. 'Thank you, Mr Redbourne,' he said coldly. 'Billy's getting a good education here – better than any school-learning could give him – and he'll go as far as he needs to go.'

'Even so,' I said, taken aback by the severity of his tone, 'there would be certain advantages. With the right kind of schooling—'

'How do you think the boy would fare, cooped up in a city classroom, learning by rote things that'll draw him from the soil he's rooted in and give him nothing worth having in exchange? Who knows what damage he might suffer?'

'I shouldn't have made the offer if I hadn't believed it to be in Billy's best interests.'

Preece's gaze relaxed slightly, though his voice was still hard. 'I believe you mean well, Mr Redbourne,' he said, 'but you've no call to concern yourself with such matters. It's not your place.'

Billy rose silently, draped his shirt across the back of his chair and slipped away into the sunlight. I stared at the floor, rigid with misery. 'You're right,' I said at last. 'I shall leave tomorrow.'

We set off early, Preece and I on ponyback, Billy loping easily beside me, one hand on the bridle. I had been touched by the boy's insistence on accompanying us and felt under some obligation to make conversation, but neither he nor I seemed able to strike the right note, and we soon lapsed into silence.

I was still far from well – frail and feverish, my eyes confused by the riddling interplay of glare and shadow on the dusty track in front of me and my mind troubled by elusive fragments of the night's dreaming. By the time we reached the station, I was already exhausted. I remember Preece helping me down from the pony as though I had been a child, and holding me lightly by the arm as we made our way to the platform.

He had allowed ample time, and we had a good half-hour to wait. We sat in the shade, Preece on one side of me and Billy on the other, our talk sporadic and constrained, while the heat intensified around us. I stared down the track into a distance creased and distorted by the quivering air, and imagined the long, hot miles ahead.

It seemed to me that I had never known time pass so sluggishly, but at last I heard the wail of the whistle, and the train steamed in with a racket that set my raw nerves jangling. Preece helped me to my feet and across the platform to the nearest carriage. He threw open the door and held it back, hovering solicitously behind me as I hauled myself in.

I pulled the door to, lowered the window and rested my elbows on the frame, queasy with the stink of grease and sulphur. Preece lifted his eyes to mine. 'I should think you'll be glad to get back to your own world,' he said.

It came to me that I should be hard put to it to locate

my own world again but the notion, glimpsed through a dull haze of fatigue, refused to come into focus, and I let it pass. 'I can't thank you enough,' I said – and the words fell dead from my lips, though I meant them sincerely – 'for all you've done for me.'

Preece took a step backward and glanced away down the track. 'I've done by you as I'd have done by any man,' he said.

There was an awkward pause. I tugged my purse from my pocket and withdrew two sovereigns. 'I must have been a drain on your resources,' I said, proffering the coins. 'I hope this will square accounts.'

He shook his head. 'There's no need.' The train jerked into motion with a squeal and clash of couplings, and began to glide slowly forward.

'For Billy,' I said. 'Take it for Billy.'

Preece made no move. Billy's face was turned in my direction, but I couldn't read his expression. Puzzlement, was it? Embarrassment? I leaned out in desperation as they began to slip away from me. 'Billy,' I cried, holding out the coins on my open palm; and then, almost beside myself with anguish, I lunged forward and tossed them on to the platform at his feet.

He didn't stoop. His father reached out and placed one hand on his shoulder. I watched the two conjoined figures dwindling away down the shimmering platform as the train gathered speed. They might have been made of stone.

IV

27

I had imagined that I should quickly recover my health once I was back at Tresillian Villa, but I was wrong: my return precipitated a nervous collapse of paralysing severity. Even as I stepped down from the buggy into the punishing sunlight I could feel some deeper dissolution setting in. True, I was able to respond to Vane's handshake with a firmness that might have passed for warmth, and as he ushered me into the house I answered or deflected his enquiries with what I imagine to have been a reasonable show of civility; but I felt that my body – my feet, my tongue, my prickling eyes – didn't entirely belong to me, and I grew sick and giddy with the effort of controlling it. As soon as I decently could, I slipped away to my room and locked the door.

I sat on the edge of my bed, hearing the sounds of other lives beyond my window – the piping of small finches in the shrubbery, the clang of a pail set down on a stone surface, a faraway lowing of cattle – and watching the lozenges of sunlight lapse slowly across the floor and walls. In a moment, I kept telling myself, I shall rise to my feet, wash, change my clothing and go downstairs; but the moments passed and I barely moved. Just once, hearing Eleanor's voice drift up from the garden, I was stirred into action: I leaped up, crossed to the window and looked out. She was out of sight beyond the corner of the house, and too distant for me to be able to distinguish more than the occasional phrase of what was evidently a slightly irritable conversation with her father. 'You should have called me,' I heard her say at one point, her voice sharp with accusation; and then Vane's light bass cut in, cool and placatory, and the two of them moved away.

A little before sundown I heard footsteps approaching along the corridor, and then a gentle rapping at my door. I sat tight, said nothing.

'Charles?' Eleanor's voice again, very soft and close now. I imagined her out there listening for my reply, her cheek resting against the varnished wood. I held my breath. My heart lurched in my chest.

'Charles, shall you be dining with us? Mrs Denham needs to know.'

The mundane detail – that casual reminder of a world in which meals are served at set hours by capable domestics – steadied me a little. 'I'm afraid not,' I called. 'I'm rather indisposed.'

There was a long silence before she spoke again, urgently now, dropping her voice to a low whisper. 'Come to the door, Charles. I want to see you.'

I eased myself back and laid my head on the pillows. 'I'm in bed,' I said. 'I'll see you tomorrow.'

Another pause and then, so quietly I could barely hear her: 'I'm glad you're back.' She turned, the fabric of her dress brushing the door, and I raised my head and strained forward to listen as her footsteps died away down the corridor.

As darkness began to fall, the rapping and whispering began again: *Open the door* – the words repeated two or three times as I rolled over on to my side, burying my face in the pillows. *Yes*, she breathed, and an instant later, her voice so close behind me that there could be no doubt of it, *I'm with you now*. A little sigh, and then the pressure of her body against my back, the warmth of her mouth at my ear. *There's nothing to be afraid of*, she said, and because it was my mother's voice I heard then, my mother's reassurance echoing back to me across the years, I turned, whimpering, and let her draw my head to her breast. *Hush*, she whispered, rocking me gently in her arms, and the sound stirred me and set my hands working at the soft fabric of her garments, peeling back layer after layer. Easily at first, and with a subdued excitement; but as I worked on, I felt the stuff disintegrating beneath my probing fingers, clumps of feathers breaking away and drifting across the bed in smothering clouds so dense that I struggled for breath and, crying out, startled myself from sleep.

Is it possible, I wonder, to convey any sense of what followed? Not a night punctuated by terrifying dreams, such as I had experienced under Preece's roof, but a night of unalleviated terror in which I slipped confusedly between sleep and waking without finding even momentary respite from the images and sensations that stormed round or through me. It's the landscapes I remember best, and this most clearly and terribly of all: a vast tract viewed at first as though from a great height or through the wrong end of a telescope – rock and forest, swamp and river, the sunlight thickening in a brooding sky. As I stare – and I know already that something frightful is about to happen – I see below me, dead centre of my field of vision, a lick of orange flame springing up like a flower. I raise my head and another starts up towards the horizon and, further still, a third. I clap my hands over my eyes to protect the land from my own incendiary gaze but I can see clean through my palms, and the fires continue to break out wherever I look. And then – it's the same landscape, but in some sombre aftermath, and I'm down there now, stumbling across the hot earth – the drifts of ash, the blackened, skeletal trees, the light draining remorselessly away; and in the choking air, little tatters of soot or darkness swirling around me as I wake, sweating, and reach for my pocket watch.

If, indeed, I did wake. I looked at the dial and saw that

it was a few minutes past midnight; but how, I asked myself later, could I possibly have seen what I thought I'd seen? Not just the watch, but the entire room in daylight detail – washstand and writing table, ewer, basin and oil-lamp, all in essence as I knew them to be, but twitching and quivering with a horrible, restless energy. And something twitching, too, at the corner of my left eye, a sooty flake from the smoking waste I'd just passed through. I reached for my handkerchief and dabbed frantically at the shadow, but it slid sideways across my vision like a shutter and I was back among the blackened tree-trunks again, staring helplessly into the deepening gloom.

Beneath the confusion ran an inarticulate longing for daybreak but, in the event, I missed the moment and the sun was well up when I woke to Vane's voice, low and insistent, calling my name. I sat bolt upright in a kind of panic, clutching at the damp cloth of my shirt.

'What is it?' My pulse was racing, my mouth dry. I heard him try the handle.

'Are you all right, Redbourne?'

A simple enough question, but the answer seemed beyond me. I made my way unsteadily to the door, unlocked it and let him in. It struck me, as his eyes met mine, that he was reading the answer to his question in my face; and at the same moment I lost my balance and lurched sideways against the door-edge.

'I shall have to sit down,' I said.

He helped me back to the bed and sat beside me, eyeing my crumpled clothes. 'You're in no condition to be on your feet,' he said. 'I'll have your breakfast sent up to you.'

'I've little appetite at the moment.'

'Would you like me to send for Dr Barton?'

'It's not necessary. I shall feel better when I'm properly rested.'

He rose to his feet. 'Whatever you need,' he said with a formal inclination of his head, 'is at your disposal. You've only to ask.'

'Thank you, Vane.' I swung my legs on to the bed and sank back against the pillows as the door clicked shut.

Towards midday, as I lay staring listlessly at the ceiling, Eleanor entered bearing a bowl of broth on a lacquer tray. 'You're to drink this,' she said, without preamble, as I struggled upright. 'I've had it made specially for you.' She was brisk and businesslike, studiously avoiding my eyes, but I saw, as she handed me the tray, that her arms were trembling. She drew up a chair and perched on the edge of the seat, emphatically present but poised as if ready for retreat, her hands braced on her thighs.

'How are you, Nell?'

She glanced away, flushing faintly. 'I've missed you,' she said simply. 'Since you went I've been . . .' She raised both hands palm upward in a delicate, hesitant gesture and let them drop again. I felt a tremor pass through me, head to heel, a swift shock of pleasure and apprehension.

'I was afraid,' she continued, 'that you wouldn't come back. Just a vague worry at first, the kind of feeling you might have about anyone you care for when they're away from you. But then the dreams began, and it came to me that you were in danger. I thought you were going to die out there.'

'Dreams about me?'

'Dreams of disaster. I thought they concerned you, but I could never get close enough to see the faces. I don't want to talk about it.'

'Has your father told you about Bullen?'

She nodded. 'Drink up your broth,' she said, 'while it's still hot.'

I dipped my spoon obediently and took a mouthful. 'You're terribly thin,' she said. 'Your face is different. Sharper and harder. If I didn't know you, you'd frighten me.'

'I've not had sight of my own reflection for days.'

She stepped over to the washstand and picked up the looking-glass. I reached out to take it from her.

'Finish that first,' she said.

I supped the broth quickly but without relish. She stood over me until the bowl was empty, then handed me the mirror.

I could see at once what she meant. In part it was the beard, still at the stage at which it accentuated rather than concealed my jawline and the hollow contours of my cheeks, that gave my face its forbidding appearance; but there was something in the eyes, too, a look I didn't recognise as my own. It was as though the wilderness I'd walked through, or some essential element of it, had lodged in me, giving my gaze an unfamiliar depth and darkness. I wiped the glass nervously against the counterpane and handed it back. 'I need a shave,' I said.

'You need a bath.' She wrinkled her nose. 'Have you been sleeping in those clothes?'

'Is it so obvious?'

'I'll ask Mrs Denham to arrange it.' She returned the mirror to the washstand and picked up the tray. I could feel her drawing off, slipping away from me into a world I wasn't yet fit to face, and I leaned anxiously after her as she moved towards the door. 'Will you come back?' I asked.

'Later. I'm working on something out in the barn. I want to keep at it while the idea's still clear in my mind.'

'A painting?'

She shook her head. 'You'll see,' she said. 'When you're ready.'

I had expected to feel better for my bath and change of clothes, but in fact I returned to my room in a deeper state of exhaustion. Not only that, but the fluttering tag of darkness was back, dancing away at the margin of my vision. I strained to take it in, swivelling my eyes or turning my head to find it always just out of range, a faint shadow flickering in sunlight like an inverse will-o'-the-wisp, simultaneously elusive and insistent. I spent the afternoon in a state of morbid anxiety, and though I heard Eleanor's knock I didn't respond immediately.

'Charles, it's Nell.'

I rose to my feet and let her in. Another bowl of broth; a slice of buttered bread on a white porcelain plate. 'I'm not hungry,' I said, scanning the tray.

'You must keep your strength up. How can you get better if you don't eat?' She stepped past me into the room and motioned me towards the bedside chair. It seemed pointless to resist.

'Does your father know you're looking after me like this?' I asked.

She handed me the tray and drew up the other chair, setting it directly in front of my own, a little closer than seemed necessary. 'Of course,' she said.

'Has he no objection?'

She glanced towards the door, silent for a moment, her lips compressed. 'I don't need my father's permission to visit a sick friend,' she said at last. Something in her words, or perhaps in her defiant tone, caught me off guard: the room blurred suddenly, and I set the heels of both hands to my eyes in a vain attempt to stem the tears.

'Do you have many friends?' she asked. 'In England, I mean.' She was watching me closely, I sensed, but her voice gave no hint of distaste or embarrassment. I shook my head, still fighting for self-control.

'Suppose you were ill at home,' she continued. 'Who would visit you there?'

I shrugged, fumbled for my handkerchief. 'I have a manservant,' I said.

'That's not what I meant.' She leaned forward in her chair, her head tilted to one side. 'What's the matter with your eye?' she asked.

'The darkness?'

An absurd question. She frowned, visibly puzzled. 'The twitching,' she said. 'At the corner.' She reached tentatively towards my face, her hand raised in the air before me as though in blessing.

'I don't know.' It crossed my mind that I might tell her about my dreams – about the burning and the desolation – but I couldn't think how to begin. 'It's been troubling me since last night.'

It was the simplest thing – just a continuation of that interrupted forward momentum, the fingertips coming to rest lightly against the outer edge of my eyelid, the side of the palm against my cheek – but I think I knew even then that there was power enough in that touch to alter the course of a life. I stiffened, froze.

'Does it hurt?'

I felt the tears well up again and, as I struggled to speak, the tray tilted on my lap and slid forward and the whole lot crashed to the floor. I sat in a kind of stupor, staring at the debris – the plate broken into half a dozen angular shards, the bowl spinning on its side, the thin broth spreading out across the polished boards; and then, as though the accident had given me permission, I began to cry without restraint.

She made no move to rise. Instead, she leaned closer and pressed my head to her shoulder, slipping her other arm around my own shoulders. She held me to her as my sobbing intensified; continued to hold me as it subsided. I felt myself drift on the rise and fall of her breathing, light as a leaf on a tidal swell. 'No,' I murmured, drawing away a little, breaking her hold.

'What is it?' she asked.

I gestured weakly towards the debris. 'All this,' I whispered. 'This mess. This damage.'

'But not only this?' She was gazing into my eyes with an expression of such searching intensity that I began to tremble. 'Tell me,' she said.

I have never talked to anyone as I talked to Eleanor that afternoon. I spoke with desperate eloquence, hearing the words spill out as though from someone else's lips, mapping out a world of irreparable hurt and loss. I recognised the element of confusion in my breakneck narrative, but I could see at the same time how everything was linked: the heron flapping helplessly in the dust, Billy stumbling sideways before dropping from sight over the cliff edge, the slender arms of the dead wallabies spread wide in mute entreaty, Daniel walking out into the pelting night, the black girl's averted gaze as I pocketed her bracelet, the flames spreading outward from beneath my hands to consume a fragile, extravagant wilderness. Each thread seemed to lead ineluctably to another, and I was still talking when the gong sounded for dinner.

'I must go,' she said, rising from her chair.

'Nell, I'm sorry. Your clothing . . .' She followed my gaze, holding the skirt wide to inspect the damage: a long, greasy stain running diagonally from knee-level to hemline.

'It's nothing,' she said. 'Nothing that soap and water won't remedy.' I bent forward awkwardly, making to gather up the fragments of porcelain at her feet, but she prevented me. 'Leave it,' she said. 'I'll send one of the girls up to attend to it.'

'I've taken up so much of your time. It was good of you to listen to me.'

'I listened because I wanted to listen.' She crossed to the window and raised the sash a couple of inches. 'A little air,' she said, putting her palm to the aperture, 'now that it's growing cooler.'

A faint breeze rustling the leaves, the hum of insect life from the flowerbeds below. She turned to face me, framed against the softening light. 'You're not to worry,' she said quietly. 'There's no cause.'

I remember her words precisely, but the words were only part of it. Standing there in front of the window, her cropped hair forming a jagged aureole about her head, she seemed at once abstracted and concentrated, as though she were communing with a world beyond our own; and fanciful as it might appear, I saw her at that moment as something more than herself – a priestess, perhaps, called upon to interpret some profound insight for the benefit of suffering humanity – and heard her simple words as a form of absolution. I felt my breathing ease, my spirits lighten and lift.

I should have been glad to prolong the moment, but she turned abruptly and made for the door. 'Shall I get the girl to bring you some fresh broth?' she asked. I was silent, caught off balance, trembling between worlds.

'Charles?'

'That would be nice. Will you come back later?'

'Tomorrow.'

The tremor was starting up again at the corner of my eye, the flickering wisp of darkness re-insinuating itself. 'Nell,' I called.

'What is it?'

'Did you understand what I was trying to tell you about Daniel?'

She paused, one hand on the door-knob. 'You loved him,' she said, 'in your own way. The harm wasn't in the loving.' She threw the door wide and the curtains billowed inward from the windowsill, lifted on a draught so sweet it might have come fresh from Eden's fields.

28

Vane came to my room several times over the next few days, but on each occasion his demeanour suggested that the visit was little more than a courtesy, while I, for my own part, must have made it plain enough that I had no interest in prolonging our stilted exchanges. I was vague and easily distracted – by the creak of a floorboard in the corridor, the murmur of voices from the hallway – and Vane, who was, after all, no fool, could hardly have failed to realise that it was Eleanor I wanted to speak to.

I don't think I was capable of such insights at the time,

but I see clearly now how strangely our roles had changed. Excitable, irreticent and prone to fits of weeping, I clamoured incessantly for Eleanor's attention during her visits while she, listening intently or speaking with gentle gravity, drew me patiently back to a world I had ceased to care for. I sensed a fine judgement at work there: she seemed to know what I needed before I knew it myself, and showed considerable skill in countering my irrational resistance to her suggestions. I remember in particular how adroitly she brought me round, on the evening of my fourth day back at the villa, to her view that it was time for me to leave my sick-room and get out of the house. I was not, I told her peevishly, well enough to do so, but she was insistent.

'I'm not asking you to go far. Take breakfast with us tomorrow, and then come down to the barn with me. You'll feel better for the change of scene.'

'And worse for the journey. I've only to stand and my legs start shaking.'

'The more reason to set them moving. I'll wake you at seven tomorrow.'

'Eight o'clock would suit me better.'

'I shall be taking breakfast at half past seven.'

'I shall come down,' I said grudgingly, 'and perhaps take a turn round the garden. I very much doubt that I shall be able to accompany you to the barn.'

I saw her smile very faintly, as though with satisfaction at something accomplished, before rising from her chair. 'We can discuss that over breakfast,' she said.

*　　*　　*

The clock had barely struck the half-hour when I came down the next morning, but Vane and Eleanor were already at breakfast, eating in silence at opposite ends of the table. Vane rose as I entered, extending his hand in greeting.

'Welcome back to the land of the living,' he said with a brittle smile. 'It's good to have you with us again.' He seated me in the chair beside his own and poured me a cup of coffee. 'What will you have?'

I settled for a slice of toast. 'We'll soon build you up,' said Vane, sliding the butter-dish towards me. 'Soon put the flesh back on your bones.'

I looked down at my wrist, so thin and frail against the dense weave of the linen tablecloth, and wondered with a flash of panic whether I should ever find my place again in the solid world of everyday things. I took up my knife and began to spread the butter, trying to disguise the trembling of my hands.

There was a light tapping at the door, and a maid-servant entered. 'Post for Mr Redbourne,' she said, holding out a letter.

'Leave it there,' said Vane brusquely. The girl placed the letter on the sideboard and withdrew, but she had no sooner gone than Eleanor rose deliberately to her feet, crossed the room and retrieved it.

'Charles might want to read it now,' she said, addressing her father over my head as she set the letter beside my plate.

The air seemed to thicken around us. Eleanor stood at my side, leaning a little inward, her body so close to mine that I felt, or imagined I felt, the warmth of it on my own skin. Vane's face, I saw, glancing up, was rigid with suppressed fury. I picked up the letter and slipped it into my inside pocket.

'It's from my uncle,' I said. 'I'll read it later.'

Eleanor stepped away and returned to her place. She sat down, rolled up her napkin and slipped it into its silver ring; then she leaned back, folding her hands demurely in her lap. Vane ate slowly, chewing each mouthful with a thoroughness that seemed in some obscure way to be directed at, or against, his daughter, but at last he pushed back his chair and we all rose together.

As we reached the french windows, I stood aside to let Eleanor pass, and was about to follow her out when Vane plucked at my sleeve. 'Might I have a word with you, Redbourne?'

Eleanor stopped in her tracks and turned to face us. 'Charles has promised to come down to the barn with me,' she said. 'I have something to show him.'

'And I,' said Vane coldly, 'have something I wish to say to him. Perhaps you'd be good enough to leave us alone for a few minutes.'

I sensed that Eleanor expected me to respond. What should I have said, though, caught there between father and daughter on the sunlit threshold? I said nothing, and after a moment Eleanor stepped back. 'I'll wait for you on the path,' she said. She flung away and strode off down the slope, her skirt swaying with the vigour of her movements.

Vane watched her until she disappeared from view behind the long curve of the shrubbery. 'Let me advise you,' he said, 'not to let my daughter monopolise your time. I shouldn't like your convalescence to be hindered by any demands she might make on your resources.'

'I believe,' I said carefully, 'that she has my best interests at heart. It's difficult to judge such matters but I suspect that her attentions have, if anything, hastened my recovery.'

'Indeed?' He drew out his cigarette case but paused on the point of opening it, and returned it to his pocket. 'There's something else,' he said. 'Your correspondence with your uncle . . . The fact is, I'd be grateful if you'd avoid any mention of my domestic difficulties when you write. I mean, I hope you won't touch on the matter of Eleanor's illness.'

'I wouldn't dream of it.'

He gave me a crooked smile. 'You're a good man, Redbourne. I shall be sorry to see you go.'

I could hear the struts and slats of the veranda ticking softly as the sun heated them. Vane placed his hands on the rail and stared out across the garden, his shoulders hunched.

'As soon as I'm strong enough—'

'Please,' he interrupted. 'You mustn't imagine that I'm hurrying you on your way. You must take your time. I won't hear of you leaving a moment before you're ready.'

There was a long, awkward pause. 'If you don't mind,' I said at last, 'I shall go and find out what Eleanor wants to show me.'

Vane turned slowly towards me. I imagined from his

expression that he had something more to say, but he drew himself up stiffly and strode past me into the house.

I was weak, certainly, and the path to the barn was more heavily overgrown than I remembered, but the walk was not the ordeal I had imagined. At breakfast I had managed to swallow a few mouthfuls of Vane's strong coffee, and now my spirits lifted as I followed Eleanor down, a little hesitantly but without great difficulty. My senses had been refined by my illness, the sense of smell above all, and I remember snuffing the air in a state of febrile excitement, almost overwhelmed by the heady mix – the subtle perfume of Eleanor's hair and clothing, flower-scents wafted from the garden, the heavier undertones of vegetation bruised by my boot soles, the rich smell of cattle-dung rising from the meadows below.

And then, as she pushed back the barn door, the tang of freshly cut eucalyptus wood. I could see at once what she had been up to in my absence: just inside the doorway, in the middle of a scatter of chippings, stood a pale upright form some three feet in height, vigorously rather than cleanly sculpted, its contours unmistakably feminine.

'Is this what you wanted to show me?' I asked, stooping to examine the piece. It was evidently unfinished, its surfaces still rough, but it was apparent to me that Eleanor had discovered, whether in the medium or elsewhere, a new and exhilarating source of inspiration. The figure was incomplete, like a piece of damaged

Greek statuary – headless and all but limbless – yet charged with vitality. Above the truncated thighs and the broad curve of the buttocks the waist narrowed and twisted sideways and backwards, the torso drawn taut against the sustaining fullness at its base; the armpits were exposed and hollowed and the breasts and shoulders raised, as though the missing arms were reaching for heaven. Not strictly naturalistic yet suggestive of a deep understanding of natural forms, it was a remarkable achievement, and all the more so in that Eleanor appeared to have had only the most basic implements at her disposal: ranged on the floor behind the sculpture were a rusted saw, a broad-bladed gouge, a large iron file and a primitive mallet crudely fashioned from a length of reddish timber.

She squatted down among the chippings and lifted her face to mine. 'There's no one else I can show it to,' she said. 'And even you . . . I couldn't be sure you'd like it. You do like it, don't you?'

'Very much indeed.' I wanted to reach out and touch the figure but some sense of the gesture's subtler implications held me back. 'It's a wonderful piece.'

'There's more to be done, but only surface work. The lines of the carving are all there, almost exactly as I envisaged them when I began. And you know, Charles, all the time I was working on her I knew she was going to come out right. I can't explain it very well, but it seemed to me that she was lodged in the wood like a tree-spirit, and that if I just let the grain guide my blade I should find her. Does that make sense?'

'Of a sort, yes.' I straightened up and stepped back for

a longer view, conscious that she was scrutinising me as carefully as I was scrutinising her handiwork; and it was at that moment that I recognised the connection between what I was looking at and the stumpy totem she had shown me in the hayloft. It was far from obvious, because the relationship wasn't traceable in the form itself but in what lay beneath the form – some dark, illicit knowledge of appetite and power.

'Yes, of course,' she said, when I delicately touched on the matter. 'From the moment I walked into the shop and saw her there, I knew I wanted to make something as strong and beautiful as she was. But you can't just copy someone else's work. I had to come at it my own way, and I could only do that when the time was right. This is the right time. And this,' she added, unbuttoning the cuffs of her blouse, 'is only the beginning.'

I dragged a chair to the doorway and, as she worked, sat staring out into the light, lulled into a state of reflective ease by the rhythmical rasp of her file. At long intervals she would break off and we would exchange a word or two but, perhaps divining my mood or perhaps simply absorbed in her task, she left me largely to my reveries. My thoughts ranged widely but I found them returning repeatedly to the walled garden at the Hall, an admired ornament to the estate in my father's time but pitifully neglected in my own. With its cold-frames smashed, its peach trees blighted and its espaliers unpruned it had become, over the years, an emblem of my own despair. Yet Preece had fashioned his garden out of raw wilderness; all I needed to do was to restore order to a plot of fertile land cultivated by my ancestors for more than a century. Yes, I should take the garden in hand, and the orchard too; and then, why not set new fruit trees in the meadow beyond? And beyond that again? I imagined the slope as it might appear in some future spring, clouded with blossoms, or glowing red and gold in late summer as the fruit sweetened on the boughs.

I lost track of the time, but it must have been close to midday when I eventually roused myself and rose unsteadily to my feet. Eleanor was on her knees in front of the figure, her back turned towards me so that I saw, with a hot, tender shock, the small bones of her neck above the collar of her blouse. Her sleeves were rolled back to her elbows and she held the file loosely in her left hand. As I watched, she ran the flat of her other hand with a long caressing movement down the figure's skewed flank and across the belly, dislodging a shower of pale dust; and with the action I experienced a surge of giddy exultation so intense that I reeled sideways against the warped boards of the door.

Eleanor looked round sharply. 'What's the matter?' she asked.

'Nothing,' I answered, steadying myself as best I could. 'Nothing to speak of.'

Back in my room that evening, I opened the top drawer of my writing-desk and took out the aboriginal girl's bracelet. For Eleanor, I thought, shifting its small weight in the palm of my hand. I slipped it into the pocket of my outdoor breeches but I had no sooner done so than I began to wonder how she might construe such a gift, and I spent the night in a foolish agony of indecision, sleepless through hours of darkness so miserably protracted that it seemed the dawn would never come.

29

As my strength increased over the following days, Vane's temper seemed to worsen. I stayed out of his way as far as circumstances allowed, taking short walks around the estate or reading in the shade of the trees at the end of the lawn while he, for his part, made no attempt to bridge the widening gulf between us. It was clear that he would have liked me to maintain a similar distance from his daughter for the remainder of my stay, but that proved impossible. Although I made a point of avoiding the barn, I was unable to prevent Eleanor from seeking out my company elsewhere.

'You can't send me away just because he doesn't like seeing us together,' she objected one morning, as I tried to reason with her. We were standing on the lawn in full view of the house, and I glanced up anxiously at the veranda as she spoke. 'He's not there,' she said, registering the movement, 'and even if he were, our friendship's no concern of his.'

'You're his daughter and I'm his guest. We each have certain obligations to him.'

'I've no such obligation.'

'All daughters have a duty to their fathers.'

'Only when their fathers have honoured their own obligations. I owe him nothing. And sometimes,' she added after a thoughtful pause, 'we have to think of our duty to ourselves.'

I considered the phrase. 'Surely,' I said, 'you don't mean that we should all be allowed to do exactly as we want?'

'Not quite. I mean that there are times in our lives when what we want is so important that we can't allow ourselves to be knocked off course by other people's wishes, especially when those people may not have our best interests at heart.' And then, turning to look me full in the face: 'I know what I want, Charles. What do you want?'

The directness of her challenge caught me entirely off guard. What I experienced then was a faint, sweet aftertaste of the exhilaration I had known in the barn as her hand moved smoothly over the swelling contours of her own creation, but I could find no way of translating the sensation into an appropriate answer to her question. 'I don't know,' I answered lamely.

'Maybe you should find out.' She gave a little laugh. 'That's your homework,' she said. 'I'll ask you again next week.'

'I may not be here next week, Nell. As soon as I'm strong enough I shall travel to Sydney and book my passage home.'

I saw the smile fade from her face. 'But you can't go yet,' she said. 'You've hardly seen anything of the country.'

I wanted to tell her that I had seen more deeply into the country than I had either expected or wished, but I thought the claim might sound presumptuous. 'I've learned a lot,' I said simply.

'There's always more to learn.' She turned and looked out across the valley before swinging back to face me again. 'There's something in particular,' she said. 'Something you should see before you go. I'll take you there this afternoon.'

'Listen, Nell, your father—'

'I'll deal with my father. We'll leave after lunch.' She broke away with a little shake of her shoulders and marched up the slope towards the house.

Despite Vane's absence from the table, or perhaps in part because of it, our conversation over lunch was horribly constrained. Eleanor was visibly unsettled, her features taut and her movements nervy and graceless, though the impression of imbalance was offset by something in her eyes and in the set of her jaw.

'He's taking lunch in his study,' she said tersely, in response to my query. And then, as I debated whether to question her further: 'John will have the ponies saddled up by the time we've finished.'

The remainder of the meal passed in near-silence, but as we rose from the table Eleanor's spirits seemed to lift, and by the time we had ridden through the gates and out on to the track she appeared to have recovered not only her equilibrium but something of the girlish insouciance that had struck me so forcibly at the beginning of our acquaintance. I remember her urging her pony forward with little whispered endearments, her mouth at the creature's ear, and then turning to me with a smile of such childlike simplicity and openness that I scarcely knew how to respond.

We had been travelling for perhaps half an hour when the slope above the track abruptly changed character – the trees stark and black, the ground beneath them strewn with charred branches. A faint bitterness rose from the ashy dust stirred by the ponies' hoofs. I know this landscape, I thought, feeling the hairs rise on the back of my neck. 'Where are we going, Nell?'

'We've arrived.' She reined her pony to a halt and slipped nimbly from the saddle. I dismounted more gingerly.

'You wanted to show me this?'

'I want you to see how the bush grows back.' She led me off the track and across the soft scatter of charcoal to a small group of eucalyptus saplings. 'Look at these.'

What I had registered initially was a scene of devastation, the ravaged landscape of my fevered nightmares. Now, looking more carefully, I saw that the damage was only part of the picture. From the base of each sapling sprouted a ring of fresh shoots, while the blackened trunks had erupted at irregular intervals with similar outgrowths, vigorous tufts of translucent green foliage flushing to red where the leaves were newest.

Eleanor reached out and brushed one of the tufts gently with the palm of her hand. 'You see?' she said. 'Hardly more than two months ago, the whole of this hillside was ablaze. From the house you could see the glow of it two nights running, and the sky grey with smoke by day. Now the land's healing itself. It always does.'

I was struggling to control my emotions, staring at the luminous foliage, half blind with tears. 'What I'm saying,' she continued after a tactful pause, 'is that you've done nothing to the land that the land itself can't mend.' Her head lifted suddenly and her eyes narrowed. I turned, following her gaze, to see what had distracted her.

Two figures were moving slowly towards us down the track, a man and a woman, both walking with a terrible languor under the weight of the tattered bundles they carried on their backs. Watching their approach, I sensed that the woman was gravely ill: her head hung low and her bare feet dragged in the dust. She was quite young, I realised as she drew close, but her features were stiff and hollow, the bones prominent beneath her dark skin. Her arms swung loosely a little forward from her sides, the wrists as thin as a child's below the frayed cuffs of her blouse.

Her companion was almost as thin, but evidently not as frail. He held his head as high as his burden allowed, walking with grim concentration, his eyes fixed fiercely on the track ahead of him. As the two of them drew level with us I called out a greeting, but they pressed on without so much as a glance in our direction.

Our actions are not always entirely explicable, even in retrospect, but I can see clearly enough how one un-satisfactory encounter with the indigenous people of the region might have stirred memories of another. I cried out, I remember, then started forward and stumbled after the couple, tugging the bracelet from my breeches pocket as I went. I can't imagine what they must have thought of me as I fell in alongside them, jabbering excitably, thrusting the thing towards them. Had they seen it before? Did they know the girl it belonged to? Could they get it back to her? Would they take it anyway? As I stopped to draw breath I saw the man shake his head from side to side, slowly but emphati-cally, his tangled locks sweeping the sides of his gaunt face. He might have been answering any or all of my questions but his eyes steadfastly avoided mine, and I interpreted the gesture more generally as a refusal to have anything at all to do with me. Disconcerted, I stepped back and rejoined Eleanor.

'I had an idea they might know her,' I said. 'The girl who owned the bracelet.'

'It's not impossible. But look at them, Charles. They've cares enough of their own.' She stared down the track, following the couple's painful progress for a moment before turning back to me. 'Let me see it,' she said.

I held out the bracelet in the palm of my hand. 'It's

beautiful,' she murmured, taking it up between her finger and thumb and examining it closely. 'So delicately made.'

'She didn't want to part with it. We forced her.'

'You told me. Bullen threatened her. Threatened them all.'

I was watching the movements of a thickset grey lizard as it hunted among the stones at the far side of the track. 'Yes,' I said, 'but the fault was mine. If I hadn't wanted it—'

'You saw the beauty in it.' She draped the bracelet across the back of her hand so that the spines fanned out as they had against the dark skin of the girl's wrist. Something in that subtle collocation startled and moved me, bringing the words to my lips before I had time to consider them. 'Will you have it?' I asked.

The stillness was so profound that I could hear the tiny snap of the lizard's jaws as it took its prey. 'No,' she said after a moment. 'No, I can't.' My expression must have betrayed me for she reached out and touched my forearm like a mother comforting a disappointed child. 'I mean,' she said gently, 'that it doesn't belong to you, and can't belong to me.' She held up the bracelet so that the yellow feathers trembled and glowed in the sunlight. 'We'll leave it here.'

'Do you think she'll find it?'

She shrugged. 'What's important,' she said, 'is that we don't keep it.' She bent one of the fresh eucalyptus shoots towards her and slipped the bracelet over the tip, easing it down until it hung close against the blackened bark of the trunk. 'You'll travel more lightly without it.'

'I shall be going back almost empty-handed. My uncle's letter asks how the collection is progressing. I'm steeling myself to report the truth – that the sum of my endeavours is a few dozen insignificant specimens, most of them taken within shouting distance of my host's front door. I set out with grander designs.'

'If you stayed on, you could organise another expedition.'

'I've no stomach for it. The fact is, Nell, that I'm coming round to your position on the matter – the grasping, the killing. It seems to me that I've done enough damage.'

'But I don't want you to leave. Not just yet.'

The ponies were jostling one another, tetchy and restless, eager to be moving. 'I must,' I said. 'I want to get back to England. I have plans for my estate.'

'Then take me with you,' she said, the colour rising to her cheeks.

I felt my own face grow hot and my heart quicken. 'You know I can't do that, Nell. You must see how such a course of action would compromise us, you as well as me.'

'Not if we travelled as man and wife.'

Her phrasing was sufficiently ambiguous to leave open in my mind the possibility that she was suggesting some kind of subterfuge. She must have read the uncertainty in my eyes, because she stepped forward and took me by the wrist, looking intently into my face. 'I mean,' she said, with careful emphasis, 'that we might be married.'

I stood speechless, listening to the wind whispering among the black branches overhead. She leaned close, so close that I felt the touch of her breath against my throat as she spoke. 'Mightn't we?'

Sheer madness, I thought, beginning to tremble the way I'd trembled out there on the cliff face that evening as I jigged and spun at the rope's end above unfathomable space; but her gaze was so clear and sane and the pressure of her hand on my wrist so tenderly compelling that it was not, in the end, unduly difficult to give her the answer I hardly dared believe she wanted.

30

Eleanor was in favour of broaching the subject with her father on our return to the villa that evening, but I held out for a more cautious approach. Nothing of our intention, I insisted, was to be revealed to Vane, either directly or indirectly, while I remained in the house as his guest. It was apparent to me that Eleanor was unconvinced by my arguments, but she complied with my wishes.

Early next morning I rode into the city and paid a month's rental on a set of rooms in a small but reasonably well-appointed boarding-house within easy walking distance of the harbour. I had intended to be back at the villa in good time for lunch, but my mount was slow and fractious, and by the time I entered the dining-room Vane and Eleanor were half-way through their meal.

'There's soup in the tureen,' said Vane, scarcely troubling to glance up. I helped myself and sat down beside Eleanor. As I picked up my napkin she reached out and placed her hand on my wrist – just for the barest instant, but I could see from her father's expression that neither the gesture nor its significance had been lost on him. I should have preferred to leave my announcement until the end of the meal, but it was clear that I now had no choice in the matter.

'I've been to arrange my accommodation,' I said. 'I shall be living in lodgings in the city for the next few weeks.'

'You'll get a berth easily enough,' said Vane. 'I doubt whether you'll need to stay as long as that.'

'The fact is that I may need to stay a little longer. Longer, that is to say, than I would if it were simply a matter of booking myself on the first available passage. There's something else – I mean, I don't intend to leave at once because—'

It was absurd. A man of middle years and some sophistication, and I was blushing like a schoolboy, mumbling my words, searching hopelessly for the elegant phrases I'd prepared during the morning's ride. 'Because what?' snapped Vane. 'Because you want to wed my daughter?'

I nodded, simultaneously relieved and humiliated by

his intervention. 'Yes,' I said. 'I should like to ask for Eleanor's hand in marriage.'

'I'm not a fool,' he said. 'Do you think I couldn't see what was going on under my own nose?'

I leaned back in my chair and drew a deep breath, steadying myself. 'There was no intention of deceiving you,' I said quietly.

Vane grunted. 'Eat your soup,' he said, 'before it gets cold.'

'And your answer?'

In the stillness that followed I could hear the servants' voices rising from the scullery; slopped water, the clank of an iron vessel. 'You have my permission,' he said at last. He pushed away his plate, flung down his napkin and, without another word, stalked out of the room.

Once away from the villa, I quickly established a healthy regimen: a brisk walk to the harbour each morning upon rising and then, after breakfast, a longer excursion, sometimes through the bustling thoroughfares of the city but more often to a quiet spot on the shoreline where I would sit and gaze at the ocean, lulled by the sound of the breaking waves. In the afternoons I would retreat to my rooms to read or write.

Eleanor was almost constantly in my thoughts, but in a distant, rarefied way, as though she were a figure from a half-remembered dream. My future wife, I would think, repeating the phrase to myself like a charm in the hope of calling her before me in slightly more substantial form, but the girl herself – the moving, breathing creature – seemed always out of reach. The letters I sent her reflected something of my perplexity: detailed but reticent, solicitous but without warmth.

I had been in the city for more than a week before I heard from her. Her letter, which I took to have been supervised or even dictated, informed me simply that she and her father would call on me at eleven o'clock the following morning to discuss the wedding. I tore the envelope apart in the hope that she might have slipped some small note into its recesses, but there was nothing to be found.

They arrived punctually, Vane rapping on the front door with his cane as the clock in the hallway chimed the hour. It had struck me that our discussion might be more agreeably conducted in the open air than in the confined space of my dingy sitting room and Vane fell in at once with my suggestion that we should stroll down to Farm Cove, though he showed no sign of wanting to initiate conversation. Eleanor walked between us, talking nervously and almost incessantly about nothing in particular, and it wasn't until we were within sight of the shore that her father turned to the matter in hand.

'I'm not planning a grand celebration,' he said bluntly. 'Aside from the Merivales, you know none of our neighbours, and it's a little late in the day to be making introductions. In any case, Eleanor has expressed her own preference for a modest affair.'

'I shall be grateful for whatever you see fit to arrange.'

He raised his hand in a brusque, dismissive gesture. 'A dozen or so families from the neighbourhood will be invited back to the villa for luncheon after the ceremony. I'll have trestles and an awning set up on the terrace, and there'll be no shortage of food or drink, but that's as far as it goes. I've no doubt you'll be marking the occasion in your own fashion on your return to England.'

'I'm sure,' I said, more truthfully than he might have supposed, 'that I shall be unable to better your own arrangements.'

There were other matters, all of an essentially practical nature and requiring little more than my acquiescence. Eleanor seemed subdued, staring at the ground in silence until her father brought up the question of best man. 'I've sounded young Merivale on the subject,' he said. 'I know he'd be glad to do it.'

I sensed Eleanor's agitation even before she spoke. 'You had no right,' she said. 'That was Charles's business, not yours.'

'I'd thought of it myself,' I said quickly. 'I'm delighted to have the matter so neatly resolved. I shall write to him this evening.'

'Then I'll take that as settled,' said Vane.

Eleanor stepped up close, taking me by the elbow. 'I should like a word with Charles,' she said, leaning across me to address her father. 'A word in private.'

Vane glared at her but she was already walking me away from him, towards the shoreline. 'It's out of the question,' she said, barely waiting to get beyond her father's hearing. 'What are you thinking of?'

'I don't know what you mean.'

'You can't ask William to be your best man,' she said. 'Don't you see? You'd be rubbing salt into an open wound.'

'He's entitled to refuse.'

'William's too much of a gentleman for that. If you ask him, he'll feel honour-bound to accept.'

She continued to press her case but I held out, citing both the wisdom of humouring her father and the absence of any other candidate. 'Besides,' I said, 'if your father has put the idea into his head, I might well give offence to both parties by failing to follow up.'

There was a long pause. 'You may be right,' she said at last.

'Thank you, Nell.' I drew away, anxious to rejoin Vane, but she called me back.

'Not yet,' she said, and then, so softly I could hardly make out the words: 'I've something more to say.' She gazed out over the foreshore to where a flock of small waders dipped and scuttled at the water's edge. 'That business with my father,' she murmured. 'It went on for years.'

I knew that she was giving me the opportunity to release myself from our hastily framed compact and felt obscurely touched by the gesture. I should have liked to take her hand but refrained, inhibited by Vane's presence at our backs.

'You must forget the past,' I said. 'You're about to begin a new life. A new life in a new world.'

She shook her head. 'We carry our past with us,' she said. 'I have my hopes for the future, but I don't expect to forget.'

I glanced over my shoulder. 'Your father's waiting,' I said.

'Do you hear what I'm saying, Charles?' She reached

out and gripped my sleeve, shaking my arm vigorously as though to rouse me. 'Do you understand?'

The birds rose and wheeled as one, their wings flickering against the rippled shine of the water. 'We can talk about it later,' I said. I turned, breaking her hold, and began to make my way back to where Vane stood stiff as a statue in the midday glare.

In the event, Merivale carried out his duties throughout the ceremony and the succeeding festivities in such exemplary fashion that I found myself wondering, as the luncheon drew to a close, whether Eleanor might not have exaggerated the extent of his interest in her; but as we rose from the table I saw him look towards her with an expression so unguardedly tender and desperate that it seemed impossible she should not be pierced to the heart by it. I glanced sideways, half fearful of surprising her in some small act of betrayal, but she was listening with rapt attention to her neighbour, her slender neck and shoulders twisted away from us, and it was my own heart that smarted for the young man and his wrecked hopes. I took him by the arm and walked him down the slope of the lawn towards the citrus grove.

'Eleanor has told me,' I said gently, 'that your own feelings for her—'

'My feelings are of no account. But I should like you to know, in case you have any doubts on the matter, that the indiscretions were all mine. Nell gave me no reason to suppose that my clumsy pursuit of her would ever be rewarded. On the contrary, she made it plain that I was wasting my time. But she was never cold, Redbourne, never unkind – though perhaps it would have been better for me if she had been.'

'You must feel free to write to her – to write to us. And should you ever find yourself in England . . .'

He shook his head, as though the possibility were too remote to be entertained. 'I like you, Redbourne,' he said. 'I like you very much indeed, and I don't mind telling you that I had some notion when we first met that we should come to know one another a good deal better in due course. I believed, to be frank, that you were the man my sister had been waiting for, and nothing' – he came to a halt and looked back up the slope to where Esther and Mrs Merivale stood talking together in the shade of the awning – 'would have given me greater pleasure than to have welcomed you into our own family.'

Was there mischief in that little speech? Nothing deliberate, I thought, scanning Merivale's open features, but I found myself profoundly unsettled by his words. I had voyaged to the far side of the world, ostensibly in the service of science but actually, as recent reflection on the matter had made increasingly clear to me, in quest of a wife. Not an unworthy venture in itself, of course; but what gave me pause at that moment was the thought that I had travelled all that distance only to snatch at the first opportunity that presented itself. What other vistas might have opened up before me if I had waited longer or explored more widely? And what had determined my choice? A wild song, the meeting of eyes across a shadowed drawing-room, a few small kindnesses offered at a time when my spirits had been at their lowest ebb and my judgement clouded – were these adequate foundations for a marriage?

'Thank you, Merivale,' I said. 'And thank you, too, for standing alongside me today. A lesser man would have refused.'

'I considered it an honour. But you mustn't imagine that my duties have been entirely easy for me.'

'All the more credit to you for discharging them so ably.'

'Ably enough, no doubt, but not as gladly as I could have wished.'

'You're a young man,' I said consolingly, 'and, if I may say so, an extremely eligible one. My mother used to say that weddings are like troubles – they never come singly. Allow me to hope that the next will be your own.'

He gave me a wan smile. 'I've never wanted anyone but Nell,' he said simply. And then, turning abruptly away: 'Perhaps we should rejoin the others.'

As we walked back up the slope Eleanor came hurrying towards us, half stumbling on the cumbersome folds of her gown. 'You can have no idea,' she laughed as she joined us, 'how much I'm looking forward to wearing my everyday clothes again.' She wriggled her shoulders, playfully suggesting the irksomeness of the gown's heavy fabric, and threw back her head, exposing the long line of her throat.

It wasn't a wanton gesture – indeed, there was a kind of innocence about it – but neither was it a ladylike one. And though I was stirred by it, my pulse quickening as I gazed, I felt it, and her words too, as a subtle affront. 'Mrs Redbourne,' I murmured, half jocular, half chiding, as I grasped her arm and drew her to my side. I felt her lithe body stiffen against me.

Merivale shifted uneasily, tugging at his cuffs. 'We're in for a storm,' he said, nodding towards the darkening horizon. 'It's a blessing it didn't blow up an hour earlier.'

There was a huddle of guests in front of the veranda, all waiting, I surmised, to bid us farewell, but as we approached the terrace Esther and her mother stepped briskly forward to intercept us. 'I'm sorry,' said Mrs Merivale, reaching for Eleanor's hand, 'that we've made so little of our last opportunity to speak with you before you leave. The truth is, my dear, that the right words seem so hard to find. It's the happiest of occasions, of course, but you'll forgive me – and I hope Mr Redbourne will forgive me too – for telling you that I've shed tears at the thought of your going, and that I've no doubt I'll shed more when you're gone.' Even as she spoke, her eyes brimmed, and Eleanor, with a quick, impulsive move-ment drew her close and held her.

I turned away, faintly embarrassed, and addressed myself to Esther. 'I'm glad to have met you, Miss Merivale, and to have heard you play. I shall treasure the memory of your impromptu recital.'

She took the compliment as a lady should, modestly but without embarrassment, her fine features irradiated by a smile of unmistakable warmth. 'I wish,' she said softly, 'that we'd had time to get to know one another better.' She clasped my hand briefly in her own, then leaned over to Eleanor as Mrs Merivale drew away. 'Goodbye, Nell,' she said. 'I hope you'll send us news of your life in England.'

'She has promised,' said Merivale. 'Hold her to it, Redbourne. And' – he turned quickly on his heel before the words were out – 'look after her.' He hurried towards the waiting carriage, his mother and sister following at a gentler pace. I stood staring after them, listening to the hollow sound of the awning as it flapped and billowed in the rising wind.

31

Vane had insisted that we remain at the villa until the morning of our sailing, but there were no concessions to our new status. My old room had been made up as before and I spent my wedding night alone, listening, between spells of troubled sleep, to the noise of the rain and the buffeting wind.

Those last two days in the house were lived in a strange state of suspension. Eleanor seemed gloomily abstracted, moving like a ghost from room to room or staring out from the veranda across the sodden lawn; and though Vane spent much of the time shut away in his study, leaving us largely to ourselves, our conversations were awkward and inconsequential. I drank more tea and coffee than was good for me and passed the hours between meals listlessly scanning the pages of Vane's farming magazines.

On the second afternoon Eleanor and I walked down to the barn to oversee the packing of her sculpture and her little cache of treasures. The rain had eased off over the preceding hour or so, but as we picked our way between the dripping shrubs it began again with renewed force, and by the time we ducked into the doorway we were wet through.

The two servants were manoeuvring the blanket-chest down the loft ladder as we entered, and neither acknowledged our presence until they had set it safely on the ground.

'That's everything from up above, Miss Eleanor,' said the older man as he straightened up. 'It's all in here, and well padded.'

'Thank you, Norwood. And there's that too.' She indicated the sculpture, scarcely advanced, I noticed with surprise, since I had last seen it.

'We've brought down a couple of old blankets,' said Norwood. 'We'll wrap it in those before we crate it up.' He crossed over to the figure and ran his hand over the smooth surface of the shoulders. 'It's a nice piece of work,' he said.

I saw the younger man smirk. Eleanor brushed past him and began to climb the ladder. 'I'm going to have one last look,' she said, glancing back at me as she hauled herself on to the platform. 'I shall be down in a minute.'

My specimens were still where I had left them, ranged on the shelves of the battered dresser over against the far wall. While the men roped the blankets around Eleanor's sculpture, I picked out a few of the more beautiful skins, laying them on the dresser's dusty surface for closer inspection – lory and lorikeets, a spinebill, the kingfisher, the chestnut teal. I took up the teal and turned it in my hands, twisting its eyeless head this way and that to catch the muted light, but the iridescence was gone and the dense breast-feathers, which I had once fancifully thought of as bearing the impress of Eleanor's fingers, were stiff and damp.

By the time Eleanor rejoined me, I was more than ready to leave and she, for her part, seemed close to tears, her face rigid with strain. 'It's all in hand,' I said. 'There's no need to stay.'

As we reached the doorway, Norwood looked up. 'What about the birds, Miss Eleanor? Are those to be packed too?'

Eleanor glanced sideways at me. I hesitated.

'Charles?'

'No,' I said. 'Get rid of them.' I turned up my collar and stepped out into the rain.

We rose in darkness next morning, and were on the road by daybreak. Vane had seated himself beside Eleanor, obliging me to sit on the opposite side of the carriage, and I spent much of the journey staring out of the streaming window, trying to avoid his gaze. He had assured me that we should be in good time, but the road had been damaged by the heavy rains, and our progress was frustratingly slow. At several points on our journey we came to a place where the rainwater, pouring in a torrent from the slopes above, had scoured a broad groove through the sandy surface, and on each occasion I held my breath, listening to the rush and swirl beneath us as we eased forward into the flood.

We reached the quayside with barely twenty minutes to spare. Vane took matters in hand at once, leaping out to collar a passing porter before I had so much as risen from my seat. While he supervised the unloading of our luggage, I paced restlessly up and down, anxious to be on board but inhibited by a sense of occasion: this was no ordinary parting, and a casual farewell, I thought, was out of the question.

Vane evidently held no such view. Turning back to us as the last of our bags was handed down, he simply gripped me by the hand and wished me well, then took Eleanor briefly in his arms. 'Write to me when time allows,' he said, as he stepped back to let us go. His voice was flat, his handsome face as blank as the grey sky above us. Eleanor gazed into his eyes for a long moment; then she lowered her head and turned away.

Once aboard, we made our way to the stern. Despite the driving rain, the deck was crowded, and though my own height gave me a good view of the well-wishers gathered on the quayside, Eleanor was unable to see beyond the massed bodies of our fellow passengers.

'I have to see him,' she said breathlessly, bobbing and weaving, searching for a gap, a vantage-point. 'I have to wave him goodbye.'

'We've said our goodbyes, Nell.'

321

'Don't you understand? It's for ever.' She ducked down and began to force her way through the crowd, moving erratically but with savage determination. I lost sight of her for a moment and then she reappeared, close to the rail, just as the ship's engines shuddered into life. I saw her scanning the quayside, her head thrust forward; and then her hand went up.

Vane had placed himself so close to the edge of the wharf that I was unable to see him from my own position until the ship drew away. The quayside crowd had begun, almost as one, to wave and shout, but Vane was standing starkly upright, a little apart from all that noise and agitation. He stared after us for a long minute and then, raising one hand in brusque salute, turned and was lost to view among the waving arms, the flourished hats and handkerchiefs.

It was clear that we were in for a rough spell. As we approached the mouth of the cove, the wind stiffened, sending the rain slantwise across the running deck, and I felt the steamer lift and lurch on the swell. The passengers began to make their way below, bracing themselves against the unfamiliar movement. I assumed that Eleanor would rejoin me but she remained at the rail as the deck cleared, gazing out over the white foam of our wake, apparently oblivious to the pelting rain. Something in her huddled posture and air of dark absorption troubled me, and I made my way towards her, moving as quickly as conditions allowed and calling her name as I went. She gave no sign of having heard.

'You'll be drenched to the bone,' I said, drawing up behind her.

She was silent, straining forward as the wharf blurred and dwindled behind the shifting veils of rain. I reached out and touched her shoulder. 'Come now, Nell,' I said. 'We should go below.'

She twisted towards me, her hands still gripping the rail, her gaze hard and angry. 'I'll come when I'm ready,' she said.

'When you're ready? What do you mean by that?'

'I mean exactly what I say.'

Ill-tempered little minx, I thought, with a dull flush of anger; a pert, cross-grained piece, and spoiled goods into the bargain. 'Do as you please,' I said, 'but I've no intention of catching my death on your account.'

As I turned my back on her the foghorn vented a long, mournful blast, a sustained note that seemed to pass through the planking and up into my shivering body; and as the sound died away, a cry went up from behind me as if in answer – a human cry, but so wild and raw that I felt my skin crawl. I stopped in my tracks and whipped round.

Eleanor had started after me and stood with her feet splayed on the tilting deck, her head thrown back, howling at the sky. Her mouth was wide, drawn down at the corners so that the sinews of her neck stood out; the skin around her eyes was creased and puckered like that of an old woman. I stepped forward and took her in my arms in a helpless confusion of pity and embarrassment, trying simultaneously to assuage her unfathomable grief and to shield her from the curious stares of the few passengers still up on deck. I remember thinking, holding her stiffly to my breast and rocking her distractedly to and fro, that I had fooled myself into marriage: the visions I had seen in the soft light of my sick-room – the loving companion, the ministering priestess – had been nothing more than the projections of my own longing.

Little by little her weeping subsided and her breathing grew more regular, and after a while she eased herself back against my cradling arms, lifting her face to mine. Her ruined face, I thought, coldly appraising the blotched skin and swollen eyelids; but as my mind framed the words she reached up and touched my own face, pressing her hand gently against the line of my jaw as though to communicate, through the flesh, matters too vast or too complex to be entrusted to language. And then, as her gaze steadied and locked with mine, I saw it all suddenly clear for an instant, knowing that what I held was the irreducible sum of things – squalor and splendour, vision and nightmare; the pathos, the pettiness and the doomed, undeniable beauty; the wise adept and the broken child. I drew her close again, feeling the delicate trembling of her body through the folds of my coat.

She took a deep, shuddering breath; then she pulled away and swung herself lightly round to stand at my side.

'I'm ready now,' she said.

ACKNOWLEDGEMENTS

A number of individuals have helped, in a variety of ways, during the writing of this novel. Particular thanks are due to Luigi Bonomi, Richard Griffiths, Stephanie Hale, Beth Hanley, Kathryn Heyman, Richard Johnstone, Keiren Phelan, Martin Thomas, Mark Tredinnick, Carole Welch, Gilly Withey and Tim Woods.

I'm also grateful to the President and Fellows of Kellogg College, Oxford, for a period of sabbatical leave in 2002; to Southern Arts and the Senate Research Fund of the University of Wales, Aberystwyth, for financial assistance with visits to Australia in 2002 and 2004 respectively; and to Arts Council England for one of their Writers' Awards in 2003.